CW01425699

For King and Country

Evelyn James

A Clara Fitzgerald Mystery

Red Raven Publications

www.sophie-jackson.com

Contents

Chapter One

Clara O'Harris was a first-rate detective.

She would have confessed to this without shame or feeling that she was being boastful. She solved mysteries efficiently and discreetly, and though sometimes the matters that were brought to her attention were upsetting, even depressing, she braved it all with the confidence that it was better to face the truth than to allow lies to fester unchecked.

But even first-rate detectives can sometimes find themselves confronted by a puzzle they cannot crack.

Such was the case with the newest patient at the Convalescence Home for ex-servicemen that Clara's husband, Captain John O'Harris ran. The patient was a man in his later years and would have only just made the upper age limit to serve in the last war. He had been a colonel and had survived four years of hell, only to come home and apparently disintegrate when faced with living in peacetime.

The colonel's wife had endeavoured to support her husband all these years as he battled his inner demons, until her own health failed her, at which point it became apparent to their extended family just how desperate the situation was.

The colonel barely ate, and he barely talked. He had to be told to do everything, from rising from his bed in the morning and getting dressed, to sitting in an armchair once he made it downstairs. If he was not watched constantly he started to weep, and more than once he had made an effort to dispatch himself – the only occasions when he had acted with independent will.

His wife was so ashamed by her husband's transformation from a forthright and proud man of the military to a virtual imbecile she kept everyone at a distance, refusing help or company. Making excuses to prevent family calling, or friends from popping by.

Her fiery resolve to take care of her husband, while noble and self-sacrificing, was ultimately a disaster for them both. The colonel's wife simply could not take the strain any longer and was currently bed bound, being tended to by her nieces, while her husband was a pickle the family were unsure how to deal with.

He might have ended up in an asylum, a fate too often enacted upon those suffering the scars of war, but he was fortunate that a great nephew had heard about O'Harris' home through a friend who had been there and found it extremely useful in his own recovery. Though the colonel was of a generation who were not easily swayed to try treatments of the mind, being more prone to dismissing such things as a weakness, the nephew proved persuasive, and after making enquiries, the colonel was brought to the home.

Colonel Augustus Bradley had entered the O'Harrises' lives without so much as a hint that he was aware of where he was. His story of his time in the war was shrouded in shadows, the trauma that had brought him to such a state hidden in his past.

He did not speak, nor make any sign that he knew he had left his own home.

He was a mystery, indeed, and one that even the experienced psychiatric doctors at the home were having a difficult time figuring out.

Patience was their motto, and so they showed remarkable patience when the colonel refused to meet their eye or acknowledge their existence.

The trouble was, while they were prepared to wait, the colonel's family were not, and they had made murmurings that perhaps the colonel was not improving because he was a useful source of income for the home.

Most of the patients had to pay for their stay at the residence, and certain cynically inclined members of the colonel's family thought O'Harris was taking advantage of their situation. If the colonel was incurable, better he be sent to an asylum than for them to keep paying for pointless treatment.

Their constant barrage of rather rude correspondence on the subject was beginning to wear O'Harris down. He knew people expected results swiftly when it came to mental health, assuming the mind should heal faster than, say, a broken leg, but it still caused him pain when people questioned his methods and his progress.

He feared that soon the colonel would be removed from his charge and thrust into a lunatic asylum from which he would never see the light of day. If that occurred, O'Harris would feel he had failed the gentleman.

The strain on her husband was distressing Clara, who had begun her own quiet attempts to assist the colonel. These took the form of sitting with him in his room, or when he was brought down to the library, and either reading to him or simply talking. She had grown into the habit of reading news items from the daily papers to try to draw him back to the world. She told him of stories of prize-winning cucumbers grown by a local schoolboy, and dolphins seen off the south coast, which had caused quite a stir. But if he even heard her, she could not tell.

The colonel was a mystery she might not be able to solve, and that depressed Clara as much as it hurt her to see her husband struggling and worrying so much. She had half a mind to speak with the colonel's family and give them a stern talking to about the nature of the mind and its recovery. But she also had this anxiety inside her that perhaps they were right.

Perhaps the colonel could not be saved.

With such anxiety on her mind, she had taken to regular afternoon strolls to bring some peace to her thoughts. She was lacking any other cases to keep her occupied, a circumstance that occurred infrequently, but always left her twiddling her thumbs.

Clara was a naturally busy person and not having something to work on was a source of irritation. Part of the reason, perhaps, she had taken to trying to fix the colonel, though she would prefer to consider that a pure act of charity and kindness.

Her walks provided her with a distraction and took her over the fields behind the home. She would leave by the gap in the old wall at the very end of the grounds and cross over a meadow, which sometimes contained lambs in spring, before reaching a stile and then following a lane past some farms, through a copse of young trees, and then back towards the home.

The entire walk took her an hour, if she hurried, if she took her time to ponder the weather or anything she saw about her, it could easily take her a couple of hours. Time that was invaluable for allowing her thoughts to settle and become her own again.

That afternoon, as the flowers bloomed in the early summer warmth, she was enjoying the feeling of the sunshine on her skin and listening to the birds singing around her. The sky was blue and there was a promise of a fine evening to come.

Tommy, Clara's brother, would be organising one of his cricket practice sessions at the home, while her sister-in-law, Annie, would be settled into a garden chair watching. She was pregnant and beginning to show. Though she refused to admit it, Annie was beginning to struggle to keep up with the housework at home and was feeling the full effects of her pregnancy. Her belly was growing, and she had swollen ankles, which she was not pleased about. Tommy was fussing about her as if a woman had never had a baby ever before in the history of the world, and all told, it was going to be a long few months as they waited for the baby's arrival in the autumn. Clara hoped they could all survive Annie's temper which was becoming strained under the pressure of being unable to do what she wanted, and being forced to sit down and rest.

Annie, much like Clara, was not good at doing nothing.

Smiling to herself as she thought of her sister-in-law, and her annoyance at being forced to step back from some of her more vigorous daily chores, Clara crossed the stile at the end of the meadow and found herself on the lane.

In the distance, she could hear the faint lowing of cows at one of the farms. She tried to catch a glimpse of them through the hedges but could not see far enough. Now humming to herself, she started to collect a selection of flowers that were growing beside the road, intending to take them back to the home and make a humble display in one of the vases.

It was then she heard a new sound.

Clara paused and listened carefully. There it was again, the urgent, high-pitched yip of a dog in trouble.

Tommy Fitzgerald had two dogs, Bramble and Pip, and Clara was something of a dog lover herself. In fact, she cared about all animals. The sound of one in distress drew her to the side of the road and then, when she could not see the dog, over the wall that banded the lane and into the field beyond.

The dog was yipping frantically, but the sound was oddly muffled. In her experience of dog ownership, Clara was aware that they could get themselves into all manner of mischief. Once, Pip, her brother's labrador, had stranded herself on some rocks at the beach chasing seagulls. Tommy had ended up extremely wet in his efforts to rescue her, only for the dog to suddenly realise it could swim and happily make its way to safety without his assistance.

Clara crossed the meadow following the noise, her footsteps encouraging the dog to bark harder, until she found herself coming to a location where there was a hole in the ground. Pulling back some dead brambles, she peered down into what appeared to be a deep gulf in the earth. In the darkness below her, something bounced up and barked happily at the sight of her.

"There you are," Clara said, leaning carefully over the hole. "Chasing rabbits, were we?"

She could not make out the type of dog trapped below, just a pair of bright eyes and the movement of a small lively body. From the high tone of the bark, she guessed it was not a big dog.

"Now, how am I going to get you out?"

Clara studied the scene around her. The ground immediately beneath her knees, as she crouched to look into the hole, was bare soil, recently dug by the looks of things. The hole seemed fairly fresh, and the clean-cut sides did not appear to offer any obvious way of climbing down to rescue the dog. Clara fancied she would have to fetch help, and a ladder, from one of the nearby farms.

"Never fear, I shall have you out of that hole soon enough," she promised the dog, standing up to brush the dirt off her skirt.

It was as she did, she heard a faint creak and felt as if the earth shifted beneath her feet. With a sudden sense of the inevitable, she made a valiant effort to get back to surer ground, only for the earth beneath her to crumble away and plummet her down into the hole below.

She landed hard on her bottom, the wind knocked from her lungs. The small dog bounded up to her and threw itself into her arms in a flurry of tail wagging and face licks. Its enthusiasm for its saviour was sweet, but rather overwhelming, and Clara did her best to gently cease its loving attentions. When the dog calmed a fraction, Clara could take a proper look at her surroundings.

Above her, the edges of some wooden planks showed where she had fallen, and earth was still tumbling into the hole.

Clara sighed to the dog, which proved to be a rather filthy spaniel.

"Well, this is inconvenient, isn't it?"

Chapter Two

Clara took stock of her position.

Nothing hurt severely, which consoled her that she had not twisted or broken anything. She had not bumped her head, which was always a reassuring outcome, and when she tentatively stood up her spine only gave a slight protest. She would be sore, but nothing worse.

Bouncing at her feet, now sniffing her shoes, and trying to convince her that it was her newest best friend, was the small dog. It was a reddish-gold coloured spaniel, the sort you would see on a shoot flushing game from bushes and retrieving downed birds. She bent down and patted its head, trying to console it as it was clearly more disturbed than she was at being in the hole.

"What stupid person put old wooden boards over this hole and then covered them with earth?" Clara grumbled to the dog. "What were they thinking? They were setting up an accident to happen as soon as those boards rotted through, which would be all the sooner with the wet earth atop them as well as beneath. People have no sense."

She took a good look at the walls of the hole. It had been dug straight down, its purpose unclear, though she did note some fragments of old clay pipe at one side which might have been used to carry water. Possibly this had been intended as a reservoir of water for one of the farms. Perhaps there had once been a stream or pond nearby that meant this was a suitable spot to gather water. If that were the case, the source of that water had long ago disappeared.

The hole was not very wide, and Clara could stretch out her arms and almost touch both sides at the same time. She scratched at the earth, finding it crumbled easily beneath her fingers and probably would not allow her to climb out. The hole was just deep enough that even with her best efforts she could not jump up and grab the upper edge, which meant getting out that way was impossible. She huffed to herself.

At her feet, the dog gave a whimper as if it sensed her despondency.

"Do not worry. They will notice I am missing eventually and come looking for me. They know where I like to walk," she promised the dog, hoping it wouldn't take either her brother or her husband too long to realise she was absent. "In the meantime, we shall just make the best of things."

As she spoke, her eyes lifted up and she noticed the beautiful sunny day was transforming before her in the way that early summer days can. In a matter of minutes, the sky was no longer bright blue but cloaked with grey clouds, and there was a real threat of rain in the air.

"Bother," Clara muttered to herself.

The pit offered no shelter from the promised shower, and she would soon be wet and muddy. Still, there was not much to be done other than to be patient and hope that it was not the middle of the night before she was found.

She located a spot on the ground that seemed dry enough and settled in to wait. The spaniel took the opportunity to clamber into her lap, tail still beating a fierce rhythm, and leaned its head as hard as it could into her chest. She took the cue and started to stroke its ears.

"Don't worry, I get myself into scrapes like these all the time," Clara assured the dog. "It always works out."

The dog gave a small sigh, as if satisfied with her explanation, and then closed its eyes. Its little body was trembling, and it was cold and damp.

"Poor thing," Clara murmured to it. "Has no one come looking for you?"

The sky finally decided to unburden itself of its cargo of rain, and water spattered down straight into the hole. Clara gritted her teeth under the deluge.

"If I ever find out who dug this hole and then put those planks across it, I shall have *them* sitting in a hole in the rain."

The spaniel snuffled as if responding to her comment, then ducked its head against her, as if hiding its eyes would make the rain less intrusive.

Clara waited out the rainstorm indignantly, sending up a few choice words to the skies above. She sometimes fancied the weather had a sense of humour. She judged the time by the sun moving through the sky, knowing roughly where it usually was on its daily journey by the time she was normally heading home.

"They must have missed me by now," she grumbled to herself.

Almost as if she had talked up her saviours, there was movement at the edge of the pit.

"Hey there! I am down here!" she called hastily.

More movement brought a face to the edge of the hole. It belonged to a nondescript fellow, wearing a flat cap and with the sort of moustache people liked to refer to as a soup-strainer. He peered into the hole and Clara did not like the way he looked at her.

"Mrs O'Harris, pleasure to meet you."

Clara tensed. While she had optimistically hoped her husband or brother might have noticed her absence by now, she had not supposed they would have rounded up a vast search party and sent out strangers to look for her. This man was unknown to her, and yet he knew her name. She felt her hackles go up at the same time as the spaniel gave a small growl.

"I think the pleasure would be greater under happier circumstances," Clara called up. "You might care to get me out of this hole."

The man nodded his head and then produced a length of rope which he unfurled down towards her. Clara was further troubled that he appeared to be so well prepared.

"Can you climb a rope, Mrs O'Harris?"

Clara glared at him.

"It has been many years since I was required to, but I dare say I shall remember," she informed him. "But what about the dog?"

"What about it?"

"Dogs cannot climb ropes, and I shall need both my hands free to get up."

"I do not see the problem?"

Clara narrowed her eyes at him.

"That is what I feared you would say. I am not going to leave this pit without my unfortunate canine friend here. Therefore, it might be prudent for you to fetch a ladder rather than that rope."

"Mrs O'Harris..."

"Stop using my name, I do not know you, and I do not care for your manner. If you know who I am, you can go and fetch my husband who will be able to extract me from this hole without causing me such aggravation."

"Do you really want to sit down there all day?" the man snapped at her, turning volatile.

"I do, if it means staying clear of you," Clara retorted back. "I find it deeply suspicious you have appeared with a rope at such a convenient moment. And you know my name, though we have never been introduced."

"I am just a kindly, helpful stranger," the man said impatiently.

"And I say, if you are so kindly, you will go fetch my husband and be done with the matter."

"Will you just climb the rope?"

"No," Clara said firmly. "And I would advise against you coming down here to try to make me. I am in a very bad mood right about now and I shall not take well to being pushed about."

"You are really..."

"Irving, that's enough."

Clara blinked at the sound of a second voice. How many people were up there? Her anxiety was rattled. She knew she was in far more trouble than simply accidentally falling into a hole. She calmed herself by taking note of the voice she had heard and impressing it on her mind.

The second speaker was well-mannered, unlike his uncouth friend. He had the smooth, quiet tones of a man who went to a public school and has had a fine education. That did not precisely make her feel more confident about his presence above her, but it did give her some sort of insight into what was occurring.

The second figure now moved towards the top of the pit, causing his companion Irving to move to one side.

"Mrs O'Harris, I must apologise for this inconvenience."

"You sound like a gentleman," Clara said to him coldly. "But gentlemen do not go around imprisoning women in holes they dug into the earth."

"Do you consider yourself imprisoned? We have offered you a rope."

"And what will occur when I accept the rope and climb out?" Clara snapped. "How many more of you are up there? Right now, I feel safer in this pit."

"I can assure you there are but two of us, but I admire your resilience and suspicious mind. It was the reason, in fact, we had to go to such lengths."

"You intend to kidnap me?" Clara demanded, wondering which of the enemies she had made over her years as a detective might now have come for her.

"It is a little more complicated than mere kidnapping," the man said, sounding almost offended she had used such a word. "We need your assistance, but we cannot allow anyone to know you are aiding us. Hence, our resort to such antics."

"You could have come to my office, if you want help," Clara grumbled.

"As I said, I could not afford for anyone to make the connection that you were aiding us. Your office is too public, and we do not wish any of your associates knowing about us."

"My associates?"

"Your husband and brother, mainly, but there are other acquaintances of yours who would be most troublesome if they learned about us and what we desire from you."

Clara made a clucking noise at the back of her throat.

"That settles it, I am staying in this pit."

"Mrs O'Harris, please try to be reasonable, I am not a criminal. Indeed, I work for the government."

"Poppycock!"

"It is not," the man said wearily. "This might seem extravagant behaviour, but we found ourselves driven to such extremes by your own rather remarkable persistence at foiling our previous attempts.

We have been watching you for weeks, now."

Clara shuddered at the confession, then she hesitated.

"I had this feeling of being watched," she said. "I thought I was being paranoid."

"You outwitted several of my men in their efforts to speak with you when you were alone. I would gladly explain all this in detail, if you would just allow me to assist you out of this hole."

Clara ignored his offer, she was thinking hard.

"What previous attempts?"

"Our first plan was simply to grab you off the street into one of our cars. That works quite well if done in a quiet place and at speed," the gentleman responded. "You, however, appeared to realise a car was following you and diverted down several busy thoroughfares. We made the effort three times and on each occasion you eluded us."

"The black car that was moving slowly down the road?" Clara nodded her head at the memory. "I didn't like the look of it. I thought something was amiss which is why I made sure to walk in busy places or down roads a car could not follow."

"Yes, you made it extremely difficult for us to reach you. Thus we had to think again."

"So, you dug a hole?"

"The hole already existed, we merely improved upon it and arranged a trap."

Clara scowled at him and crossed her arms over her chest.

"You can go and fetch my husband now, for I am done talking with you."

"Mrs O'Harris, please be reasonable."

"Reasonable?" Clara looked at him in amazement. "You are the one who has me imprisoned in a hole in the ground!"

Chapter Three

C aptain John O'Harris leaned in the doorway of his library and looked at the older gentleman sitting by the window. The man was hunched up in his armchair, almost as if on the cusp of falling out. His gaze was fixed on the floor, his hands on his knees. He neither moved, nor spoke, and might as easily have been a statue.

O'Harris sensed a presence beside him and glanced over to see that another of his long-term patients had joined him.

"Peterson," O'Harris nodded to the former private.

Peterson had been his most taxing case before the arrival of the colonel, but he had made great progress in recent months. Though he still struggled to live in the everyday world, he was slowly gaining his independence. He now resided outside of the home but returned each day to help the other men who were there. He had been trying his hardest to assist the colonel, without any success.

"You look rather worried, Captain?"

Peterson had a tendency to be over formal, which was a habit O'Harris was trying to get him out of. He did not need the youth using his rank when he was here, especially as he had been in the air force, while Peterson was in the army. O'Harris had no authority over him and wished for him to see him as a friend.

It was a work in progress.

"I suppose I am, Peterson. Colonel Bradley's case is proving somewhat more complex than I had anticipated."

Peterson turned and looked at the colonel. He was a good-looking young man who was just beginning to fill out from his youthful gauntness and turn into the man he was meant to be. He folded his arms across his chest and became thoughtful.

"I think he is making progress."

"Perhaps you are seeing something I am not?" O'Harris said lightly.

"Perhaps I am," Peterson smiled back. "But, I do believe his gaze is less rigid and he seems to know more of what is going on around him."

O'Harris fancied Peterson was seeing things he wanted to see. From his perspective, the colonel was as unmoving and quiet as always.

"You will not give up on him?" Peterson suddenly asked, an edge of unease in his voice.

O'Harris patted his shoulder warmly.

"I never give up," he promised him. "But the colonel's family are pushing for results and do not understand that these things take time. I fear they may remove him from my care before I have a chance to bring him back to himself."

Peterson became grim. Stung by the notion of the colonel's family simply giving up on him. It had been different for Peterson. He had been the one to give up, while his mother had refused to and had found the home. He was doing his best to live up to the faith she placed in him.

"I shall work it all out," O'Harris promised the lad, though he was not convinced of the fact himself. "Did you want to see me about something?"

Peterson was reminded of why he had sought out O'Harris.

"Oh, yes, we can't find Clara and she was supposed to be

conducting one of her detective classes this afternoon."

Clara had taken to showing the men the skills necessary to solve mysteries and would discuss past cases with them as a form of diversion. Her classes were proving very popular, and more than one of the men was considering a career as a private detective after their time at the home.

O'Harris now frowned to hear his wife was missing. Clara could be occasionally absent-minded when she was working a case, but she never missed her appointments with the patients at the home. She was as dedicated to them as her husband.

"She is not back from her walk?" O'Harris glanced over at the grandfather clock in the hallway behind him and saw that it was a good hour past the time Clara normally reappeared. He felt his own pang of unease at the knowledge that she was extremely late.

"Do you think we should go look for her?" Peterson asked. "We did not like to just assume, we thought perhaps she had become distracted."

"Clara would have sent word to us if she was unable to take the class," O'Harris said firmly. "If, somehow, she became caught up in a new case, she would have let us know. To have received no word suggests that something might have happened."

Peterson was upset to hear this. He thought a lot of Clara and he would never wish to see harm befall her.

"We should begin a search for her, we know the route she takes," O'Harris made up his mind. "Round up all the men you can find and tell them what we are about."

"Do you think some harm might have come to her because of her detective work?" Peterson asked anxiously.

O'Harris tried to smile reassuringly, but the truth was that was exactly what he was thinking.

"Clara's work takes her into the lion's den on a regular basis, and sometimes the lion decides to bite. It would not be the first time she has faced danger because of her work, but on this I am certain, Clara is resilient and brave, and anyone trying to do her harm is worthy more of our pity than our anger."

Peterson nodded his head, still worried but prepared to be consoled by O'Harris' words. He went to round up the men, while O'Harris sought out Tommy.

Tommy Fitzgerald was sitting with Annie in the conservatory, having a cup of tea before they headed home. Tommy was just recovering from the exertions of his recent cricket practice, his fair hair was still a little damp with sweat. He loved cricket, but his war wound made it harder work for him than it was in the past. He had to push himself to make the pace, and sometimes his hip hurt. Each summer, when they began to practice again, he noticed how tight his muscles felt, seized up after the winter off. Sometimes, he feared one summer he would not be able to cut the mustard anymore, but that was an unspoken fear he kept to himself.

It was miraculous enough he was walking again, let alone playing cricket.

"Tommy. Annie," O'Harris entered the room, and his expression immediately alerted them to something amiss.

"What is wrong with Clara?" Annie asked.

She was settled into one of the new wicker chairs the captain had purchased for the conservatory and was for once not bemoaning the need to rest. She was feeling rather jaded, and her feet were hurting. She had been leaning back in the chair, with her hands on her expanding belly, trying to enjoy the peace and quiet.

That was until O'Harris arrived with a worried look on his face.

"You cannot just assume it is Clara who is in trouble," Tommy rebuked his wife.

Annie raised an eyebrow at him.

"Who else would cause John to look so distressed? That expression on his face is the one he has when he is worried about Clara."

"She is right," O'Harris said. "I *am* worried about Clara."

"I would say, told you so, but I do not feel this is the appropriate moment," Annie pulled herself into a more upright position in the chair. "What is the matter?"

"Clara went out for her afternoon walk, as usual, and has not returned. She is over an hour late," O'Harris confirmed his own assessment of his wife's lateness by glancing at the mantel clock in the room.

It tallied with what the grandfather clock had already told him.

"Clara gets absorbed doing things," Tommy said, trying to mitigate his fears.

"She was supposed to be teaching a class when she returned from her walk," O'Harris explained. "She would not miss that, not without sending word of why she could not be here."

"He is right, Tommy, Clara would never do that," Annie was pulling herself up higher in the chair. "Something has happened. What mischief has she gotten herself into now?"

"I am organising the men into a search party for her," O'Harris explained. "But I thought I should tell you what is happening."

"I shall come too," Tommy stood up.

"I would rather you stayed here in case she does return," O'Harris said. "And Annie should not be here alone."

"I am not an invalid, you know," Annie huffed indignantly.

"Sorry," O'Harris was abashed by his mistake. "But I do think it is best if Tommy remains here. Clara may have had an emergency which has delayed her. If she returns while we are searching, there should be someone here to find out what has occurred."

"Yes, of course," Tommy nodded his head. "She did not seem worried about anything when she left?"

"No, and she is not working on a case, either," O'Harris shrugged his shoulders. "But that does not mean trouble cannot find her."

"Clara is a magnet for it, rather like jam to wasps," Annie sighed heavily. "Now she is no longer at home, I do not have the opportunities like I used to, to pick up on her thoughts and determine if something is bothering her."

"I would have noticed if something was bothering her," O'Harris said, hurt she thought he might have missed something significant.

"You would have noticed if Clara had noticed herself," Annie explained to him. "Sometimes, Clara doesn't even realise something is amiss, but she knows it deep down and I see it on her face and the way she butters her bread."

"Annie there surely can be no secret code to the way my sister butters her bread," Tommy groaned.

"There is, and it is just the sort of thing O'Harris should know. I should have told him about it sooner. When something is bothering Clara, but she is not yet sure herself what it is, she stops buttering her bread from the centre outwards but rather butters from the corners inwards. And she does so much slower and in a thoughtful way. Honestly, it is subtle things like that which are so important to observe."

O'Harris glanced at Tommy, horrified he might have missed something.

"I can't remember how she buttered her toast this morning at breakfast."

"Ignore her, old man, she has these theories, but it is not for you to observe the different ways your wife butters her bread and work out what that means."

"I am right here, Thomas Fitzgerald," Annie scowled at her husband. "And do not dismiss my insight so readily. For instance, I know when you are worried about your hip by the way you sit unevenly in your chair, as if trying to protect it. That is why I always place an extra cushion to one side of your seat when I notice you doing it."

With that observation, Annie pointed to the seat Tommy had just departed. Tommy glanced and saw the extra cushion he had not even noticed her discreetly putting there, but which had indeed helped him to take the weight off his injured leg.

He grimaced as he realised how stupid he had been.

"Sorry, Annie," he said.

"Sorry, Annie," O'Harris repeated.

"Oh, don't look so maudlin," Annie sighed at them. "We all know what Clara is like. She will be fine, but you best go looking for her before she does something terrible to whoever has delayed her."

O'Harris nodded his head and then departed hastily. Annie watched him out the door, and when she was sure he was out of sight, she turned to her husband.

"Tommy, I am worried about Clara."

Tommy knelt by her side and gave her a hug.

Chapter Four

"I consider your behaviour uncouth and unworthy of your appearance of a gentleman," Clara informed the figure above her. "I am always open to being spoken to by those who need my assistance, but not after being forced into a pit."

"This might seem unnecessary, but I assure you we had exhausted all other possibilities."

"The telephone?"

"We could not risk any conversation being overheard," the gentleman shook his head.

"A letter then?"

"Too easily intercepted."

"Having someone call at my house?" Clara said.

"We did not want anyone to see us talking with you, we could not take the chance. You have to understand, this is a matter of grave importance. I could go so far as to say the security of the nation may be at stake."

"Now you are spouting nonsense," Clara snorted.

"I am not, Mrs O'Harris, and I would gladly elaborated on this situation, if you would clamber out of the hole and join me."

"I take this walk every day, you could have met me here on the road," Clara said, determined to have her say.

"We could have done," the gentleman nodded. "But you have an alarming habit of becoming aware of when we are following you and you have avoided my men twice already."

Clara paused as she considered his words.

"Twice?" she reflected on her last few walks. "There was that day I saw two suspicious individuals sitting on the wall near the stile and so I changed my route to avoid them."

"And fell into conversation with a passing labourer who you asked to escort you home."

"He wanted to talk about his wife with me," Clara corrected. "She still cannot remember what she did with her favourite teapot, and it is driving them to distraction."

"The second time we attempted to intercept you, Irving quietly followed you once you were beyond the stile, and you then headed off to the nearest farm."

"I dislike being followed," Clara stated. "I was acutely aware of his presence."

"Yes, we have discovered you are quite adept at avoiding us," the gentleman groaned. "It might almost be imagined you are more proficient at this business than we are."

"And what business, precisely, are you in?" Clara demanded.

The gentleman paused for a moment, then he gave a quiet mutter to himself, conceding defeat.

"We are in the espionage business, Mrs O'Harris. We work for the government, looking into matters that could threaten national security."

"I have a hard time believing that."

"It is the truth, and I could show you some identification to prove it, if you would just get out of that hole."

"I am comfortable in my hole," Clara countered. "I am not comfortable around you."

"Fine," the gentleman sighed, and then he dropped something into the pit.

Clara watched as a paper fluttered to the ground at her feet. She reached forward and picked it up. The first thing she noticed was the official stamp embossed on the head of the paper, then she took account of the address written in the upper right which stated this had been sent from offices in Whitehall. Lastly, she read the letter, which was a simple statement that the gentleman above her was working on behalf of the government and with the full authority of the Prime Minister and His Majesty.

"You are Mr Wimpole," Clara said, finishing her reading.

"I am, and as you can see, I am not a criminal, nor a threat to you."

"The latter remains to be seen," Clara said coldly. "I still do not see why you had to set this trap."

"I have already explained, traditional routes of reaching you were impossible, due to the risk of being intercepted or overheard. We wanted to quietly remove you from the town so we could speak in private. Bundling you into a car would have been ideal and has worked for us in the past."

"It would not have been ideal for me," Clara snapped.

"In any case," Wimpole ignored her. "When that failed, we resolved to catch you on your afternoon walk, but your robust cynicism prevented our attempts from succeeding. Running out of time, and fearing you would become even more cautious after our failures, we set out to lay a trap. Mr Irving came up with this notion of a dog in a hole, postulating, quite rightly as it has turned out, that you could not resist a call for help."

"Your horrid man put this poor dog in a hole just to catch me,"

Clara glowered. "And now you want my help? You make a poor show of winning my trust or compassion, Mr Wimpole."

Clara was holding the spaniel in her arms, close to her.

"In hindsight, we perhaps underestimated how you might feel about such a thing," Wimpole apologised. "But we are desperate, Mrs O'Harris, and that has us throwing caution to the wind."

"Desperate. National security. Danger. You have yet to tell me what all this is about and how I might aid you? I am no spy."

"Not yet, Mrs O'Harris, but the whole purpose of this subterfuge is to recruit you as one."

"No," Clara said firmly. "I do not involve myself in such nonsense. I am not one for subtlety or lies. I seek out the truth, and that is all I have ever done."

"Then you shall remain a seeker of truth, but you will seek that truth on our behalf," Wimpole said, sounding exasperated. "We have thought long and hard about this, Mrs O'Harris, and resolved ourselves that you are the only one who can do what we need done."

"I am even more amused by your statement!" Clara laughed. "I am the only one who can act as a spy for you?"

"Not precisely, we think you are the only one who can convince the person we wish to spy for us to agree," Wimpole explained.

"How diabolically convoluted!" Clara snapped. "You must have better things to do with your time."

"No, indeed, Mrs O'Harris, we do not, and this is the most important thing to us at this instant. When I say you are the only person we believe can help us, I mean it and I cannot take your refusal for an answer."

Clara stared at him hard.

"Then you do intend to kidnap me?"

"If it comes to that, I shall, yes," Wimpole replied. "But I would rather you joined us willingly."

Clara settled herself back in the pit.

"Fortunately, I have the patience to remain here until someone I like comes to my aid," she informed him.

"Sir, we have tried your way, now it is time for mine," Irving snapped from the shadows alongside his master.

"If that little man tries to come down here, let him know he shall have a rock about the head before his feet touch the ground!" Clara replied, wondering where she might magic such a stone from.

"Irving, it will not be necessary. Mrs O'Harris is a reasonable person, who shall be willing to help us once she understands the seriousness of this matter."

Irving made a sound as if he were not convinced, or possibly he was annoyed he was not to be allowed to deal with Clara. She was making a mental note that as soon as she had the chance she would turn him in to Inspector Park-Coombs.

"Mrs O'Harris, let me begin again," Mr Wimpole spoke. "We need you to come with us in secret to speak to someone who we need to work for us. This man is refusing to aid us."

"What a surprise," Clara muttered. "Have you shown him the same hospitality as you have me?"

"He is refusing to accept that his help could very well save this country from a grave emergency," Wimpole ignored her question. "But we believe he will listen to you. We believe there is a threat over this country from people who wish to see our king dead and our country in turmoil. You have encountered such anarchists once before and foiled their assassination attempt."

"I did," Clara agreed. "Not because I was forced to, though."

"You did so because it was the right thing to do," Wimpole concurred. "Well, now we need you to do the right thing again. There are people in power, who have wealth and influence, who have been caught up in this conspiracy to dismantle the monarchy and, in turn, the government. These people are difficult for us to reach and while they are at large, they present a constant danger."

"If you cannot reach them, then how can I?" Clara replied.

"You cannot," Wimpole answered. "But we have someone who can. Someone we have a hold over which makes him as trustworthy a person as we can find under the circumstances, and also who has the cunning to serve our purpose. However, he is refusing to assist us in this matter, despite our attempts at persuasion. We feel he needs something to spark his conscience, someone who can speak to the better man within him."

"Me?" Clara wondered who it could be they wished her to speak to.

"You, Mrs O'Harris. We have been watching this man for years and each time he comes into contact with you, we have noticed something. He does not behave in the way expected, and he almost appears to want to do the right thing. Thus we have hope that you may be able to persuade him to do as we ask."

"Surely this hold you have over him is enough to do that?" Clara asked.

"No, it is not. It means he will listen to us, but we need to be sure that when the time comes he behaves in a fitting manner. He could easily agree to aid us and then turn the tables as soon as we give him some freedom."

"So, you don't trust him?" Clara frowned. "But you think I can persuade him to do the right thing?"

"It is going to be a tad more complicated than that, Mrs O'Harris," Wimpole was sounding apologetic again. "Along with you being a good influence on him, we fancy you might be the one person he cares enough about to actually be interested in their wellbeing. He owes you a favour or two and so we are hopeful he will do our bidding as an insurance that you shall be released when the time comes."

"Wait!" Clara glared at him. "You are saying you are going to hold me hostage?"

"Not if you freely cooperate with us," Wimpole promised her.

"I refuse to play this game!" Clara told him. "I am not your puppet! Government authority or no government authority, I am not coming with you!"

"Oh, Mrs O'Harris, why could you not be more reasonable," Wimpole groaned. "I really do not have the time for this."

"Now, sir?" Irving asked.

"Now," Wimpole sighed.

"Now what?" Clara was ready to take on Irving if he tried to get down the rope.

But no one appeared over the side of the pit, instead, a canister was throw over the edge and started to spew out smoke. Clara put her sleeve over her face, her eyes prickling with tears as the smoke overcame her. She started to cough, and the spaniel whined, running to a corner of the pit and trying to bury itself in the earth.

Clara kicked the canister as far away from her as she could, but it was already too late. She felt a little light-headed and it was becoming harder to breath. She turned her gaze back up to Mr Wimpole and called him a name that would have made Annie shudder.

"Now, now, Mrs O'Harris, language," Mr Wimpole tutted at her. "This would have been so much easier if you had just helped us willingly."

Clara coughed hard, her eyes burning, the world was fading around her. She wanted to swear at them again, but she could not speak.

Then she was falling into blackness and all concerns departed her.

Chapter Five

F orming a search party to look for Clara was easy enough, seeing as she was good friends with everyone in the home. Not only did the guests (as O'Harris preferred to call his patients) volunteer, but so did the staff. Eventually, a suitable number were chosen to spread out along the route Clara must have taken that day. It was now drawing into the dusky evening, not late enough to be dark, but dimming into that low grey light that signalled the end of the day.

O'Harris was worried about finding his wife before the night came on. Searching for someone after dark was infinitely harder. If she had had an accident that prevented her from calling out to them, they would have to search every inch of the fields and hedgerows looking for her.

There was also the possibility that she had suffered a mishap near one of the farms and been taken into a local home, but if that were the case, and Clara was able to speak to her helpers, he was sure she would have sent a message to the home to let them know where she was.

He had to assume that whatever had happened to Clara had caused her to be so incapacitated she could not get word back to her husband. Every step along the road O'Harris took he hoped to catch a glimpse of her making her way home, looking annoyed and embarrassed by whatever mishap she had found herself in, ready to tell him all about it, and complain over dinner about her bad luck.

But she did not appear, and with each minute that passed with no sign of her, O'Harris' anxiety increased. He told the men to fan out and form a line as they searched across the fields to be sure they missed nothing. They used to do something similar in the war when looking for wounded during brief ceasefires. You never knew where a man might have fallen and then found himself unable to respond to calls. O'Harris had every faith his fellow searchers would do a sound job, but he felt it was beholden on him to find Clara first, and nothing anyone could say would convince him otherwise. It was his duty to discover her and bring her home safely.

He would not cease looking until he had his wife back.

About half-an-hour had passed when they reached the copse which Clara usually rambled through. O'Harris had accompanied her once or twice on her walks when he had some free time and knew her route well. He regretted he had declined to go with her that afternoon, saying he simply had too much work to do. It had been an excuse as O'Harris had never been one for idle walks, but how he wished he had put down his paperwork and followed her. Then she would be at his side and this nightmare would not be unfolding.

The trees of the copse were in full leaf and blocked out most of the remaining light of the day. O'Harris had brought a torch, and he now found it necessary to flick it on so he could look into the densest undergrowth. Each time he did so, he was fearful of catching a glimpse of a shoe or a hand.

It was as he was peering under some brambles that he heard a faint whimpering sound.

O'Harris automatically tuned into the noise, which was somewhat overshadowed by the movement of men all around him. He paused and listened intently, slowly pinpointing where it was coming from.

He moved through some deep bushes and nearly tumbled headfirst into a pit in the earth which was virtually hidden in the shadows of the evening. By luck, his torch beam had shone on the edge of a broken plank of wood, and he had come to a stop before he took a treacherous step into empty air.

From the depths of the hole he heard a sharp bark, followed by a howl so mournful it would have broken the heart of any dog lover. O'Harris peered into the pit, casting his torchlight down into the darkness and illuminating a very dirty spaniel at the bottom.

He was disappointed to see no sign of Clara, but the dog being present caused him to halt and reconsider for just a moment. He knew what his wife was like, he knew if she had heard the dog's whimpers she would have gone to any lengths to try to rescue it. Could this lost dog be somehow linked to her vanishing?

He cast the light of his torch around the pit further, and noticed how the planks at the edge had broken very recently, their white splinters like raw wounds indicating their suffering.

How curious.

It appeared someone had stumbled into this pit, perhaps looking for the dog. The wooden planks did not look as if they would have broken beneath a light-weight spaniel. But a person could easily have been too much for them.

Whether he was seeing what he wanted to see, or being too imaginative in his hopefulness, there was only one thing to do, and that was rescue the dog.

"Hey there, I need a hand!"

O'Harris' call brought several men to the scene, and he had to quickly issue a warning to avoid them falling into the pit.

"This thing is lethal," someone bellowed and O'Harris could not agree more.

Whoever had dug the hole ought to have their head examined, it was a death trap for animals and people.

"We shall worry about seeing it dealt with after we rescue that poor dog."

If the men wondered that O'Harris would stop his search for his wife to help a dog in a hole, no one mentioned it. They were probably all acutely aware that Clara would never forgive them if they simply abandoned the animal to its fate to search for her.

O'Harris was still wondering if the dog was connected to his wife's sudden absence; it was a curious coincidence, if nothing else.

They debated for a while how to get the dog out of the pit. It was too deep for a man to jump down into and then climb out again. They would need a rope or a ladder. O'Harris sent two of the men towards the nearest farm, while he instructed the others to carry on their search. He remained at the side of the pit, something nagging at his guts as he looked down at the dog and it wagged its tail at him hopefully.

"Sir?"

O'Harris glanced up to see Jones beside him. Jones had once served as ground crew in the RFC at the same time as O'Harris was a pilot. When the war was over, he found himself jobless and O'Harris had hired him to drive and maintain his extensive car collection. Though O'Harris liked to drive, and rarely required a chauffeur, it was useful to have the fellow around to move the cars from one place to another, and to drive Clara.

O'Harris had yet to find the courage to allow his wife to drive his cars. He couldn't quite bring himself to let her take one for a spin. The problem was, as that day was demonstrating too clearly, strange things happened to Clara, and there was no knowing what might occur to her on just a short drive down the road. He might never see the car in one piece again.

"Jones, there is something peculiar about all this."

O'Harris circled his torchlight around the edge of the broken planks. Jones had his own torch which he had brought along in his pocket, and he now flicked it on and observed the pit alongside his friend and employer.

"Looks like those planks broke recently."

"Yes," O'Harris nodded. "And I cannot help but wonder if they broke because Clara was here. Maybe she heard the dog and came to aid it, and in doing so she fell into the pit."

"Then, where is she?" Jones asked the obvious.

"Perhaps someone else came along and rescued Clara but left the dog behind. Which would most likely mean she is badly hurt and unable to protest the animal not being aided along with her."

"A troubling thought," Jones agreed.

He was carefully casting the light of his torch around the edges of the pit. At that moment, the spaniel moved from the spot it had been hovering in, and Jones' torch glimmered on the edge of something.

"What is that?" O'Harris pointed.

Jones had moved his torch, but now carefully brought it back and fixed it on the spot where they had both seen something shimmer. The torch did not have a huge distance to its beam, and it was struggling to disperse the shadows of the pit, but they could both clearly make out something cylindrical on the ground.

"I don't like the look of that," O'Harris shuddered. "Reminds me of a smaller version of the gas shells they liked to throw at our boys in the war."

Jones was frowning as he studied the object, but at the top of the pit they were too far away to make out what it really was. They had to wait impatiently until the others finally returned with a ladder from the farm.

Along with them came the farmer, who had heard the tale of a missing woman and was concerned as well. He knew Clara from the times she went past his fields and waved to him; he was upset to think misfortune had befallen her.

"Whose land is this?" O'Harris asked him as the men began to feed the ladder into the pit, being careful to not drop it on the spaniel, which was now bouncing around at the bottom excitedly.

"Ivy Farm," the farmer explained. "But the pit was never like this before. It was an old badger set that was dug out when a terrier disappeared down it and got stuck. But it was nowhere near as deep as this."

"And the wooden planks?" O'Harris pointed out the broken planks.

"No one would be stupid enough to put wooden planks over a hole like this. They will rot through and make it more hazardous than before. Sheep are grazed in this area, imagine one of them tumbling down there."

The farmer shuddered at the thought.

O'Harris was feeling a similar shiver of dread as he imagined all too vividly Clara falling down into that hole.

The ladder was finally in position, and he was determined to be the first down into the pit. He shimmied down and was warmly greeted by the spaniel, which jumped up at his legs and then virtually propelled itself into his arms. It was filthy with mud and obviously agitated about its misfortune. He clasped it under one arm, then went back up the ladder until he was high enough to pass the dog to one of the men. The spaniel never stopped wagging its tail as it was handed across and then placed on the ground next to the pit. It then ran around happily greeting its saviours.

O'Harris dropped to the bottom of the hole again and took a good look around. His eyes were pinned on the strange object he had spotted with Jones. He picked it up and saw it was indeed a metal canister which looked suspiciously like something that would emit gas or smoke. There was embossed writing on the top which proved to be instructions describing how a pin had to be removed to activate the device.

"Jones," O'Harris called the man's name and, once he was looking at him, tossed him up the canister.

"That is suspicious as hell," O'Harris said through gritted teeth.

Jones examined the canister as O'Harris did a circuit of the hole to look for anything else that might indicate where Clara was. Then he returned to the top of the pit and looked around him at the search party.

"I can't ignore the possibility any longer," he said to the anxious faces all around him. "That canister is the last piece of the puzzle to convince me of the thing I had been most worried about. I think Clara has been kidnapped."

Chapter Six

C lara felt groggy and a little sick.

Her throat was sore and there was a scratchiness when she swallowed that she did not care for. She was desperate for a glass of water.

Opening her eyes cautiously, she took in her surroundings.

She was not sure what she had expected, but it had not been a rather well-appointed bedroom with tall windows that allowed in the evening air – unfortunately, they were also barred, and with the best will in the world, Clara was not going to be able to contort herself through the gaps.

She examined the space for a while, taking in a rather nice antique dressing table and regency chair with a pale burgundy covering, along with a taller freestanding mirror, overhead chandelier, and a wardrobe of colossal proportions.

Clara was lying on a bed which was overflowing with pillows and blankets. The only real inconvenience in this entire scenario was that someone had taken the precaution of handcuffing her.

Clara was rather offended by the action, though from a practical perspective, she had to admire the wisdom of her captors. Clara was notoriously uncooperative with people who upset her, and she would have done all in her power to escape. The precaution was certainly wise, even if it did increase her anger.

She climbed off the bed, taking a few moments to recover her equilibrium when she was upright, her head still suffering the aftereffects of being gassed. She wondered what they had used to knock her out. Having a good working knowledge of the deleterious effects certain gasses could have on the body, in particular the lungs, which she had sadly acquired nursing men invalided home from the front, she was somewhat anxious at what might have been used on her.

However, aside from the scratchiness in her throat, she did not feel any terrible side effects of the misadventure, and she seemed to be able to breath just fine. She had to hope her captors had the sense not to use anything truly dangerous against her. Though they did not strike her as the sort of people who would place compassion over necessity.

She took a walk around the room beginning with the window, which naturally drew her attention with its tantalising promise of a way out. She was disappointed to discover that wherever this house was, it was far away from people. All she could see out of the window were rolling lawns and distant trees. She had vaguely entertained the idea of shouting out for help, but that was clearly not going to be feasible. Who would hear her other than her captors? She checked the iron bars across the opening, just to be sure they were well cemented into place and was once again disappointed that her captors had employed rather good masons for the task.

The evening had drawn on since she was abducted, and no doubt O'Harris was now aware she was missing. Perhaps he was even searching for her?

Clara was regretting she had not had the forethought to leave something in the pit that belonged to her and would have clearly indicated where she had been. But she had not anticipated foul play, and by the time she was alert to the possibility, her captors were present, and she could not have written or dropped a note for her husband without them seeing. Still, she should have had the sense to work loose a button discreetly and leave it behind.

Clara was annoyed she had missed an opportunity to send her husband a clue. She just had to hope he had been in her company long enough to be suitably cynical and suspicious, and to fear the worst, first. Clara knew most people liked to think optimistically about things until they had information to confirm a person was really in danger, what she needed was for O'Harris to think like her, and to immediately assume the gravest outcome had occurred, bar one.

She did not want him to be worrying she had come to great harm or – a horrifying thought – that she might be dead. He ought to have enough faith in her to know that was not how Clara O'Harris (*nee* Fitzgerald) behaved in an emergency.

The window was proving a depressing dead end, despite its temptingly open panes. She moved to the dressing table and began a thorough exploration for something that might be useful as a weapon. She had no intention of cooperating with her kidnappers any more than was absolutely necessary, and was determined to make their lives a living hell so they would never consider doing anything like this again.

Whether it was true they were working for the government or not, they had no right to treat her like this, and she was going to make sure they knew it.

Sadly, the dressing table proved to be empty. It was there for show and nothing else. The wardrobe was equally disappointing as it happened to be locked, meaning she could not even consider hiding inside it, though what that would have achieved she could not say. Having explored every inch of the room and determined it was barren of anything useful, the last place she turned to was the door.

She bent down to peer through the keyhole and discovered there was no key in it, that was hardly surprising. For the sake of thoroughness, and because there was nothing better to do, she tried the handle.

Much to Clara's chagrin, the door proved to be unlocked, and it swung open onto a corridor with green striped wallpaper. Clara felt ridiculed by its unlocked state, as if her kidnappers were mocking her abilities as a detective. It had taken her too long to determine the door was her means of exit, because she had assumed they would not have left her in an unlocked room.

The next thing that crossed her mind was that if they were prepared to leave the door unlocked, they were confident she could not escape the house. She doubted they were the sorts of fellows to make obvious mistakes, and the handcuffs on her wrists told her they were well aware of how difficult she could be.

She stepped out into the corridor and glanced up and down. To her left was another window overlooking the same stretch of lawn as the one in her room. She headed towards it and tried its handles, not surprised to find that this one *was* locked. She wondered if it might be possible to break the glass with the right tool, but the panes of the window frame were compact, and she would have to shatter the whole thing from its frame to make an opening wide enough for her to slip through. Such action would alert her captors to what she was up to before she had barely begun.

She turned in the other direction and started walking along the corridor. There were doors on either side of her. As she headed past, she tried their handles and discovered they were all locked. Annoyed that her captors were endeavouring to make it extremely obvious where she was allowed to go – as if herding her like a sheep – she carried on down the corridor, promising herself that someone was going to suffer for this indignation. She was just not yet sure who that would be.

The corridor turned at the end and finished at a landing with flights of stairs running both up and down. Clara glanced up first. That route ended in a door, which when she walked to it and tried the handle proved to be locked.

Muttering unpleasant words under her breath, Clara stomped back down to the landing and then proceeded to follow the stairs downwards, finding herself in a passageway with an open door to her right and another straight ahead.

Through the door to her right, she could see a fire that was burning low and was more for effect than because it was needed. She also had the impression that there were people in that room. People who were being very quiet and waiting to see what she did. Like a sinister game of hide and seek, she could sense them holding their breath and anticipating she would come across them sooner rather than later.

Clara did not want to play this game, so she turned her attention to the only other door that was open. Walking towards it, briefly checking a door on her left as quietly as she could – locked, of course – she stepped across the threshold and found herself in a large kitchen. There was a vague scent of cooking lingering in the air, but it did not seem as if the room had been used recently. The range was stone cold, Clara could see that at a glance, and Annie would have been appalled that it had been allowed to go out.

But what really drew Clara's attention was the man sitting before the range, tied to a chair. She recognised him immediately, even though his head was dropped forward.

"Hello, Mr Chang."

Brilliant Chang lifted his head and looked at her with fierce belligerence, which she was pretty certain she did not deserve.

The Chinese man looked sorry for himself, with a black eye marring what was generally a charming, some might say even handsome, face. His ebony black hair, normally kept pristinely cut and oiled in place, had grown long and hung around his face. He had a savage look in his eyes that did not fill Clara with much confidence.

When he saw her, he tried to shift from his seat as if he would lunge at her, and she heard the rattle of handcuffs.

Not only were Chang's hands cuffed behind his back, but his ankles were shackled too. In short, he looked extremely miserable and sorry for himself.

"Stop looking at me that way, you're the reason I am stuck here," Clara scolded him, holding up her hands to show him her own handcuffs.

Chang had been so busy glowering at her, he had not noticed them until that moment.

"Why are you handcuffed?"

"Because I am here under protest as much as you are," Clara snorted. "I am indignant about the matter, and I shall make sure someone suffers for it."

She raised her voice on this last sentence, casting it in the direction of the other room where she was sure her captors were sitting.

Chang relaxed a fraction in his seat.

"Why have they brought you here?" he asked.

"My vague understanding is they are trying to convince you to aid them, and they think my presence will help. I have a worrying feeling they intend to hold me hostage while you do as they say."

Clara perched against the kitchen table near Chang and wished the range were alight. She suddenly had a chill running down her spine.

"Why would I do anything for you?" Chang huffed.

"Apparently, they are under the mistaken impression you have a sense of duty. They clearly do not know you like I do," Clara responded. "Care to explain this situation to me?"

Chang was about to reply, but his gaze slipped past her to the doorway of the kitchen. Clara glanced over her shoulder, though she already had a hunch who she would see. The gentleman who had kidnapped her was standing in the doorway, just behind him was his dogsbody, Mr Irving.

"It will not be necessary for Mr Chang to supply you with an explanation," the man said pleasantly. "I intend to give you one myself. I am delighted to see you are awake Mrs O'Harris. I must apologise again for the inconvenience I have put you through. Now, would you care for a cup of tea?"

Chapter Seven

Though O'Harris was satisfied he had found the cause of Clara's disappearance, he did not stop the search, just in case he was wrong.

The searchers scoured the fields for ages, looking for a sign of his wife, only to return empty handed. O'Harris met them all at the copse, where he was still turning the canister over and over in his hands. His anger was almost overwhelming as he looked at the object and thought about what might have happened. The only thing keeping his temper in check was the knowledge he must save his wrath for those who had done this to Clara. He would have no mercy upon them.

When everyone had regrouped from the search, they headed back to the Home, leaving the farmer muttering about the extra work that was going to be required to fill in the pit.

At the feet of O'Harris bumbled the spaniel, which had not left the scene even after it was rescued. It seemed to have decided it was best to stay with O'Harris and his search party, and he did not have the heart to shoo it away.

He had no idea where it might have come from, or who might be missing it. He was also wondering how it had ended up being used as bait in the pit to nab his wife.

That had to be it, didn't it?

She had heard the dog's cries, fallen into the pit while trying to rescue it, and then been taken. Which meant her kidnappers had been happy enough to abandon the dog when they took her.

O'Harris glanced down at the muddy creature that was trotting at his feet, sniffing the ground as it went. Clara was going to be furious about all this. She might have forgiven being kidnapped; she would not forgive the dog being left to die in the pit.

It was dark as they returned to the house and made their way inside. Tommy was waiting in the kitchen with Annie. Their late return had fuelled his own anxiety and when O'Harris entered alone his panic peaked. He jumped up from where he was sitting at the table, and Annie had to grab the edge of his shirt sleeve.

"Be calm," she told him firmly.

From her fraught expression, it appeared she had been instructing him in this manner and trying to contain his anguish for quite some time.

It was the last thing the pregnant woman needed, especially when she was struggling with her own fear.

"We didn't find her," O'Harris said, needlessly. "But we have a vague idea of what might have happened to her."

At that point, the spaniel blundered into the kitchen, racing around in a circle and throwing itself at the feet of everyone in greeting. It ended up on its back by Tommy's feet and he glanced down with a frown.

"Where did you come from?"

Tommy's own dogs, Bramble and Pip, were lounging in O'Harris' study, enjoying a well-deserved nap after racing around the grounds of the house all day.

"We found him in a hole," O'Harris explained. "I think someone used him as bait to lure Clara to the same place and then to kidnap her. We found this as well."

O'Harris placed the suspicious canister on the kitchen table then elaborated on the scene they had come across, and why he had come to the conclusion that his wife had been abducted.

As the information sunk in, Tommy lowered himself back into his seat. He was feeling shaken and there was a moment when he was not sure his legs would support him for much longer. The spaniel took this opportunity to settle on his feet, recognising a dog person who would be kindly to it.

"That is such a horrible thing to do," Annie said when O'Harris finished, her hands forming fists. "That poor dog, it must have been so scared."

"Annie, you might want to save some of that concern for Clara," Tommy said quietly.

Annie waved a hand at him.

"Clara is capable of looking after herself and if her kidnappers are not already regretting what they have done, they soon will be. But that poor dog is innocent in all this. When did the poor thing last eat? It looks cold, wet, and starved."

Annie rose from the table and set out to make a platter of food for the dog. The spaniel sensed what she was about and followed at her heels. O'Harris was looking confused.

"She is using the dog's plight to distract herself from worrying about Clara," Tommy explained to him. "But she is right, Clara will have no mercy on her captors."

Tommy glanced at the table where the canister sat, and a smile crossed his lips.

"Look, they had to incapacitate her to capture her, what does that tell you?"

O'Harris felt comforted by Tommy's humour, he relaxed a fraction.

"I sometimes forget how fearsome Clara is," he admitted. "But that is also why I am deeply disturbed she has been taken. Clara would not go without a fight, so they must have had to use strong methods to secure her."

"Hence this," Tommy nudged the canister. "Clara is going to be furious when she wakes up. I hope they know what they have undertaken in upsetting her."

O'Harris groaned and sat down at the table, dropping into the seat Annie had so recently vacated.

"What do I do, Tommy?"

"First of all, we contact the police," Tommy said firmly.

"Yes, I know that. But what do *I* do? I want to be out there searching for her, but where do I begin?"

Tommy was not sure what to say to him, a similar urge had come over him, but with nothing to go on they could not simply wander about the countryside looking for his sister.

"Our only clue is this," Tommy lifted up the canister and examined it. "It has a serial number embossed on the bottom, and the name of the manufacturer. If we could trace who purchased this, that might give us a clue as to who took Clara."

"That's a long shot," O'Harris pulled a face. "There has to be something else."

Tommy was not sure what to suggest. Whoever had taken Clara had clearly done so with the intention of blindsiding any would-be rescuers. She had simply vanished.

"They must have taken her away in a car," he said after a moment. "She would have been unconscious and, even if they could have escorted her on foot, it would have been too risky. Clara would have called out for help, and anyone might have accidentally spotted them."

"Then we ask around about unknown cars in the area," O'Harris understood what he was getting at. "A lot of the farmers in the area will take note of unusual vehicles driving by because of the risk of farm thefts."

"We should also ask around about strangers in the area. They had to have been here a while to set up their trap. It was too elaborate to have been done on the spur of the moment."

"And they had to do it when Clara was not around to notice what they were up to. I would suspect they dug the pit and lined it overnight, thereby avoiding attention."

O'Harris was feeling more positive now he saw a path forward.

"One last thing is the dog," Tommy said. "It had to have come from somewhere. Either they stole it or bought it, whichever the case, we may be able to find more witnesses to these people that way."

With so many avenues for investigation, O'Harris felt a sense of hope filling him. There had to be a way they could figure out who was behind the kidnapping and get Clara home.

Annie was returning with an enamel bowl filled with various cold meats she had found in the larder, and some cubes of old bread, along with some chunks of cheese. The spaniel was beside itself as it bounced around her feet, in real danger of tripping her up. She put the bowl on the floor, and it dived into the food, its sides seeming to cave in as it virtually inhaled the contents. Annie stood back with her hands on her hips and watched it.

"Poor little thing."

The two men watched the spaniel, the dog's antics a welcome distraction from their raging thoughts.

"I should ring the police," O'Harris said at last, standing up. "Inspector Park-Coombs will be very upset."

"With any luck he will put the constabulary on high alert on our behalf and have Clara home within the next few hours," Tommy added.

O'Harris gave Tommy a sad smile, appreciating his attempt at reassuring him, but finding it hard to be so convinced. He only had confidence in himself to find Clara, it was like a burden sitting upon him. He could not even explain it to Tommy, as it would mean implying he did not think the man could find his own sister. But O'Harris really felt this was upon him, and only he could do this.

He left the room to make his telephone call, leaving Tommy and Annie alone. Aside from the rattle of the bowl as the dog consumed its dinner, there was no sound in the room and the stillness felt oppressive.

"Clara would hate to think how upset John is," Annie said sadly, sitting down. "She doesn't like to worry him."

"Clara never thinks about worrying people," Tommy scoffed. "That is why she is always getting into trouble."

"No, you are wrong. She worries a great deal about others, but she never says a thing. I know she will be fretting about us all, rather than herself."

Tommy saw the anxiety finally penetrating Annie's calm façade and he reached out for her hand.

"We will find her, and then those who took her will suffer horribly," he promised her.

"I know. I know we will," Annie nodded, though her tone did not sound entirely convinced. "I am just being silly."

"No, you are just concerned and that is natural. I am worried too. But to go to such effort as these people have done, they must wish to keep Clara alive and that is something."

Annie looked alarmed. Until that moment it had not crossed her mind that Clara's life might be in danger. Tommy realised his mistake and quickly tried to take back his words.

"I didn't mean she was in danger like that. I was trying to point out these people clearly wish to take care of her, and her wellbeing is not in question."

Annie shook her head.

"I have never felt so scared as I do in this moment," she said quietly. "I know Clara has been in scrapes before, but usually I only learn about them afterwards, when everything is back to normal, and people are safe. Right now, we have no idea where she is, or who has her, and it terrifies me."

Tommy squeezed her hand tighter.

"Clara is tough, and she takes no nonsense from anyone," he said firmly. "I think the people who really need to be afraid are the ones who have captured her. They shall be suffering far worse than us at her hands."

Annie managed just a wisp of a smile at his words.

"Clara is pretty horrible when she wants to be."

"And she will be fuming they left the dog behind. She will show no mercy for that."

As if on cue, the spaniel ceased attempting to lick out every last crumb from the bowl, which was clean anyway, and bounded over to Annie and Tommy. It crouched down and wagged its tail at them in an appeasing fashion. Tommy reached down and stroked its little head, and it rolled over onto its back.

"Oh, that thing is filthy," Annie tutted. "It will need a bath."

Tommy tickled the dog's chest.

"He," he said, fussing the dog. "*He* will need a bath."

Chapter Eight

"I must apologise again for this inconvenience, Mrs O'Harris, but it is really the fault of our friend here," Mr Wimpole declared in a distracted fashion.

"You do not care at all about my inconvenience," Clara responded. "But I shall be sure to make you very sorry for what you have done."

Chang gave a low chuckle.

"She is right about that. There is no mercy from that woman when you upset her."

Mr Wimpole was unmoved.

"This whole matter could have been easily resolved if Mr Chang had felt more patriotic toward the country which has supplied him with such opportunities. That is hardly my fault."

Chang sneered at the rebuke.

"Perhaps, Mr Wimpole, now you have me in your charge, you would elaborate on this threat to the nation you are so concerned about," Clara demanded, her gaze stony as she studied the man. "I ought to at least know why you are so determined to keep me here and disrupt my life."

"Very well, Mrs O'Harris, an explanation is perfectly reasonable and hopefully you will then see your way forward to persuading our friend here to assist us," Wimpole vaguely pointed at Chang. "This matter goes back many months and has required a great deal of observation from my particular department. We have been investigating the people involved in this scheme for over six months and are now reaching a point where we could press our case home if we were just able to get one last crucial piece of evidence."

"Here is the part where I come in," Chang grumbled.

Clara held up her hand for silence.

"You are not explaining, Mr Wimpole, you are telling me what you want Chang to do without giving me the reason behind it. Try again."

Wimpole looked at Clara, exasperated. Behind him, Mr Irving twitched as if he would like to do more than merely handcuff Clara. She had already decided he was the more volatile out of the pair, but that did not necessarily make him the most dangerous.

"I was endeavouring to explain," Wimpole protested.

"You very clearly do not understand the meaning of the word. Let me outline the matter for you so we have a full understanding. I want to know what this national crisis is, not some vague mutterings about a threat to our country. I want to know what you *actually* mean. Are we talking war or something else?

"Secondly, I want you to explain to me why Brilliant Chang, a notorious criminal not renowned for having any shred of honour or any concern for his adopted country, is suddenly the only person you think capable of saving this nation. I might add, it rather looks to me as if you are clutching at straws, especially as you have kidnapped me in the hopes this will somehow lead to Chang agreeing to your plans.

"Personally, I think it more likely Chang will use me as a means to escape you and disappear for good."

Chang was grinning as she described his character, unfazed by her deprecating words. Wimpole gave him a sour look.

"Mr Chang was hardly our first choice, but we find ourselves here out of necessity," Wimpole sighed, then he glanced at Clara. "The threat is indeed deadly enough to possibly bring about another war. Germany suffered a severe battering at our hands, but to suppose they were truly defeated is to misunderstand their resolve or character. It is early days, but there are new political movements forming in the country, some of them are Communist and emulate the new Russian way of governance, while others are still an unknown quantity.

"We have little influence over politics in another country, but we do observe and wonder what it shall mean for us. In the meantime, we find ourselves with a more obvious threat in the form of a handful of secret British organisations which supported the German cause during the war and are actively working to aid Germany in any future conflict."

"But the war is over," Clara pointed out.

"The fighting is over, but the tensions that brought about the war remain and truly, with the right catalyses, we could see ourselves straight back to the horrors of the previous decade. It is not something anyone cares to think about unless they have to. My department is responsible for rooting out subversive groups who might be trying to encourage war and exploit any political discord within this country to leave us vulnerable in a future conflict."

Clara frowned. Wimpole's words shook her. It was over a year since she had foiled an anarchist plot to blow up the King, but she still vividly remembered how it made her feel to know some of her fellow countrymen were prepared to go to such lengths to have their opinions heard.

"How serious are these threats?"

"It is hard to say," Wimpole replied. "It may be the threats we know about are not the ones we should truly fear, and that there are worse secrets we have no knowledge about. But we can only go with what we have, and one of the biggest threats at the moment, is a movement among some of the manufacturers in this country who benefited financially during the last war, who believe another conflict would serve to significantly increase their profits."

"That is horrible!" Clara was appalled. "Are you saying there are some people who see war as a business opportunity?"

"That is rather naïve of you, Clara," Chang said, amused by her words. "You should know, as well as anyone, that people without morals are quick enough to look to profit over their own conscience."

Clara did know that, but she did not wish to mention it to Chang.

"A number of manufacturers became extremely wealthy, extremely fast, during the war, due to contracts for weapons, vehicles, and other supplies that were necessary for the conflict," Wimpole explained. "These same people are not happy with the smaller profits they have returned to now our country is at peace, and they want to change that. They have formed a conglomerate and are working secretly to try to stir up political unrest that could lead to war. They are not concerned who that war might be with, either. They are encouraging tensions in Ireland, as well as South Africa and within Europe.

"Their end goal is simple, generate a war that enables them to sell their products and make a fortune. They are extremely dangerous, because they not only have political clout, but the wide-ranging influence necessary to produce another war."

"Why have they not been arrested?" Clara asked.

"Because they have not done anything wrong, at least nothing that we have evidence for," Wimpole explained. "Talking about politics and business is not illegal. If we could prove they were sending important information to contacts abroad, we could then argue they were participating in espionage for a foreign nation, but that is where we find ourselves stumped."

"And where they want me to come in," Chang had a nasty grin on his face. "They have been trying for months to get one of their people into the inner circle of these individuals without success. They need someone who already has access and who could move among them without raising alarm."

"A man like you?" Clara raised an eyebrow at him.

"Turns out, people who like making guns and other weapons of war, are also rather fond of being off their head on my drugs," Chang winked at her. "I suppose it is how they sleep at night."

Chang was a sophisticated criminal; it was how he had first crossed paths with Clara. He sold drugs to the upper classes and walked in the circles of the rich and famous. He had other criminal businesses, and Clara did not care to pry into them too deeply for the sake of her sanity, but his primary one remained selling all manner of narcotics at steep prices to those with the money to pay for them, and the lack of sense to avoid them.

"You really find yourself with Chang being your only option?" Clara turned her penetrating gaze on Wimpole.

"Tragically, that appears to be the case," Wimpole sighed. "We have endeavoured to turn others already within the organisations, but our biggest struggle is finding someone who can move freely between the various players without raising suspicion. Equally, we need someone who is capable of keeping a secret and not giving themselves away. All these factors have led us to conclude that Mr Chang is our only possible option."

"And what do you want Chang to do?" Clara asked.

"We need him to get inside the private homes of the people in question and look for documents that would give us hard proof of what they are doing. We need evidence they are selling secrets to our enemies in order to trigger a war and put us at a disadvantage. Only then might we be able to crack down on this threat."

"That is a lot of maybes and mights," Clara observed. "I can see why Chang is hesitant."

"Thank you, Clara," Chang grinned at her. "I forgot how agreeable you can be."

"Don't get cocky," Clara growled at him. "You are still not my favourite person, and if you can be of use to this country and prevent a war, you should do all in your power to do just that, without needing extra persuasion."

"I would be harming my own business," Chang spluttered. "Not to mention risking my life and reputation. You think I will be welcome at the homes of the rich and famous if I am caught snooping around someone's office and stealing papers?"

"We all have to take risks to protect our country and the fragile peace we find ourselves in," Wimpole scolded him.

"And what exactly are you doing to protect it? Other than disrupting my life," Chang huffed. "And kidnapping young ladies who have nothing to do with any of this."

"He does have a point, in that regard," Clara added. "I am not happy about being here."

"You refused to aid us!" Wimpole snapped at her.

"I was stuck in a pit in the ground, at your mercy, and you failed to offer me any sort of explanation as to what precisely you desired from me," Clara retorted. "That hardly inspired trust."

"You could have had a little more faith," Wimpole grumbled. "I showed you my papers."

"You did, and I was not impressed by those either," Clara replied. "I value the truth over all things, and your actions seem more like the sort of thing a rogue like Chang would do rather than men working for the government."

"Steady on!" Chang snapped.

Clara ignored him.

"Now I am here, my understanding is that I am supposed to be leverage to convince Chang to work for you? Perhaps supply him with a nudge to his moral compass that will have him suddenly discover he has a trace of honour in his soul?"

Chang was sniggering under his breath as she berated Wimpole.

"You seem to assume Chang holds me in higher regard than his own wellbeing or his business," Clara said. "Which I can assure you is not the case. Chang has no regard for me, other than as a nuisance who occasionally proves useful to him."

It was at these words that Chang stopped sniggering, and Clara felt her gaze drifting towards him. He looked deeply uncomfortable.

"Unfortunately for you, Mrs O'Harris, your dim view of Mr Chang is not entirely accurate," Wimpole had a new smile on his face. "We have been watching Mr Chang for a long time, and when we learned of his association with you it drew our interest, especially as on more than one occasion Mr Chang has gone out of his way to protect you."

Chapter Nine

C hang looked sheepish, which was not an expression Clara ever imagined seeing on his face. She gave him a hard stare, waiting for confirmation of what Wimpole had just said, and wanting to know precisely what was going on.

Why would Brilliant Chang, a notorious criminal, and a man Clara had regularly clashed with, be protecting her?

Chang said nothing.

"It seems our Asian friend is not inclined to explain himself," Wimpole declared snootily. "I shall, therefore, elaborate on the matter. Mrs O'Harris, you have found yourself involved in some interesting cases over the years, and some of them have had a wider impact than you were probably aware of at the time and have made you a few enemies you have never even heard of. You have solved a police corruption case, involving our friend Chang here, which caused a number of constabularies to reassess their own people and revealed some alarming problems with individuals happily taking bribes from criminals.

"The result of these investigations means that many in the criminal world no longer have an insider in the police force and this is disagreeable to them. Then there was the matter of the criminal gang

Chang's sister attempted to set up here in Brighton. It had a lot of influence, and your destruction of the gang left behind people who have a grudge against you.

"Lastly, there was the matter of the airship that you investigated and discovered that one of our peers of the realm was supplying information and technology to the enemy. He was one of those very people who would desire another war to suit their needs. Your unravelling of that masterplan made you some very high-status enemies."

"Talking about that airship case, I was in contact with a gentleman who was involved in the secret service, and I should like to speak to him again about this current affair," Clara wished she had thought of that before. Captain Steadfast had worked with her to reveal the secret airship base and would surely be furious at her being imprisoned here.

"The gentleman you are referring to does not work for our department," Wimpole said quickly.

"And what department is that, precisely?"

Wimpole gave a cough, indicating he was not going to reply to that question.

"My point is that you have made some dangerous enemies, and these people would be inclined to cause you harm or, at the very least, manoeuvre you out of the detective business, just so they could get on with their nefarious schemes. Chang hears about their plans through his business associates and, I dare say, he has people specifically listening out for any mention of your name in the wrong places. We have found on multiple occasions that when someone has discussed the possibility of coming after you, he has intervened and ensured they did not."

Clara's gaze returned to Chang, who was making a determined effort not to look at her. She found it hard to believe the self-centred, virtually heartless criminal could care that much about her wellbeing that he would put himself in harm's way to prevent anything happening to her.

Yet, she did not doubt what Wimpole was saying. He had brought her here for a good reason, and he must be pretty confident Chang would be moved to help them if he thought she was in danger to have done that.

"Stopping evil men intent on causing me harm and working for you because you intend to detain me for a while, are rather different things," Clara said to Wimpole. "You cannot keep me here indefinitely. People will already be looking for me."

"Quite correct, we cannot keep you here indefinitely," Wimpole told her, his face hardening as his expression grew sinister. "We shall have to move you, and we have the power and discretion to make you disappear, Mrs O'Harris, if we choose to."

"That is criminal!" Clara snarled at him. "It is underhand!"

"And what is your point?" Wimpole laughed. "This is an underhand business, and for the sake of the safety of this country I would cause to disappear a dozen women like you. Mr Chang is fully aware of how far I would go to ensure his cooperation."

Clara reflected on how far Wimpole had already gone and felt a shudder running down her spine. There was something about the man, something that bordered on madness, that she didn't like and which troubled her deeply. If she could not get herself out of this pickle swiftly, she fancied he would do exactly as he said and take her somewhere no one would ever find her.

Her attention bounced back to Chang.

"Chang, we need to talk."

"I hoped you would be that way inclined," Wimpole almost clapped his hands in delight to see his plan coming together. "We shall give you some privacy, come along Irving."

He departed the room with his dogsbody, though neither closed the kitchen door. Clara watched as they retreated to the room they had come from, then she sat down in one of the chairs by the table.

"What a mess," she groaned.

"I can't believe they caught you," Chang snapped at her suddenly. "What could they have done to manage that?"

"They set up a trap with a dog in distress," Clara shrugged.

"Really? How stupid can you be?"

"And how did you end up here, Chang?" Clara snapped back at him, not in the mood to be berated by the criminal.

Chang immediately fell silent and refused to reply. Clara took a deep breath, knowing she was going to have to be the reasonable one in this conversation or else they would get nowhere.

"It doesn't matter how we ended up here, what matters is how we escape," Clara glanced around the kitchen, aware that there were mechanical means for listening in on conversations. That was how a lot of information was gathered in the war – put two people together, seemingly alone, and let them talk freely while someone listened to their conversation at a distance.

"How do you propose we escape?" Chang asked sullenly.

"I don't know as yet, but now there are two of us, which is better than just one," Clara sighed. "Of course, you could just do as they say and then this would be over and done with."

"You cannot mean that?" Chang looked at her, appalled. "You heard what they want me to do!"

"Some people would do it just for the sake of aiding their country," Clara pointed out, knowing this would not go far with Chang. "If I thought I could help stop a future war in which millions of young men might be hurt or die, I would do all in my power."

"And that is why they caught you with a dog in distress," Chang grumbled at her. "They are asking me to put my life on the line. The risk is enormous. If I were discovered, it would not just be the end of my business, it would be the end of me. I am very precious about staying alive, as you may recall."

Clara made a gruff noise at the back of her throat, unimpressed.

"Talking about the greater good and honour with you is rather pointless," she conceded. "But I should have thought your professional pride would have made you want to at least try."

"Professional pride?" Chang snorted.

"Yes, they think you are the only person capable of doing this. Are you saying they are wrong, and you are not as sly, cunning, nefarious and double-dealing as they suppose?"

"If you are trying to flatter me, you are falling short," Chang barked.

"Then you are saying you couldn't do it?"

"Do not try to trick me, Clara! I shall not be played that way."

Clara narrowed her eyes at him.

"I think I could do it," she said quietly.

Chang's own eyes widened in surprise.

"You wouldn't dare!"

"I have never been one to sit around and wait to be rescued, not really my style," Clara remarked airily. "For a start, it is rather boring. It seems to me, finding out this vital information that could save the country would be much more productive, and I would be saving myself in the process."

"You have no concept of the danger you would be in!"

"I actually have a pretty good idea, and this is not my first time dealing with dangerous people who are spying on our nation," Clara responded. "It seems to me, it would be my duty to find that information."

"Do not be a fool!" Chang hissed at her, and there seemed a genuine hint of concern on his face.

Clara was pleased by that, with any luck he believed her threats, which were at least partially true. She *would* prefer to be the one to act, rather than sit around and wait for someone else to succeed on her behalf. She never was good at giving over responsibility to others.

She had only been toying with Chang, trying to convince him, when she voiced the idea of going in herself to find these secrets, but now it was occurring to her that it might not be such a bad thing after all. She could sort this mess out, be free of Wimpole and get on with her life again.

A bit of action suited Clara and she was a little too confident in her own abilities at times to see the potential perils of her suggestion.

"Clara O'Harris, you must desist in this notion at once!" Chang insisted, his tone fierce. "You have no idea the people you will be facing, the power they wield and the danger you would be in if caught."

"I would not be caught," Clara said confidently.

"You are sitting alongside me because you fell for a puppy in peril scam!" Chang reminded her.

"I should point out to you that they attempted on several other occasions to catch me, and I avoided all those attempts. They had to be extremely cunning and devious to finally lure me into trouble, and I shall not be fooled that way again. Next time I become aware of a dog in distress, I shall make sure the ground is not covered with rotten planks to cause me to tumble."

Chang, who had no idea how the process of the dog trap had actually worked, frowned at her and tried to think of something to say. It turned out, trying to reason with Clara was almost as difficult as trying to reason with him.

"You have to consider the alternatives," Clara said at last. "What are they going to do if you continue to refuse? I don't suppose they will do me physical harm, but I do believe they will make me disappear somehow, and probably you as well. We shall never be heard of again. I have seen how that can happen."

Clara was thinking of the zeppelin case from the year before, where a man had apparently disappeared off the face of the earth and no one could trace him. The poor fellow had been imprisoned for years, until he made a final desperate act to escape which ended in disaster.

"All the time we are sitting here, your business is at risk of being taken over by one of your rivals," Clara added. "How long before someone takes charge, assuming you are dead and your whole organisation is taken from you?"

Chang gritted his teeth as Clara struck a nerve. She was right, sooner rather than later someone would attempt to replace Chang as the head of his criminal organisation, assuming he was either dead or had left the country.

"The longer you sit here in sullen silence, the worse it is for you," Clara persisted. "Your stubbornness is admirable, and I would have done very much the same in your shoes. In fact, it pains me to suggest you work with our captors, but it is the only option left to us if we wish to escape this trouble."

Chang sniffed haughtily, trying to come up with a response that would knock Clara's sound argument down in flames and failing. At last, his shoulders slumped, and he groaned to himself.

"This is terrible."

"No, it is not," Clara replied. "It is inconvenient, and we can resolve inconveniences. Now, are you agreed we must cooperate with these people, at least for the time being?"

Chang caught the insinuation in her words as she hoped he would.

A sparkle returned to his eyes.

"You have something in mind?"

"I merely think helping them is our duty, and is really our only option," Clara replied, before she gave him a wink.

Chang's smile grew.

"For the first time since you arrived in this kitchen, you have said something truly sensible," Chang chuckled.

Clara was offended, but it was not the time to argue. The important thing was that they were beginning to work together and there was hope ahead. She smiled back at the criminal.

"Perhaps, it is time we asked for Mr Wimpole to return and to accept his proposal?" she suggested.

"Perhaps it is," Chang agreed.

Chapter Ten

I nspector Park-Coombs arrived at O'Harris' home flustered and agitated. He was badly dressed, having been at home when the call came about Clara being missing. He had been lounging around in his pyjamas and dressing gown after taking a long bath, hoping for a quiet night and an early bedtime. The arrival of a constable on his doorstep with the news Clara had gone for a walk and never returned filled him with such panic he had buttoned his shirt up all wrong, and he had odd shoes on his feet.

"Captain O'Harris!" he declared at the sight of the man opening his front door. "Has she returned?"

"No, Inspector, and we are confident she has been kidnapped," O'Harris said bleakly.

He showed the inspector through to the kitchen while explaining to him the events of the day. He left out no detail, no matter how mundane, and concluded with the story of the discovery of the gas canister.

Inspector Park-Coombs found Tommy and Annie in the kitchen, he nodded to them, his brow pulled deep into a frown and then picked up the empty canister lying on the table.

"Nasty business," he winced to himself, then heard his words and knew the effect they must have on the others. "Clara shall be fine. She is the sort of person who always gets herself out of trouble."

"I wish I could feel so hopeful, Inspector," O'Harris mirrored his frown. "My wife has never disappeared like this before. She would have fought tooth and claw to avoid being kidnapped."

"Hence the need for such drastic measures," Park-Coombs indicated the canister in his hand. "Her kidnappers had a good idea of how difficult Clara was likely to be."

"You must search the entire county!" Annie declared suddenly, her own anxieties finally overwhelming her.

Tommy reached out for her hand and clasped it.

"The inspector will do everything he can," Tommy promised her.

"I shall leave no stone unturned," Park-Coombs swore to them. "Now, have you considered how *you* might go about investigating this case?"

"We have a few plans," Tommy said, then he outlined the ideas he had already discussed with O'Harris.

"I shall ask among my constables to see if any of them have noticed unusual cars in the neighbourhood," Park-Coombs replied once he had finished. "I have several boys who patrol around the countryside and might have seen these cars on their routes. They can also ask around at the local farms, for further witnesses. As for the missing dog, no one has reported an absent spaniel to us, though that is not to say someone is not looking for the fellow. People do not always think to report lost dogs to the police."

"I take it you have had no reports of strangers about the area acting suspiciously?" O'Harris asked.

"That is one thing that is curious," Park-Coombs said. "I do recall a report from a local farmer about two individuals he saw lurking near his fields. He did not recognise them, and farmers are always wary about strangers near their land, out of fear of robbers."

"We should speak to this farmer!" Tommy said urgently. "Right now, see if he can tell us anything more."

Park-Coombs attempted to calm him, but saw it was a fruitless effort, and in truth, he wanted to speak to the fellow as well. In his experience, you could not waste time in a missing person matter when it was plain the victim had been kidnapped. He agreed, therefore, to take Tommy and O'Harris to the local farmer so they could speak to him again about what he saw.

Annie reluctantly agreed to stay behind. She was looking exhausted, both emotionally and physically and O'Harris insisted she must go up to the master bedroom and get some sleep. Annie did not want to concede to the fact she was desperate for rest, saying she would feel awful trying to sleep while Clara was in danger, but Tommy slowly convinced her it was for the best. She had to think of the baby and needed all her strength for whatever lay ahead.

Exhausting herself would not help Clara.

Annie finally agreed, though not without a considerable show of reluctance. She wished them all good luck, and extracted a promise they would report any news immediately to her, even if it meant waking her. With their sworn oaths made, she headed upstairs.

Outside, O'Harris had fetched a car, and the inspector and Tommy were bundling into it. Park-Coombs knew the way to the farm, and it did not take them longer than ten minutes to reach it. The farmer's fields stretched around the tail end of Clara's walking route, where she would pass on her way home.

They found the farmer in his kitchen, about ready for his bed – farmers preferring early nights to compensate for their early mornings. He looked at them through tired eyes, while his wife and daughter fussed in the background, thinking that there was some emergency on the farm. It took several minutes of Park-Coombs explaining the matter before they calmed down and realised there was no need for them to begin making plans for staying up all night.

The farmer's wife had to be stopped from boiling up a kettle and several pans of water – in her experience, most farm emergencies required copious amounts of boiled water. When everyone was finally settled around the old farm table, the inspector was able to begin asking them the questions he needed answered.

"Mr Sargent, I want to know about the men you saw the other week near your fields?"

Mr Sargent had been a farmer since he was old enough to feed the cattle by himself. He had inherited his farm from his father, who had inherited it from *his* father. Sargent was now in his fifties; a scrawny man whose appearance belied the strength he had in his body when the need arose. He loved his farm, and he protected it with a hawk's eye for anything suspicious. When he had spied two men lurking near the wall of his back field he had paid them close attention.

"They weren't locals, I know everyone around here," he began. "They were dressed in dark trousers and wearing jackets, like they had wandered out from the city and did not know what to do with themselves. They were not dressed as labourers, that is for sure, though it might also be said they were not dressed as typical farm robbers. Still, I did not like the look of them."

Sargent reflected back on that day when he had witnessed the two men, and the unease that had stirred in his belly.

"They were just talking and smoking, watching the road rather than me. I had cattle in that field at the time. I took a while longer than normal to feed them and check the herd, so I could keep my eye on the men. They never moved and never seemed to notice me."

"What time of day was this?" Tommy asked when Sargent came to a pause.

The farmer based his timings on the events of his day, not possessing a pocket watch. He was like his grandfather before him, living his life by the sun arcing through the sky and listening to his belly to know when it was time for his meals.

"It was the afternoon," Sargent answered. "I had gone to check on the cattle and give them some extra feed as several are in calf. I always do that after my lunch at one o'clock."

"The same time Clara goes for her walk," O'Harris observed.

"I know your wife, sir," Sargent said uneasily, suddenly feeling the need to put on his best manners around the captain and his friend. Everything felt so serious with the police involved. "She is a nice lady, always waves at me and says hello as she passes by."

"That is Clara, all right," O'Harris pulled a forlorn smile onto his face. "Did you see her that day?"

"No," Sargent shook his head. "I was at the field at the right time for her to go past, but all I saw were those two men. They hung around for a couple of hours. I know because I kept coming back to check. It must have been between four and five when they finally left, as I remember hearing the distant chiming of the clock in the church tower a few miles away. You can hear it clear as day if the wind is blowing in the right direction."

"They had to have been waiting for Clara," Tommy decided. "But why did she not appear?"

"Maybe she did not go for a walk that day?" Park-Coombs

suggested.

"What day was this?" O'Harris asked Sargent.

The old farmer blew out his cheeks as if he had been asked to perform an extremely complicated sum. He considered for a while, before supplying an answer.

"I think it was the Wednesday before last."

O'Harris did his own mental calculations and frowned.

"She went for a walk that day, I am sure of it."

"Knowing Clara, she probably didn't like the look of those men any more than Mr Sargent did, and decided to give them a wide berth," Park-Coombs rumbled. "Just a shame she did not mention anything about them when she returned home."

They fell into silence at this statement. Sargent looked despondent to have been of so little help.

"I hope you find her," he said. "She is a nice lady."

"It is awful to think of a woman being whisked away like that," his wife chimed in from behind him.

She was clutching at her daughter, a grown woman herself, who was trying to extract herself from her mother's grasp, embarrassed by the display of emotion.

There was nothing more to be done at the farm. Sargent saw them out with further wishes for success and they headed to the car.

"Someone was spying on Clara," O'Harris said bleakly when they reached the car. "Why did she not tell me?"

"Maybe Clara did not realise?" Tommy suggested.

"Or she thought she could handle the matter by herself," Park-Coombs said sourly.

They all froze at his words. He shook his head.

"I shouldn't have said that. Clara has a good head on her, she is more sensible than that."

But the words had been spoken, and they spun in all their minds. Had Clara been foolish enough to think she could deal with any threat against her alone?

And if so, what did that mean for her eventual capture?

Chapter Eleven

Clara called for Wimpole to return, saying they had come to a decision. He had an irritating smile on his face as he entered the kitchen, assuming Clara had finally convinced Chang to do as he was told. She wished she could have said something to wipe that smile from his face, but the truth was they had decided to agree to his arrangement.

"Mr Chang is willing to undertake the task you have asked of him," Clara told him, taking a good look at Irving as he lurked in the doorway.

He had a sinister habit of glowering at her, and she had not forgiven him for abandoning the spaniel when he had brought her out of the pit. She had seen no sign of the dog, and she knew they had had no intention of saving it. She narrowed her eyes at him.

When this was over, he would be the first person she came for and would make sure he was arrested for his actions.

"I am overjoyed to hear that!" Wimpole declared, once again narrowly avoiding clapping his hands together in delight.

Mad, Clara reminded herself, quite mad.

Whoever he worked for, she hoped they had a better grasp on their sanity than he did.

"There is no time to waste, I shall have you released at once so you can begin to make the arrangements," Wimpole beamed.

"There is one other thing," Clara spoke before he could get carried away. "I am going with Chang."

Wimpole looked stunned, even Chang was surprised. Clara had not mentioned this idea to him when she had convinced him he had to cooperate with Wimpole.

"Mrs O'Harris, that is unacceptable. You are to remain here to guarantee Mr Chang's good faith," Wimpole said sternly.

"I would rather go with him and guarantee his 'good faith' in person," Clara replied. "I am not fond of sitting around and doing nothing. Besides, you have explained to me the seriousness of this matter, the consequences to the country in the event of failure. I cannot, in good conscience, ignore such a threat and wish to do my part."

"How noble," Wimpole said, looking unsure of himself. "But you will be going into territory where you are known as a detective."

"People may know my name, but how many know my face?" Clara asked him. "I doubt many do, and with some cosmetic adjustments, I believe I can avoid anyone realising who I really am."

"You are stark, raving mad!" Chang snapped at her.

"Yes, probably," Clara shrugged at him. "But I am not going to just sit here and wait for you to sort things out. I could not bear it."

"Mrs O'Harris, I couldn't allow such an action, even if it is heroic," Wimpole interjected. "Should anything happen to you, I would never forgive myself."

Clara pinned him with a gaze.

"You had me fall into a hole, gassed me, and now have me sitting here handcuffed, threatening to make me disappear. Rather late to suddenly develop a sense of responsibility for my welfare."

Wimpole was stung by her words. He did not seem to know what to do, it was Irving who broke the tension.

"Send her," he said to his employer. "She will keep Chang honest, and she will only be a nuisance if she remains here."

"Mr Irving, you understand me so much better than I had thought," Clara responded to his suggestion with a grin.

Irving cast her a dirty look. They were enemies, of that she was sure. He had decided he hated her probably around the time he had had to go to the effort of constructing the pit to ensnare her, and things had not improved when they had met and conversed.

She fancied he would not care if she were caught on this little escapade and ended up dead at the hands of dastardly people.

"Mr Irving, it is really unspeakable to place a woman in such danger," Wimpole blathered, oblivious to the contradiction in his statement.

Chang tutted in his seat.

"You will never get around her, just give in to the stupid woman," he snapped. "With any luck, she will get herself in so much trouble everyone will be completely distracted, and I shall be able to steal the documents you want."

"I was not going to refer to my behaviour as troublesome, but I do believe I shall be a worthwhile addition to this scheme," Clara added. "Chang will have more chance of success with a comrade to back him up."

Wimpole was too astonished by the suggestion to speak. Of course, he could still refuse, and with Clara handcuffed what could she do about it?

But Clara had a look about her of someone who could cause an awful lot of bother if she did not get her way, and the slight smile on her lips hinted to Wimpole that she was already contemplating how difficult she could make his life.

"Send her and be done with it," Irving hissed in his master's ear.

Clara made a note of his behaviour, reflecting that Wimpole seemed very obliging to his subordinate and might not be the true master of the events unfolding before them.

"I wish I could be so indifferent to the matter," Wimpole said to Irving, in a whisper loud enough for them all to hear. "But she is a woman."

"She is a problem," Irving snorted. "And she might just have a point about being able to help Chang."

Chang shot a look at Clara, which implied he didn't like people thinking he needed any help. Clara would have folded her hands across her chest and looked pleased with herself if she were not wearing handcuffs.

Wimpole took a long, deep breath.

"Very well," he said. "I suppose the lady might be a good addition to our scheme and I know that Mrs O'Harris is a woman of her word and will promise to do her utmost to find the evidence we need, and not simply try to escape us the second an opportunity presents itself."

He pinned his eyes on Clara, as if he would have her make that promise there and then. Clara was amused that he really thought she would be a woman of her word, when her promise was extracted under duress.

"Of course," she responded to him, doing her best to look serious. "You have persuaded me this is a matter we should all be concerned about. We do not want to face another war, and if by risking my life I can prevent such a calamity, I will gladly do it."

Clara could feel Chang's eyes burning into her, but she was glad he did not make his usual snide remarks at her statement. She needed Wimpole to believe her.

"Please, Mrs O'Harris, if you would give your word that when you leave this property you will do all you can to retrieve those documents?" Wimpole asked.

"I swear, when I leave this property, I will go to any length to recover the documents you require," Clara replied without hesitation.

Irving gave her a nasty look, and she suspected he doubted her, but he did not contradict her.

"Then, it is just left for Mr Chang to give his word that he will do the same."

Wimpole turned his attention on Chang.

Chang was clearly simmering under the weight of his fury. He sucked in his lips, as if he feared he might explode and tell them all what he thought about their 'honour' and giving his word. But his eyes shifted to Clara, and she sensed he knew she was right; if he wanted to get out of this house before his entire organisation was taken over by one of his rivals, he had to play this game.

With great reluctance, as if the words caused him pain to speak, he finally relented.

"I swear I shall aid Clara in all her efforts."

Wimpole studied him for a long while, perhaps wondering whether to ask for more, but had the sense to realise he was already pushing his limit as to what Chang would agree to.

"Very well, this is rather delightful. Two willing agents, not just one!" Wimpole saw nothing amiss in his use of the word *willing*. "The timing is, indeed, perfect. This weekend Lord Selby is hosting a party at his house, and we suspect it is a ruse to discuss with his fellow conspirators their plans for the future. We think it would be a prime opportunity to find evidence proving their plot. I believe, Mr Chang, you have a standing invitation to any of his parties?"

Chang looked less than pleased at Wimpole's knowledge.

"You are correct. I can attend any of his gatherings I wish, as long as I bring along suitable entertainments."

"Then you will attend with Mrs O'Harris, who we shall supply with a fake identity," Wimpole's eyes were starting to sparkle again as he thought about the plan. "The guests will be arriving the day after tomorrow, enough time to make our final arrangements. I cannot tell you how relieved I am that you have chosen to do this. It will all be worthwhile and will save so many lives."

Chang grumbled under his breath that the only life he was interested in saving was his own.

"What potential back-up might we have in case of an emergency?" Clara asked Wimpole calmly.

Wimpole blinked at her.

"Back-up?"

"Surely you will be ready to send in the cavalry if we require it?" she asked. "If something goes wrong, and we are discovered, you will be able to rescue us?"

"You will be on your own," Irving told her.

"You will not be watching us?" Clara demanded, acting alarmed.

"We shall be nearby, ready to receive you when you have the papers," Wimpole told her. "But there are no knights in white armour to come to your aid if you are revealed. I am sorry, but if you are caught you are on your own."

Clara hardened her gaze at him, but in reality she was pleased with this information. If there was no back-up, that meant there was no one to chase them down when they made their escape. If only Wimpole and Irving were to be present, then there was a good chance they could be long gone before either realised what had happened.

"I rather feel this is a poor show," Clara sighed at Wimpole. "But it is all we have and so we shall make the best of things."

"You are most obliging Mrs O'Harris, and I do really regret I could not speak with you in a more convivial manner in the first instance. I should have preferred to have made a better first impression."

Wimpole gave her a smile that was worrying because it seemed sincere.

"Might we dispose of the handcuffs now?" Clara asked.

Wimpole looked about to agree when Irving intervened.

"The handcuffs remain. No telling what you two might do without them."

Clara shrugged her shoulders at him.

"It was worth a shot."

Chapter Twelve

L ittle could be done that first night Clara vanished, though
Park-Coombs instigated another search of the area, hoping to
find overlooked clues. It was not until the following morning that they
could begin their enquires in earnest.

O'Harris and Tommy split up, dividing the local area between
them, as they set out to ask people about strangers, suspicious cars,
and a lost dog. They hoped someone would be able to provide them
with a clue as to what had happened to Clara and set them on her trail.

Annie opted to go with Tommy, point-blank refusing to stay
behind any longer. There was nothing he could do to deter her, and
so he agreed.

Jones would act as their chauffeur around the countryside, taking
them in one of the cars to wherever they needed to go. O'Harris
would drive himself. He set out alone, his mind churning with anxious
thoughts about his wife and how she must have spent the night. He
hoped whoever had taken her had treated her kindly and that she was
warm and dry. But his imagination was prone to offering up other
suggestions, that filled him with horror when they popped into his
head.

The first farm he came to was one he visited regularly to purchase eggs and milk for the home. He knew the farmer, Mr Miles, well and often stopped to chat with him. That morning, he hoped Miles would be able to offer him more than a discussion on the rising price of cattle feed and whether it would be a good harvest that year or not.

Miles was in his cattle barn where he had some yearling calves he was bringing on. He was in the middle of doling out feed and hay to them when O'Harris rolled into his yard. He glanced up, recognising the rumble of the car engine, but knowing it was an odd day for O'Harris to be there.

His yard dog, Marbles, charged at the car barking his heart out and trying to nip the wheels. He never succeeded in his efforts, O'Harris was always too cautious to give the dog time to act. O'Harris climbed out of the car, only for Marbles to change from guard dog to his oldest, dearest friend and bounce up at him, putting his paws on the captain's clean trousers.

O'Harris absently stroked the dog's head then headed over to Miles, who had emerged from his cattle barn and was leaning on a rusty metal gate, awaiting him.

"What can I do for you this morning?" Miles asked, a hint of concern on his face.

Farmers do not like things that are out of routine, they always consider them a bad sign.

"Sorry to disturb you so early," O'Harris said, his heart hammering in his chest as he realised the words he must now say. "But, I believe my wife has been kidnapped and I need your help."

Miles straightened up like a ramrod had been shoved down his spine. He called Marbles away from his pestering of the good captain and turned his full attention on O'Harris.

"That is a very serious matter, you ought to come inside for a cup of tea."

"I don't have the time."

"You need to make the time, you look pale and ill from the worry of it all," Miles said firmly. "Have you eaten this morning?"

O'Harris shook his head, he had not had the patience to wait around for breakfast.

"Then you will come in and my Nettie will make you something. You need to keep your strength up if you want to find your wife."

Miles would hear no further protests and escorted O'Harris into his home, calling out for his wife as they entered.

"Nettie! Put the kettle on, and be ready to make another breakfast, we have an emergency brewing, and this man needs his strength."

Nettie, Mr Miles' wholesome if somewhat plain wife, peered through the narrow door of the kitchen and saw who their guest was.

"Captain O'Harris, whatever can be the matter?"

In the face of their concern and generous kindness O'Harris began to weaken. He somehow managed to make it to the kitchen table to sit down in a chair before his legs gave way beneath him.

"Tell Nettie how it is," Miles encouraged him.

O'Harris sucked in a gulp of air as he went to repeat the words that seemed to choke him, and which he hoped he would never get used to saying.

"My wife, Clara, went for a walk yesterday afternoon and never returned," he explained to them. "We went out looking for her and found some alarming indications that she was kidnapped, but we do not know why."

"Goodness," Nettie Miles gasped in horror at the news. "You need bacon and eggs, and lots of toast."

Nettie was rather similar to Annie in that she believed no disaster ought to be faced on an empty stomach. She set about cooking this food for O'Harris as he continued to explain to her husband how he could help them.

"We have spoken to Mr Sargent, and we know there have been men lurking about the area. Strangers. We believe people have been watching Clara for a while and if we can work out who these men are, and where they are currently residing, we might just find her."

"A fair plan," Miles nodded his head. "I remember Sargent mentioning some strangers to me. He saw them lurking by his cattle field and wanted to know if I had seen anyone, but I had not."

O'Harris was immediately disappointed that Miles had not seen the men. He nearly dropped his head into his hands. He feared this could be the pattern of his morning.

"I might not have seen strangers going about, but I have seen some cars I didn't recognise," Miles continued, noting the captain's despondency. "I saw them on several occasions, each time they were driving north along the road that runs outside my yard. They were black cars with white wheels. I don't know what type, I can't tell cars apart like I can tell tractors apart, but I would say that they were newish cars. They had that sleek look to them that the cars from before the war did not."

"Were they saloon cars?" O'Harris asked, but this only drew a frown from Miles, so he rephrased his question.

"Were they very long?"

"Yes, very long. And they had a solid roof, not like those sports cars I have seen driving about with no roof at all. I always wonder how the people inside don't get drenched when it rains. Oh, and they had what looked like a stripe of silver running all down the sides, like a line."

O'Harris noted this detail. The cars sounded expensive, but who would have them and what were they doing driving them around the back roads of Brighton?

"They were always clean too," Miles added, proving he had paid greater heed to the cars than O'Harris had supposed. "You notice things like that when everything is covered in mud. Even though they drove past several days in a row, each time they were as shiny and clean as the first. The driver must have cleaned them every night to achieve that."

"Did they drive past yesterday?" O'Harris asked urgently.

Miles nodded his head.

"I was just coming back into the yard from my rounds of the fields. It was around four, and I saw the pair of them drive past the gates. Didn't think anything of it, of course, not as I had seen them most days doing the same."

"Do you think those people in the black cars have taken your wife?" Mrs Miles asked, placing a plate of food before the captain.

O'Harris' excitement at hearing her husband's information was now dimmed as he realised what it meant.

"I think they did," he told Nettie.

She nodded, her face sympathetic as she wiped her hands on her apron.

"Eat up, you are going to need all the energy you can get to chase after them and find Clara," she said firmly.

Though O'Harris felt as if he had no appetite, he was too polite to refuse to obey, and once he began on the food he discovered his treacherous body was indeed hungry and the nourishment was welcome. It seemed wrong to be eating a hearty breakfast when he did not know if Clara had been given any food or water by her captors, but his growling belly reminded him that Nettie was right – he needed his strength to find Clara.

"I shall keep my eyes peeled for those cars," Miles promised him. "And I shall let all my lads know, and the neighbours. Might be possible for someone to follow them the next time they drive past.

They can't go fast down the lanes and a quick runner could keep up with them by cutting through the fields.

"I would be truly grateful if you could do that," O'Harris said, at last feeling as if there was a ray of hope in the darkness.

Nettie placed a cup of tea before him, adding three spoonfuls of sugar before he could protest.

"Is there anything else I can do to help?" Miles asked.

O'Harris paused.

"I don't suppose you know of anyone losing a dog recently, do you?"

"What sort of dog?" Nettie asked.

"A brown spaniel," O'Harris replied. "We found it trapped in a hole where we think Clara was snatched. We have a theory that someone put the dog there to lure her to the place."

"How cruel," Miles, a devoted dog lover, muttered. "Poor creature, and your poor wife for being snatched when she was acting out of kindness."

"I don't know of any missing dogs," Nettie told him. "But I do know that there is a squire a couple of miles away who always has lots of spaniels and is ready to sell them to anyone who comes calling. He breeds them like rabbits for use on the shoots but has far too many. Maybe the spaniel came from there?"

"Maybe," O'Harris said, and then he asked for directions so he could go to speak to this squire himself.

He had extracted all the information he could from Mr and Mrs Miles, and he had delayed their daily routine for long enough. He thanked them for their help and for the breakfast and tea. They, in turn, promised they would do all they could to aid him and spread the word about his missing wife and the suspicious strangers.

With their promises ringing in his ears, O'Harris returned to his car and set out for his next destination. Marbles chased his car out of the yard, before being summoned back by its master. O'Harris turned onto the road that the black, unknown cars had been using day after day and wondered if Miles had witnessed the very vehicles that his wife had been abducted in.

O'Harris grimaced at the thought. More to the point, how had he been so oblivious to these strangers in the neighbourhood? Why had no one mentioned the cars and the men lurking in the area?

If only they had known!

But what would they have done? It was not illegal to drive a car down a road or to stand smoking in a lane. While it was possible these incidents were connected to Clara's disappearance, just as easily they could be a coincidence.

O'Harris slapped his hand on the steering wheel of the car. There had to be a solution to this matter he was not seeing. He would find Clara and there was no point berating himself for failing to realise she was in danger sooner.

He just had to concentrate on the here and now and seeking her out before any harm could truly befall her.

He just hoped, whoever had taken Clara, she was giving them hell and making them bitterly regret ever daring to kidnap her.

Chapter Thirteen

Mr Wimpole proved to be something of a natural at disguises. He began with the simplest but most dramatic of Clara's transformations – dying her hair. Clara had mousy brown hair, that often reddened to a pale chestnut in the summer. Mr Wimpole saw to it that within an hour she was changed to a platinum blonde. Clara was so stunned by the new and extremely vibrant colour that she had to stare at herself long and hard in a mirror to convince herself she was the same person.

That was when things took a difficult turn, for Mr Wimpole insisted it must be cut as well and styled like a lady from a fashion magazine. That would mean giving it a shingle, so that it flopped in rippling waves from the top of her head to just below her ears.

Clara was not happy with the idea. She liked her hair long and kept it back in a plait when she was working. It might not be all the rage at that period in time, but Clara had never fancied she had a face that suited the bobbed styles that were the trend among certain ladies.

Mr Wimpole was lurking about her with a pair of scissors, trying to persuade her as she contemplated her new colour in a hand mirror, that she needed to have her hair cut. Clara was refusing, and as she had been granted the liberty of the removal of the handcuffs, there was a real danger of Clara putting up a fight and accosting Wimpole with the hand mirror if he tried to force the issue.

It was Chang's intervention that finally resolved the matter.

"No woman hanging on my arm at a party would have long hair," he said in a casual tone.

He had *not* been granted the liberty of the removal of his handcuffs, so was sullen, and doing his best to smoke a cigarette with his wrists manacled.

Clara narrowed her eyes at him, but Chang merely shrugged.

"You wanted to be involved," he reminded her. "Stay here and keep your hair long, but if you want to take part in this mission, then you will have to cut your hair and look as though you follow the latest fashions."

Clara knew, deep down, that he was right. Her disguise would only work if she truly transformed herself and became someone no one would recognise. Clara O'Harris was known for her long, dark hair, which she did not wear in a fashionable bob. Her alter-ego had to be as different as was possible from that.

Resigning herself to her fate, and reminding herself her hair would grow back, she allowed Wimpole to get to work with the scissors. She was mildly bemused at how competent he proved, not just that, but he seemed to take pleasure in styling her hair. He had sent Irving out for the chemicals he needed to add a shingle to her bob and used them with confidence.

When he was done, Clara was surprised at how glamorous she looked and how professional a style Wimpole had given to her hair.

"You appear to be a rather expert hairdresser," Clara remarked to him.

"Actually, I like making wigs," Wimpole explained, grinning. "Handy for the work we do, and they all have to be styled just like real hair."

Clara once again found herself wondering just who this strange gentleman was who liked to style hair and worked in a world of secrets. That itch at the back of her mind – the one that reminded her about the hint of madness she had seen in Mr Wimpole – came back to her. At what point might Mr Wimpole's eccentricities be seen as the first signs of lunacy?

There was no time to worry about it. She just had to get this all over and done with and find her way back home.

The next task was selecting her an outfit that would be fitting for the party she planned to attend. Chang suggested something dazzling and a little overdone for the evening, while during the day it should be a more high-class affair – a nice coat and fur stole, with shiny black patent leather shoes. He painted a picture of how he envisioned Clara to look as she lingered on his arm.

Clara pulled a face at him, feeling he was enjoying himself a little too much. Chang merely smiled.

Wimpole gave instructions to his assistant Irving, who seemed to find nothing strange about being tasked with finding women's clothes. He departed and returned a few hours later with quite a selection. Clara wondered where he had found them, and how he had paid for them. The day outfit he had picked out was a smart dark green dress, with black decoration, over which was a burgundy jacket with shiny brass buttons. The stole was mink, and Clara disliked it immediately. She had always felt it was wrong to adorn oneself with a dead animal in such a manner. This one still had the head and paws of the creature it had been made from attached, so that when it was draped around the shoulders it looked as though it was a living thing just resting there.

Clara was horrified by the thing with its glassy eyes, but yet again she knew she was going to have to swallow down her concerns for the sake of getting herself and Chang out of the house.

The evening dress Irving had picked was just as concerning, but for different reasons. It was cut from a dove grey fabric that shimmered in a way that made Clara think it was satin. It had a smooth nap to the surface and when it caught the light it almost glowed. Sewn onto it were silver sequins forming an elaborate leaf pattern, which seemed to focus specifically around the chest area. Clara was a tad concerned about that, along with the rather swooping neckline.

Not to mention that the skirt appeared to be made of thin silver tassels, and when she took a closer look she realised the fabric actually stopped just above her knees. If she moved her legs in the wrong way, or was not careful when she sat down, she would be exposing a great deal more flesh than she was accustomed to.

Chang was enjoying seeing her bemusement and unease at the outfits. He had a broad grin on his face but was at least distracted from his own woes.

"No one will recognise you in that," he pointed his cigarette at the silver evening gown.

"I would not recognise myself," Clara sighed. "Still, needs must."

"We are not quite finished with your appearance, Mrs O'Harris," Wimpole interceded just as she thought they were done, for the time being, with her transformation from private detective to glamour girl.

"What else could you possibly have in mind?" she asked anxiously.

"We have yet to discuss your make-up, it is unthinkable that a lady who would travel with such clothes, and with hair so bleached and shingled, would not also be concerned about her facial features."

Clara felt her stomach drop.

"Oh," she said, not knowing what else to offer.

Clara never wore make-up, though she did possess a handful of items that had either been gifted to her or she had bought on a whim. Somehow, she had never found herself getting into the habit of waking each morning and ornamenting her face like other women did. She was always rather preoccupied with other things.

Now Mr Wimpole produced a case of make-up products, and she did not have the heart to ask where he had acquired them. She had a worrying feeling they probably belonged to the gentleman in question.

"I think a darker shade of pink would suit your complexion," Wimpole produced a tube of lipstick and used a brush to apply the colour to Clara's lips.

She glanced at herself in the mirror, seeing the plea in her eyes to stop this madness. She apologised to herself, as the ordeal persisted.

Mr Wimpole picked out a pale brown shade for her eyelids, which he mixed with a darker violet at the corners to create the effect he desired. He used mascara and eyelash curlers that he warmed by the fire to enhance her eyes. Then he dabbed a little bit of a blush colour onto her cheeks before standing back to admire his work.

"There is just one thing," he observed after contemplating her for a while. "We shall need to pluck your eyebrows."

"What?"

"I think we shall be able to get away without dying them, as they are quite a pale shade of brown, but they do need to be plucked to improve the shape."

Clara found herself looking to Chang for help, though she knew she was not going to get any. He merely smiled at her in amusement.

What was the point in arguing?

Clara sat down in a chair as instructed by Mr Wimpole, closed her eyes and braced herself as he set about her eyebrows with a pair of tweezers.

Clara had always thought she had nice eyebrows, not ones that required a great deal of attention. They were not too big, and they sat in a shapely manner on her face, but apparently Mr Wimpole found them wanting.

His tweezers plucked and pruned, pulling out hair after hair, while Clara grimaced and puckered her mouth. Chang chuckled behind her, and she determined she was going to have to repay him for his amusement. After all, she was doing this for his sake.

The torture complete, Clara once again looked herself over in the mirror, noting the redness around her eyebrows.

"Are we done?" she asked hopelessly.

"You shall have to learn how to do this all yourself, no knowing how long it will take you to retrieve those documents," Wimpole told her.

"We are only there for the weekend," Clara protested. "Surely, the make-up will last that long?"

Mr Wimpole gave her an astonished look; the look of a man who has suddenly realised he knows more about the workings of cosmetics than the woman before him. Panic skipped across his face at the thought that Clara was going to have to be left to attend to her appearance alone once she was inside the house.

"Don't worry, I can do her make-up," Chang sniggered.

Clara glanced in his direction. He tilted back his head and took a long drag on his cigarette.

"I have spent a lot of time with women who adorn themselves, and I might have occasionally aided them with their appearance," he explained to Clara. "I imagine I know more than you do, at least."

"I am beginning to question the soundness of this plan," Wimpole was frowning. "Perhaps, on second thoughts, Chang should go in alone."

"Chang will not have the same chances if he goes alone. He needs an accomplice," Clara insisted, refusing to entertain the notion of being abandoned at the house alone with her future left residing in Chang's hands.

"She will be fine," Chang dismissed Wimpole's concerns. "Clara is nothing if not resourceful."

Clara was not sure if that was a compliment but opted not to dwell on the matter.

"Are we at last done?" she asked of Wimpole.

The man nodded his head.

"You are truly transformed Mrs O'Harris, however, you shall need a new name. One that will complete your disguise."

"Judy Barlow," Chang said without hesitation.

"Where did that come from?" Clara asked him.

"She was a girl I knew a long time ago," Chang said with a shrug. "But no one will recognise the name."

"I suppose it is as good as any," Clara grumbled to herself.

Taking one last look in the hand mirror she resolved herself to the coming adventure.

"Hello Judy Barlow," she said to herself. "Try to look more confident than I feel, would you please?"

Chapter Fourteen

B y four in the afternoon, O'Harris, Tommy and Annie found themselves back at the house, having exhausted their first set of possible leads in the investigation. They needed to regroup, discuss what they had each learned, and determine a new course of action.

O'Harris found his brother-in-law and his wife in the kitchen once again, drinking deep cups of tea and looking as anxious as when they had set out that morning. They glanced up sharply as he entered, hope in their eyes, which flickered out the second they realised he was not accompanied by Clara.

"It was too much to suppose you had found her," Annie sighed. "But I really hoped you would walk through that door with her."

O'Harris shook his head. He had been hoping something similar as he drove home, that he would enter his house and find Clara with her brother and friend, regaling them with her adventures while they were apart. He had painted such a vivid picture in his mind of that scene that he had almost convinced himself it would become reality.

If only wishing for something hard enough would make it happen.

"What did you find out?" O'Harris asked, pulling out a chair from the kitchen table and sitting down.

A moment later, the cook who worked in the kitchen, making sure the home's residents were well fed, placed a cup of tea and a cheese sandwich at his elbow. She murmured that he should get his strength back and O'Harris supposed she was right.

He had not eaten all day, since leaving the farm of Mr Miles, and it now occurred to him that his stomach had been growling at him for a while. In his daze of fear and anger, he had completely ignored it. He took a bite of the sandwich and a sip of the tea, discovering he was ravenous.

"We toured the local farms, as we agreed," Tommy explained while O'Harris consumed his sandwich. "We found a few more witnesses who had seen the men lurking in the area. One gentleman, who is a stockman over on Ivy Farm, recalled that Clara had stopped to talk to him one day when she caught sight of the men. She had observed to him that they were new to the area, and she did not care for them. They both agreed they could be looking to rob some of the farms.

"Clara then joined the stockman as he walked back to the farmhouse to tell everyone about the strangers, and the possibility of trouble in the future."

"Clara thought they were watching the farms, not her," O'Harris shook his head. "It was a logical assumption, I suppose, but I wish she had considered the possibility she was the one at risk."

"Clara would never have given that a thought," Annie told him. "She always assumes any trouble she can handle herself, and that no one is a serious threat to her."

"My sister has a sense of self-confidence that is quite remarkable," Tommy added. "Considering the things she has been through, or perhaps because of them. I would almost say that confidence makes her reckless, though it also has a tendency to get her out of those same situations she stumbles into because of it."

"I hope you are correct in this instance," O'Harris said sombrely.

"She isn't dead, you know," Annie told them both firmly, looking between their sad faces. "They would not have gone to such effort simply to murder her. They wanted her alive."

"Annie has a point. If they wanted Clara dead, they had opportunities aplenty to deal with her and disappear. No, they wanted her alive," Tommy grimaced at what that could mean for his sister.

"Let's go back to what you have learned," O'Harris said, deciding he did not want to linger over speculating on Clara's fate.

Whatever had happened to her, the important thing was they continued their investigation and located her.

"Aside from the stockman who had witnessed the men lurking in the lanes, several people had witnessed smart, black cars driving around the area," Tommy continued. "They said they looked new, and expensive, and had white tyres."

"That fits with what I was told," O'Harris agreed. "Those cars were seen driving through the area around the same time each day, coinciding with Clara's walk."

"I feel it is safe to assume the cars are connected to her disappearance," Tommy agreed. "Our next question is whether we can trace them and find Clara that way?"

"They must have been based somewhere nearby," O'Harris said thoughtfully. "I was told they were clean every time they drove past Mr Miles' farm, which means someone was washing them every morning. That had to be done where there was access to running water, like a garage or stableyard."

"Someone must have rented the car owners a suitable space to keep them, as they are not locals," Tommy nodded his head. "That is another clue to follow up. Maybe if we trace where the cars are being kept we shall find Clara."

"There is something else," O'Harris added. "I was advised by Miles that there is a local squire who breeds spaniels and other gundogs for the local shoots. He always has a surplus available for sale. I went to ask him if he had sold anyone a gingery brown cocker spaniel in the last week or so."

"I know who you mean," Tommy frowned. "The fellow is more interested in making money from his dogs than for their welfare. He wouldn't give a damn who he sold them to."

"Indeed, and he tried to sell me a dog while I was there," O'Harris shook his head. "However, after I explained the situation to him, he did recall having a gentleman call on his house and ask to purchase a dog. He described him as a tall, lean fellow, with a small moustache and a posh accent. He assumed he was a sporting gentleman, though he did not seem very inclined towards dogs.

"There was another fellow with him, looked to the squire as if he was a gamekeeper. He had a surly expression and said very little while he was showing them around the kennels. But then the gentleman turned to him and said, 'Irving, you pick one, I am really indifferent on the matter.' The squire thought this rather odd."

"But not odd enough to stop him from selling one of his dogs to the fellow," Tommy clicked his tongue behind his teeth in frustration. "Did he recall anything else?"

"The fellow called Irving asked for the cheapest dog he had. He remarked that all his dogs were fine animals, the usual sort of spiel from a salesman," O'Harris shrugged. "Then, when Irving insisted, he pointed out a ginger spaniel that had proved gun shy and had been hanging around in the kennels unsold for months. He offered them the dog at a cheap price, and they took it. He never mentioned the dog was gun shy, of course, just in case the gentleman was thinking of working it at a shoot. And they never asked why the dog was so cheap."

O'Harris paused.

"Where is the creature, anyway?"

"Jones kindly bathed him," Annie replied. "And then introduced him to Pip and Bramble. Pip was delighted and they have been romping around the gardens all day. They are now all sleeping in your study."

"Bramble tried to pretend he did not exist," Tommy added. "I was told he gave Jones a dreadfully haughty look, the sort that says he would not lower himself to communing with a spaniel and then left it all to Pip."

O'Harris found himself smiling at the dogs' antics; it was welcome to have a distraction.

"Clara will be pleased to know the little fellow is safe," he remarked. "I am sure she is concerned about what has happened to him."

"Clara is probably more worried about the dog than herself," Annie huffed. "Though it was horrible they just left the poor beast to die in that hole."

"It does not say much for these people," Tommy agreed.

They all became quiet as they reflected on what that could mean for poor Clara.

"At least we have a name now," O'Harris brought them out of their doldrums.

Clara would not linger in despair if she were searching for any of them, she would spend her time more productively.

"Who is this Irving fellow?" Tommy pondered. "Sounds like he is the dogsbody for this gentleman."

"They paid in cash, which offers us no further leads," O'Harris added. "It would have been too convenient to discover the gentleman had paid by cheque."

"But we do have more information we can ask people. We know that this gentleman and Irving bought a dog and must be connected to the cars in the area. Someone has to know where they have been living while they plotted to snatch Clara. It seems to me this did not happen swiftly," Tommy was thoughtful. "If I was a kidnapper, where would I take a person I had just trapped in a pit and gassed?"

O'Harris was silent as he considered the question, it proved to be Annie who spoke up.

"In my magazines, whenever a young lady is kidnapped and it is not in a city, she is taken to somewhere remote in the countryside. A large country house or a farm, where no one will see her."

Annie read a lot of magazines that featured women's stories, some of these were of the melodramatic kind, but O'Harris thought, in this instance, she had a point.

"They would be renting somewhere they could keep the cars out of sight," Tommy said. "How many properties like that in the neighbourhood?"

O'Harris considered the question.

"I would argue not that many, at least not that are empty and available to rent for a short period. Some of the finer houses in the district can only be rented for a year at a time, which would be inconvenient to our kidnappers."

"We need to find an agent who rents properties around here and see if he recognises the name Irving or the description of the gentleman," Tommy decided. "I was also thinking that we explore the sightings of the car further, to determine a search area. If we can work out the rough location they appear and disappear, that would narrow our search."

"No luck finding someone who saw them driving away on the day

Clara vanished?" O'Harris asked. "Mr Miles saw them just before she must have been taken."

"No one we spoke to recalled seeing them yesterday afternoon," Tommy shrugged. "At least no one we have spoken to *as yet*, but there could be someone out there."

O'Harris was thinking about getting into his car again and driving the lanes to track down more witnesses when he was distracted by the ringing of the bell over the back door. The cook gave a puzzled look, not expecting anyone, and went to answer the summons. A few moments later, Miles the farmer entered the kitchen, looking embarrassed that he had interrupted them.

"Miles, what are you doing here?" O'Harris asked, offering the man a chair.

Miles did not sit down.

"I asked around, like I said I would, Captain," he replied. "I was deeply upset about what happened, as was my wife. I spoke to as many people as I could think of, and I have some information that might be important, which is why I walked all this way to see you."

Annie had risen and was pouring out a cup of tea for the farmer. He looked parched from his walk, but the paleness of his skin seemed more out of concern that Clara was missing than from the exertion.

"What have you learned?" O'Harris asked, trying not to sound too eager.

Miles took a deep breath.

"I think I might know where the kidnappers are hiding out."

Chapter Fifteen

Just after five, Clara and Chang were escorted to a black car. Wimpole was looking excited and wide-eyed that at last his plan was in motion. Irving was sullen.

For the first time, Clara witnessed the extra guards the men employed. The two burly fellows attempted to look intimidating as she walked past to the car where Wimpole was holding the door open for her.

Clara paused and looked them both in the eye.

"You were the fellows who were lurking in the lanes when I was taking my afternoon walk," she said. "If you were meant to be doing it secretly, you failed miserably. Several people in the local area saw you, along with me. We assumed you were prospective farm robbers."

Wimpole was abashed at this information, and the knowledge his men had been so obvious.

"They are relatively new," he informed Clara.

"They could do with some work on their ability to blend in. Their clothes made them stand out like a sore thumb," Clara shook her head at him. "I spotted them a mile away, not only because they were strangers, but because they did not dress like farm workers."

"It was unfortunate," Mr Wimpole admitted. "Might you get in the car, now?"

Clara obeyed, but not before giving the two men a hard stare she hoped they would remember.

She sat beside Chang, while Wimpole took up position in the driver's seat. Irving and the two thugs headed for a second car that would follow them. Clara's hands were still free, but Chang remained handcuffed, though Wimpole had been generous enough to remove his ankle manacles. Clara leaned her elbow on the sill of the car window and rubbed at her temple.

"I still feel groggy from that gas," she complained.

"It will not have a lasting effect on your health," Mr Wimpole informed her, though her comment had not been aimed at him.

"So you say," Clara grumbled.

Chang fidgeted in his seat, trying to get comfortable while also attempting to remove the cuffs without Wimpole noticing. Clara had watched him contorting his hands to try to slip off the metal cuffs for hours while they were in the kitchen. He had yet to achieve anything other than rub raw his flesh.

"Give it a rest Chang," Clara told him. "I need you to have your hands in one piece for this adventure."

Chang scowled at her and ignored her suggestion. After a moment, he managed to squeeze the thumb on his right hand so far into his palm that he could almost get his hand through the cuff. He gritted his teeth and started to pull, only to discover he had not squeezed his thumb in tight enough and was on the point of being perilously close to crushing it or dislocating it, as his hand was now wedged in the cuff.

Pulling an urgent expression at Clara, while holding down on the cry of pain and curse words he desperately wanted to say, he showed her his hand.

Clara sighed, grabbed his fingers with one hand, the cuffs with another, and yanked back, releasing his hand with a sharp pop and almost producing a scream from Chang. He managed to contain himself and simply shudder hard. Clara raised an eyebrow at him in silent rebuke.

He growled at her.

"All right back there?" Wimpole asked, his eyes flicking from the road to the car's rearview mirror.

"Nothing to worry about," Clara smiled. "Tell me where we are going again?"

"Lord Selby's shooting estate," Wimpole explained gladly, he seemed to delight in talking about the people he was spying upon. "It is not as large and rambling as his regular home, but it is certainly grand."

"I have been there before," Chang said. "It has fifteen bedrooms, and at least a dozen bathrooms, most with running cold water, if not hot."

"It has certainly been adjusted for modern living," Wimpole acknowledged. "Lord Selby has invited a number of his co-conspirators to spend the weekend, and we are confident they intend to discuss something of importance. At the very least, there should be plenty of papers around that you can purloin for us. In my experience, men like Selby leave an extensive paper trail. They like to have invoices and letters, along with documents outlining their plans. It makes them feel all nice and organised."

"And they are confident no one will find those plans in their own homes," Clara observed.

"I suppose," Wimpole nodded. "Mr Chang, you are satisfied you can attend this gathering without an invitation?"

"I told you, I have a standing invitation to go to any of Lord Selby's gatherings," Chang huffed. "You don't invite me to these things, I invite myself. That is how I work and everyone knows it."

Clara hoped he was right, otherwise they would be in trouble before they began.

"All being well, you will have plenty of time to roam the place looking for evidence," Wimpole continued. "Lord Selby is something of a simpleton, in many regards, and I should not be concerned about him working out what you are up to but do watch out for some of the others who are much more cunning."

"Who do you expect to be there?" Clara asked.

"We have heard that the Duke and Duchess of Manchester will be present. Along with a gentleman called Mr Bourton who is an influential but controversial MP," Wimpole explained. "There are likely to be others we have not identified."

"What are your thoughts on these people?" Clara asked Chang.

He shrugged nonchalantly.

"All people I have sold various substances to, along with gambled with, and had entertained by some of my girls," he explained.

"There is going to be no suggestion I am one of your girls, understood?" Clara said firmly.

"Never crossed my mind," Chang said, casting her a smile. "You shall be my own, personal date for the weekend. I never go anywhere alone."

"Except to the lavatories on the train station, what!" Wimpole laughed.

Chang's face clouded over, showing the storm of emotions deep within. Reading between the lines, Clara suspected something had happened at a train station that had resulted in Chang's imprisonment, and he was ashamed he had let his guard slip.

"We shall both be more cautious in the future," Clara remarked to him.

Chang sighed and nodded his head.

"We both let ourselves down. I am not proud that I was so easy to capture."

"I do not consider that I was easy to capture," Clara replied. "In fact, I feel I was rather difficult, all things told."

"You were incredibly difficult," Wimpole grumbled from the front of the car. "I honestly never thought Mr Irving's suggestion that we would need to disable you with a gas bomb would be necessary. I was proved wrong."

"They gassed you?" Chang asked her.

"Only way to stop her talking and telling us how she refused to cooperate," Wimpole replied before she could. "She refused to be helpful."

"You intended to kidnap me, why would I be helpful?" Clara snapped.

"You could have had a little more faith," Wimpole seemed oblivious to the fact he had trapped Clara in a pit and then informed her she was coming with him.

"Faith?" Clara scoffed. "How about you have a little faith and take off Chang's handcuffs?"

"Now, now, Mrs O'Harris, we have compromised and taken off yours."

Clara cast a look at Chang that implied she had tried her best. He was left to mutter under his breath.

"Once you arrive at Lord Selby's, you will have only two nights and two days to search the house for evidence," Wimpole continued, ignoring the simmering dislike being directed at him from the back of the car. "We shall be waiting nearby and shall instruct you on a signal you can shine with a mirror to let us know when you have the evidence."

"Or if we need to be rescued," Chang interjected.

"I told you before, there will be no rescue. Once you are inside, you are on your own. If you are caught, you shall have to use your own wits to get yourselves out again."

Clara did not like the sound of that, but she supposed she had no option. She had considered opening the car door, grabbing Chang, and throwing them both out, but she doubted they would get far. As soon as an opportunity arose, however, she would endeavour to escape.

"You have become quiet," Wimpole spoke. "I hope you are not contemplating how you might relieve yourselves of this mission?"

"I have been contemplating the many ways I would like to inflict pain on you before I let you die," Chang hissed at him.

"You are an uncouth fellow, really, is that necessary?" Wimpole sounded hurt rather than afraid.

"It is very necessary," Chang retorted. "We are not doing this because we want to, we are doing it because you have forced our hand. When this is over, I suggest you find somewhere to hide yourself, because if I can track you down, I shall, and you would not like that."

"You are not encouraging me to give you your freedom," Wimpole snorted. "Remember, that it is my good will that is the key to you surviving this escapade."

Chang let out a roar of laughter.

"Your good will? That is what this is?"

"Mrs O'Harris, please talk to your companion and have him appreciate the essential nature of this work!"

"I find that difficult to do," Clara replied. "Seeing as I have also been contemplating the multiple ways I could inflict pain upon you once this situation is over. I doubt I am quite as inventive as Chang, but I am certainly as vindictive. I have not forgotten how you treated the poor dog you used as bait to lure me to your trap. I shall never forgive you for leaving the creature to die."

"You wish to hurt him because of how he treated a dog?" Chang asked her, curious.

"I could forgive him kidnapping me, after he explained he was concerned about a threat to national security, but the dog I cannot forgive," Clara explained. "I am very particular about these things, Chang."

"There you go, Wimpole. You have lost the good graces of Clara O'Harris, and once lost, they are rarely given again."

Wimpole's eyes flashed briefly in the rearview mirror.

"Really now, we shall all be good friends after this, or at least comrades, who have done all in our power to save the world."

"If you say so," Chang chuckled.

Clara leaned back in the car seat and watched the landscape drifting by outside her window. The evening was still light enough to enable her to see the hedges and houses beyond, and she was able to work out roughly where she was. She wished she were at home, sitting in her husband's study, eating crumpets, and discussing something dreadfully mundane, like the ongoing damp problems in the conservatory. Instead, she was being driven to a location unknown to her, to pretend to be someone she was not, and find out secrets for her country.

She was not sure if she should feel proud, scared, annoyed, or simply angry. Maybe she should feel it all?

Beside her, Chang fell into belligerent silence, not even looking at her. She knew he was upset with himself, and nothing she could say would change that. She decided it was best to let him brood, while she continued to watch the landscape go by and try to work out where she was.

If she could work out her location, then she was one step closer to an escape plan. All she had to do next was actually escape.

Chapter Sixteen

Mr Miles was wringing his cap in his hands, looking deeply distressed by the news he was now bringing, even though it would hopefully resolve the mystery of Clara's disappearance and bring her safely home.

"Take your time and explain what you have learned," Annie nudged him along, the menfolk having already thrown at him a series of questions without giving him a chance to answer and leaving him flustered.

Her calm, commanding voice broke through the throb of noise and brought everyone else to a halt.

Mr Miles took a deep breath, then began.

"I walked over to Mr Parsons' property, which neighbours my farm. He lives there alone these days, just tending to his horses, but I thought he might know something. Mr Parsons happens to own a very old house in the middle of nowhere that he inherited from his uncle. He rents it out, as he does not need to reside in it. I thought, perhaps he might have rented it out recently to people with cars."

Tommy jumped up from the table.

"We need to head there at once!"

"Thomas, Mr Miles has not finished," Annie said to him sternly.

When she used his full name he knew she was losing patience with him. He sat down abruptly and promised not to interrupt Mr Miles further.

"Please, continue," Annie said.

Mr Miles obeyed.

"Mr Parsons had not recently rented out his property, as he explained to me. It needed some work doing on the roof and was currently empty. However, I fancied it might be worth going to take a look in that direction, just in case."

Miles proved to have a soundly suspicious mind that did not take the obvious at face value. For that they were all grateful.

"Mr Parsons decided to come with me after I explained the situation, though I fear he was more concerned about the possibility someone was occupying the premises without paying him, than about your missing wife, Captain. Still, he was with me, and we crossed the fields and made our way to the house.

"As it turned out, the property was just as Mr Parsons had last left it. Every door and window was locked up and there were no signs of tyre tracks leading up to it. We were both satisfied that no one was using it without his knowledge, however, before we left, Mr Parsons wanted to go inside and check on the issue with the roof. I would have left him to it, but he asked me to give my opinion on the matter and whether he would need to take apart the ceiling."

Miles shrugged, indicating the frustration of this situation and the bother it had been to him when he was busy, but also that he had felt unable to refuse.

"While we were upstairs, and Mr Parsons was pointing out the ceiling of one of the bedrooms where there was a large patch of damp, I glanced out the window and that was when I saw a dark car driving past along the nearby road. It was the same car I had seen driving past my farm, I was certain of it.

"I excused myself from Mr Parsons, and I fear he thought me rude, but I had to hasten downstairs to chase after the car. I ran across his garden and by hopping over the various hedgerows and fences I was just able to keep it in sight. It swept around a corner and then drove down a lane that leads to another house. I went as close as I dared, to assure myself the car was stopping there, and then I rushed home.

"I thought the house was occupied by a lady called Mrs Lodes and could not think why the car would have gone there. But when I made my way home and spoke to my wife, she informed me that Mrs Lodes had passed away some months back, and the house was empty. I do not know if it is being rented out, or whether the people there are residing in it illegally, but that is where the car went."

Mr Miles finished his tale, having taken a little more time over it than was perhaps necessary. Tommy was agitated and wanted to scream at the man for distracting them with talk of Mr Parsons and his damp ceilings, but O'Harris was far calmer, having taken his time to process the information.

"We must go to this house at once," he decided. "We shall take as many people with us as possible and conduct a raid on the premises."

"What if it is the wrong house?" Annie asked, nervous at his tone.

"Then we shall apologise profusely and explain what has caused our anxiety and earnest haste. But I do not think that will be necessary."

His voice dropped and a darkness came over his features that made Annie uncomfortable. She saw suddenly the visage of a man who had undertaken mission after mission in an aeroplane on the frontline, risking his life, bolting down his fears beneath a blanket of determination.

Heaven help the kidnappers when he found them.

"I can show you the way, if you don't know how to reach it

yourselves," Miles said.

"We shall need your guidance," O'Harris confirmed. "I never met Mrs Lodes nor know of her house."

"She was a bit of a recluse," Miles nodded his head. "I told my wife I might be a while helping you, and said she should not wait up for me."

The decision made, O'Harris hastened through the house to round up a number of the men to assist with his plan. He found several of them sitting in the library where Colonel Bradley was hunched up in his usual armchair. No one was paying the old colonel much attention, as he was locked in his own world, as usual.

"We think we have an idea of where Clara is being held," O'Harris told the men before him. "We are heading to the place now to rescue her and apprehend her kidnappers."

He did not have to say anything more. The men were on their feet in an instant and rushing to fetch their coats and hats to accompany him.

As O'Harris went to follow, he thought he saw the unfortunate colonel move, as if he lifted his head. The captain paused and turned to the man, but he seemed as still and silent as always. O'Harris assumed it was his anxious mind playing tricks on him.

Back in the kitchen, Tommy was itching to be going and had started to pace back and forth. Annie confined herself to preparing a hamper of food and drink items that she fancied Clara might need after being held hostage for several hours.

"She will be all right," she told Tommy as he stomped past her.

Tommy said nothing, too focused on his erratic pacing.

A short time later, the rescue party departed from the home in two cars, one driven by O'Harris, the other by Jones, and both packed with men. Mr Miles sat in the front passenger seat of the lead car and pointed out the way to O'Harris. In the second car, Tommy was sat beside Jones and barely able to contain his impatience. He would almost have preferred to run the whole way to the house, if it were feasible, than to sit in the car twiddling his thumbs.

It was now dark, and the roads were only illuminated by the headlights of the cars. They swooped down the lanes purposefully, determined to catch the fiends red-handed and to serve up their own brand of punishment before relinquishing them to the police.

O'Harris had not yet decided what he would do to the men who had taken Clara, but his temper was so high he did not think they would get away without a fist to the face. He was not a man who approved of violence, in general, but on certain occasions emotions overspilled.

Though, if Clara had her way, it may be the case that she was the one to throw the first punch.

Miles pointed out the lane which served as a driveway to the house. It was just a dark gash in the hedgerows, which had become overgrown through the years of Mrs Lodes' reclusive occupancy.

O'Harris swung in sharply, ignoring the scratching sound of branches against his paintwork, and pointed his car towards the large house they could make out in the distance. The dirt driveway was marked by recent tyre tracks, which had left an impression after some squally summer weather had drenched the area. O'Harris was gritting his teeth, his hands tight on the steering wheel as they drew closer to the house.

The property showed no signs of anyone being there. There were no lights glowing in the windows, and no cars.

Miles became agitated.

"The car pulled up right there," he pointed to the side of the house. "I swear!"

O'Harris did not doubt him. Miles was not the sort of fellow to send them on a wild goose chase, but the fact remained there were no cars there now.

O'Harris pulled up before the house, the second car coming to a halt alongside him. He turned off the engine and stared at the property for a moment. Considering a pair of strange cars had driven up to a place supposed to be serving as a hideout for criminals, there was no indication that they had been noticed.

O'Harris remained cautious. Someone could be watching from one of the darkened rooms, and that someone could have a gun. No one had exited the car beside him, though no doubt Tommy was barely able to contain himself. O'Harris finally decided that the only option was to step out of the car and see what happened. He braced himself and threw open the car door.

A part of him was fully anticipating hearing a shot ring out. Fortunately, nothing occurred. He stood on the earth before the house and looked at the windows, suddenly sensing that the place was empty. His heart sank.

A rifle shot would have been much more welcome than this silence.

Jones, Tommy, and the others all joined him. Miles was eager to point out where he had seen the car park up. They followed him to the spot at the side of the house and saw the tyre imprints where a car had repeatedly stopped here and then turned around. There were also some speckles of oil which showed up in the beam of a torch O'Harris cast across the earth.

"Someone was here," he said solemnly. "But they have gone."

Tommy did not want to hear that. He did not want to think they were too late. He stormed over to the house and tried the front door, determined to batter it down if he needed to. He discovered it was unlocked and opened easily.

That made sense, as whoever had been here had probably not had a key and it was doubtful they much cared about securing the place after they left again. Tommy stepped into a darkened hall and tried the nearest light switch. Nothing occurred.

"No electricity," Tommy called back to O'Harris.

"We shall search the place top to bottom for any clue to who has been here, and if they were holding Clara. We need to work out where they went next," O'Harris gave his orders to the men who had followed them.

Torches were distributed among them, though there were not enough for one for each man. They would have to work in pairs.

O'Harris and Tommy formed up, and Miles joined them. The three of them slowly made their way through the house. They soon discovered that a number of the internal doors were locked, and there was no sign of the keys. O'Harris was not quite prepared to suggest they batter down the doors, at least not until they had exhausted their efforts in locating the house keys.

With Tommy and Miles, he made his way through the house to a kitchen at the very back. The faint aroma of cooking indicated the place had been in use recently. There was a lamp sitting on the kitchen table. Tommy lit it with some matches he was carrying in his pocket and the glow it produced helped them to see the space.

Sitting next to the lamp on the table was a bundle of keys, clearly for the locked rooms they had walked past.

O'Harris picked them up and almost threw them down again. Clara had been here, he was sure of it, but now she was gone. He looked around the room, wishing to see some sign of his wife, something that proved she was safe and well.

It was Miles who found their first clue. He had spotted something on the floor and picked it up. It was a clump of long hair that had been recently cut and fallen under the table, where the half-hearted efforts of whoever had cleaned the place had failed to touch it.

"That's Clara's hair," Tommy winced, looking sick at the sight of it. His eyes shot to O'Harris. "They cut her hair!"

Chapter Seventeen

The drive seemed to take hours, and Clara was sick of being stuck in the car. Her kidnappers had failed to provide her with much in the way of sustenance aside from a couple of rather bad cups of tea and a sandwich hastily made by Irving when she complained of hunger. She was still hungry, as well as tired and thirsty. Her throat still scratched from the effects of the gas, and she felt out of sorts with herself, not sure if this was also a consequence of whatever she had breathed in, or because of her situation and the toll it was taking on her nerves.

She would never admit it aloud, but she was worried about this espionage adventure and feared what might happen if she failed. She had never done anything like this before, and she didn't consider herself an exceptional actress. While her main goal of agreeing to accompany Chang was to give her a means to escape, she was well aware that she might also have to undertake some element of the mission while she worked out a way to elude the attention of Mr Wimpole and Irving. She knew they would be watching her and

Chang like hawks, anticipating treachery. Just because she was out of the house, did not mean she was free to leave.

Then there was the matter of the people she was about to meet and convince she was Judy Barlow. People who, if they knew who she really was, would be glad to dispatch her there and then.

What was she doing?

When she had been stuck in a kitchen wearing handcuffs and utterly furious with everyone, there had seemed nothing she could not do, and it had felt imperative she get out of that house and assist Chang. Now, however, she was calming down and feeling the pang of real fear.

Oddly, she had never felt particularly threatened by Wimpole and Irving. She disliked them, but she had never fancied her life was in peril with them, but the men at the house she was now travelling to were a different matter. They were men with a lot at stake, who would not take kindly to her interference.

Clara glanced at Chang, trying to draw his eyes to her. She wanted to talk to him, discuss how they could go about this, maybe even have some reassurance from him, but Chang had shut his eyes and was pretending to sleep. Whether he was as anxious as she was, it was hard to tell, and she was not sure if it would make her feel better or worse to know that he was.

After an interminably long drive, Wimpole brought the car to a sudden halt near the tall wall of a property. The wall was grey stone and towered above them, giving Clara an impression of a prison, even though she knew that was far from the case.

"We are close to the house," Wimpole turned in his seat and addressed them.

Chang opened his eyes, revealing he had never been asleep in the first place.

"We are going to leave you with this car, Chang," Wimpole spoke to him. "It would seem more appropriate you driving up to the house than appearing on foot."

"I should think so," Chang snarled at him.

"Be aware, however, Irving has made sure this car has very little fuel left in it. If you think you can drive off in this car, you will be sorely disappointed. It has maybe a couple of miles left in the tank if that. Not to mention you will be watched constantly by my men."

"Nice to know you trust us," Clara snorted.

"I imagine the feeling is mutual," Wimpole grinned at her. "There is one last thing, because I am sure you have both considered the possibility of escape. I want to make it plain that is not an option. While I am inclined to be gracious towards you, Mrs O'Harris, as you are technically an innocent in this whole affair…"

"Thank you for at last noticing," Clara snapped.

Wimpole ignored her.

"I shall not offer the same leeway to Mr Chang. If we see you leave the house and appear to be attempting to escape, you will be shot. I have given all my men orders to ensure you do not leave this place alive, other than with the documents we require and in one of our cars."

Chang merely smiled at him, though if a smile could ever be more sinister and hateful was debatable.

"I had expected as much," he replied.

"We have to behave responsibly," Wimpole said, sounding haughty now. "You are a known criminal, one who has caused the police a good deal of trouble. I imagine few would weep over your passing."

"I do not care for your antics, Mr Wimpole," Clara told him coldly. "It strikes me that this business of secretly protecting the nation's safety brings out the worst in people."

"I confess to being ruthless," Wimpole agreed with her cheerfully.

"But I see the bigger scheme of things. We are all just pawns in a much larger game and one life is insignificant in the saving of potentially millions."

"I think you are missing the point," Clara replied. "Those millions are made up of those individual one lives. To show disregard for one, is to show disregard for all."

"Then, I must correct *you,* Mrs O'Harris and say that you are missing the point," Wimpole was unmoved. "But, no matter, you know your instructions. When you recover the documents, you shall make your way to the pavilion at the rear of the house. In the event of an emergency after you have acquired the documents, you can use the phrase 'frogspawn' to summon our help, but do not use it frivolously."

"Frogspawn?"

"A codeword you are unlikely to use under any other circumstance and thus be mistaken for requiring assistance, Mrs O'Harris," Wimpole shrugged at her. "In the event you fail, and end the weekend without the information we desire, you shall depart the house after all the other guests in this car and stop at this spot. We shall then collect you and plan when and where to try again."

Clara narrowed her eyes at him.

"I was not aware that there would be further missions. I thought the agreement was Chang does his best at this gathering and then be allowed to go free."

"That would be rather foolish on our part," Wimpole tutted at her. "If such was the arrangement, what would stop Chang from simply biding his time, enjoying the party as if it was any other, and then walking out at the end saying he did not have the opportunity to steal anything? No, you will both be required to help us until such a time as you succeed."

"Or get caught," Chang had his usual playful smile on his face, the one that suggested he was not taking anything terribly seriously.

"There is that possibility," Wimpole concurred. "In any case, you know your instructions and what the potential consequences of disobedience might be."

"I will be expected to have travelled here with certain supplies," Chang mentioned, looking sly.

"You will find a suitable array of your usual products in the boot of this car," Wimpole informed him. "Judicial use of them might very well aid your efforts to secure those papers."

Wimpole glanced between the two of them.

"Any questions?"

Clara had plenty, but none of them she expected to receive an answer to. She confined herself to scowling at him.

"Good," Wimpole declared. "Come on, then, time we switched places."

Wimpole exited the car before opening the rear door for Clara and showing her to the front passenger seat as politely as if he were her chauffeur. Meanwhile, Irving appeared from the second car, and Chang finally had his handcuffs removed. He was then shoved behind the steering wheel of the car by a mean-faced Irving. He was grinning from ear-to-ear, apparently more amused than upset by the performance. Clara did not share his nonchalance. Her stomach was churning with nerves and she sorely wished she had never opened her mouth and insisted on going with Chang.

She had been overconfident, thinking they could slip away once they were free from the immediate threat of Wimpole and Irving. She had underestimated her captors and was now paying the price.

"You look rather scared, Clara," Chang observed as he started the engine. "Might I suggest you work on that? It would not pay for you to turn up among my friends looking as terrified as a cat in a dog kennel."

"I am having a hard time feeling anything other than fear," Clara said, though she knew he was right and made a concerted effort to take deep breaths and regain some of her composure. "I feel like I have stepped out of the frying pan and straight into the fire."

"You asked to come along," Chang reminded her.

Clara hated that this had been her choice. Sometimes she allowed her temper to speak for her and get her in over her head.

"It seemed a good idea at the time," she snapped.

"Well, it is better than sitting in a kitchen in handcuffs," Chang rubbed at one wrist as he pulled the car forward and took them a short distance down the road, before turning through a large pair of metal gates.

"Do you think they would shoot you?" Clara asked.

"Yes," Chang said, and his smile slipped. "I don't think Wimpole is working for people who much care about the consequences that happen to pawns like me."

He was reiterating what Wimpole had said earlier; that they were pawns in a larger game.

"Who exactly do you suppose they work for? The government?"

"Not any branch that can be held accountable. Probably something more secret, and free from restraint. I have no doubt they are working for the benefit of this country and to keep the nation safe, but that does not make me feel any kindlier towards them."

Clara had to agree with his statement. The last twenty-four hours felt as though she had stepped into a nightmare, and she could not really comprehend what was occurring. A part of her vaguely hoped she was somehow dreaming, a consequence of the gassing she had suffered, and she was not really about to play spy at all.

But her rational self knew that she was really here and had made the choice to aid Chang.

"Try to behave like the sort of woman who would hang off my arm," Chang said, as they approached the house in the distance.

"I am going to assume that means being rather giggly, prone to saying silly things, and unlikely to cast scathing glances at people."

"You can have a bit of brains, I like my girls to be able to keep up, but don't behave like a detective."

"Right," Clara said, wondering how she could achieve such a thing.

"And don't be nervous."

"Easier said than done."

"Would it help if I said I will look out for you?" Chang turned his gaze briefly on her, and just for an instant, she could have sworn there was sincerity in his eyes.

Then he was looking back at the driveway and the moment was passed.

"It might help, a little," Clara conceded. "Though I am rather good at looking out for myself."

"Of course you are, never doubted it," Chang chuckled. "I would never question how remarkably talented Clara O'Harris is for keeping herself out of trouble."

Clara was not amused by his teasing.

"My name is Judy Barlow."

"Of course," Chang grinned. "Don't worry, Judy, I will look out for you."

Chang slipped her a wink, just as they pulled up before a massive mansion. Clara did not have time to consider what his manner meant, as she found her attention absorbed by the structure before her and the number of people milling around.

Her stomach knotted painfully again, and suddenly she was very glad she was there with Chang and not alone.

Which was the oddest thing in the world to ever cross her mind.

Chapter Eighteen

The discovery of the lock of hair, presumably cut from his wife's head, left O'Harris in a daze. He did not know what it meant, nor how to feel about it. Tommy was equally upset, but able to maintain some of his composure, at least long enough to issue the house keys they had found to the main search party so that every room in the property could be searched.

"Why would they cut her hair?" O'Harris repeated.

"I don't know," Tommy admitted. "But at least it is only her hair."

He heard the words as they spilled out of his mouth and regretted them at once. He winced.

"What I mean is, it does not look as though they hurt her."

O'Harris was not listening, he tossed the strands of hair on the floor and began to search the kitchen for further clues in a belligerent manner. Mr Miles watched quietly from a corner, afraid that it was his discovery of the hair that had triggered O'Harris' ire and worried the captain's wrath might fall back on him.

Tommy followed O'Harris around the room.

They observed that two chairs had been left pulled out from the table and one had odd marks scratched recently into the legs. Tommy knelt to observe them, using the torch O'Harris had abandoned once he had the lamp.

"There are scratches on the tiles here," he said. "Looks like something hard has gouged into them. Same with the legs of the chair."

"What could that be?" O'Harris asked, focusing his efforts now onto looking for more clues.

He would have to process what was meant by the lock of hair at a later date, right now his priority was finding Clara.

Tommy fingered the scratches.

"I don't know, but it appears something was around the legs of the chair, there is a circular cut. What is hard enough to cut into tiles, though?"

"A really sharp stone?" O'Harris suggested.

Miles had wandered back over, having heard the discussion, he leaned over the table.

"I have marks on my kitchen floor like that," he said quietly. "I made them by accident when I was cleaning some chains I had on the farm. They had gone rusty, and I was trying to oil them. I dropped them on the floor, and they dragged, leaving scratches like that. Nettie was furious."

"Chains," Tommy hissed, looking at the marks again. "Did they chain her up?"

O'Harris growled under his breath.

From outside the room, they heard someone shouting for them. They followed the noise and made their way to a sitting room a short distance from the kitchen. One of the men was stood by the fireplace.

"There are shards of paper in the hearth," he said. "Looks like someone had a fire here recently."

"Fish them all out, maybe they will tell us something," O'Harris instructed.

The man set to work, and Tommy helped him. The papers were badly charred and dangerously close to disintegrating into ashes. Most of them were unreadable, but one caught Tommy's eye.

"This is the address for a very fancy dress shop in town," he said, examining the paper he had come across. "I think this is a receipt for clothes. Women's clothing."

The man helping him had found some other scraps of paper from the same receipt and when they laid them out on the nearest flat surface it appeared Tommy's assumptions were correct. It was a receipt for several items of women's clothes, most of the list was unreadable but they distinctly could see the words 'evening dress' listed among the items.

"How bizarre," O'Harris said.

"Clara's hair was cut, and they bought her new clothes. Could it be they are trying to disguise her?" Tommy suggested.

"I can read something on this paper too," the man at the fireplace remarked.

They both turned to him.

"I think it is the remains of a letter, and it says quite plainly that there is a gathering at Lord Selby's home this weekend, beginning today."

O'Harris took the scrap the man had found as the fellow went back to searching for more.

"He is right. Lord Selby's name is obvious, but what does this mean?"

"Could they have taken Clara to this party?" Tommy said. "It would explain the need for an evening dress."

"But why? Clara would not be attending willingly. If they kidnapped her to take her to a party, it is the most ridiculous thing I have ever heard."

Tommy had to agree with him. None of the things they had found made any sense.

The fireplace proved to have nothing further to offer them, despite the diligent efforts of the searcher who poked through it. It appeared a lot of papers had been burned recently, but only the few pieces they had already discovered had survived the inferno.

The other searchers were having a similar result. Aside from finding a bedroom where it appeared someone had been sleeping recently, they had not found any further clues. The house had plainly been abandoned, and the kidnappers had moved on.

Perhaps they had moved on to Lord Selby's house?

"Where does Lord Selby reside?" Tommy asked O'Harris.

The captain's aunt and uncle had moved in more prestigious circles than the Fitzgeralds and he might have knowledge of where the gentleman lived.

"I don't know," O'Harris admitted, looking miserable at his failure.

"We have another lead, that is what is important, old man," Tommy consoled him.

They regrouped in the kitchen. Everyone was weary and upset that they had not found Clara. Miles had vanished, but no one had noticed, it was only when he suddenly reappeared in the kitchen that they realised he had been absent.

"I thought we might all need a drink," he said, showing them a bottle in his hand.

It was a partly consumed bottle of whisky.

"You have been rummaging in Mrs Lodes' cupboards," O'Harris said, though not with any rebuke – he fancied that drink.

The next task was locating suitable glasses for everyone, and in the process of doing so Tommy opened a cupboard and discovered there was a rubbish bin inside. The bin was almost empty, though a few items remained in the bottom. There was nothing important in the bin, but it was what it represented that sparked a new idea in Tommy's mind.

"We should search the rubbish bins!" he declared.

O'Harris glanced in his direction.

"They might contain something. The people who have been living here in secret must have disposed of their rubbish, right? We found none of it in the house aside from the scraps of burned paper. Maybe there is something in the outside rubbish bins?"

O'Harris needed little encouragement to begin the search once again. Heading outside through a back door, they explored around the house until they came upon two metal rubbish bins. One was almost overflowing with waste and must have been filled by the recent occupiers of the home.

O'Harris did not have the patience to search through it in a nice fashion. He kicked it over instead, scattering the contents on the ground and letting everyone have the chance to pick through it.

They found a lot of cigarette butts and ash, along with food waste. But also among them were some curious items. First, there was an empty container for hair dye, platinum blonde to be precise. O'Harris studied it with a frown, wondering who had used it and why. Could there be a woman involved in this kidnapping, which would explain the evening dress so recently purchased?

Another item in the waste caused him greater concern. It was a man's handkerchief with blood upon it, just small speckles as if someone had been punched in the nose or mouth. There were initials embroidered onto the edge of the handkerchief.

B. C.

"Who do we know with the initials B and C?" Tommy said as the handkerchief was held up before them by one of the men.

O'Harris blinked rapidly, his tired mind working fast. A number of names were slipping through his head but only one seemed to be the sort of name you would connect with the kidnapping of Clara O'Harris.

"Brilliant Chang!" Tommy and O'Harris said together, as they both realised what the initials were hinting at.

"He is just the sort to go around kidnapping people," Tommy growled. "Maybe he needs Clara's help and thought the only way he would get it was by kidnapping her?"

The handkerchief seemed to be the final piece of the puzzle. Why it was bloody they did not care to ask, but it had to mean that Chang was behind all this.

"That fiend!" O'Harris snapped. "Clara has always been too generous to him in the past. He must have snatched her away!"

"But why?" Tommy asked the obvious. "And does this have something to do with the letter about Lord Selby's party?"

"It must," O'Harris declared, mainly because he was desperate for that to be the case.

Otherwise, they had nothing to go on and no idea where to look next. "We have to find where this Lord Selby lives and pay him a visit."

They were all agreed it was the only thing they could do. They had searched the house from top to bottom and come up with a handful of new clues, but the only thing that hinted at a new location was the letter about Lord Selby. Who the man was, and why he would interest Chang, and why Chang would want to take Clara to him, was a mystery they could not explain with the evidence before them.

They finally left the house, their investigation complete. In the morning, they would let Inspector Park-Coombs know about the place, so that he could go and do his own digging around. Maybe he would find something they had failed to spot?

In the meantime, they were all feeling exhausted, and with no knowledge of where to go next, the only prudent option was to return home and to sleep for the few hours left of the night. Clara would not benefit from them being exhausted, even if it was hard to consider sleeping when she was missing.

They headed for the cars; a sombre pack of searchers who felt they had failed the one person they had come to aid.

O'Harris drove Miles home before he headed back himself. He thanked the farmer for all his efforts, which had led them this far. Miles wished he could have done more and admitted to feeling guilty that he had not tried to enter the house when he had seen the car there. Maybe, if he had, he would have found Clara and been able to rescue her. Instead he had run for home, doubting what he was seeing, and only after speaking to his wife thinking it would be a good idea to speak to Captain O'Harris.

What if that delay proved to be a fatal error?

O'Harris tried to convince him he had done the right thing, but Miles still headed to his house looking glum and clearly wondering if he had condemned Clara to her fate.

O'Harris drove the short distance home, struggling to keep his attention on the road. Annie was waiting for his arrival with a cup of cocoa. She had already given one to her husband and the other men who had been in the car driven by Jones. Now she made sure that O'Harris received the same.

The cocoa was welcome, but it felt as if it was a consolation, an attempt to soothe them after their failure.

O'Harris drank his too fast, burning his tongue and not caring.

Then he headed upstairs to his bed – his bed that suddenly felt empty. He fell onto it fully clothed, reaching out to the spot where Clara should have been.

His resolve broke at that moment, as he stared up at the ceiling and thought of his missing wife. He clutched at the blanket where she ought to have been lying, and the tears pricked at his eyes.

In the darkness of the night, he prayed pitifully to see his wife again.

Chapter Nineteen

"Lord Selby, it is always a pleasure to attend one of your gatherings," Chang beamed brightly at the older man who stood before him.

Lord Selby stood a good head over Chang, and had the most impressively bushy white eyebrows Clara had seen in some time. He was a well-built man who was slowly running to fat, with the watery red eyes of someone who drank a little too much and did not get enough sleep.

"May I introduce my lady friend, Miss Barlow?" Chang motioned to Clara who had politely stood a pace behind him.

She would normally have been standing at his side, introducing herself as a matter of principle, but she doubted Judy would have behaved in such a manner. Judy would step back and allow Chang to do all the work, while watching the men around her shyly.

"What a divine young lady," Lord Selby fawned over Clara's hand, taking it and kissing the back of it.

Clara did what she hoped was a suitably silly giggle and ducked her head modestly. Clara was not generally doted on by older men in this regard. She rarely had them kissing her hand and calling her divine. Clara was certainly pretty, but her figure was a little too curvy for the fashion of the day – though she had to admit, Irving had picked a dress out for her that was rather flattering, and she felt rather beautiful in it.

It was just that, on the whole, men found her rather intimidating and seeing as she was often meeting them during the course of an investigation, when they were either a suspect, victim, or witness, she rarely had them kissing her hand.

Lord Selby held onto her fingers a little longer than she was comfortable with and had an appraising look in his eyes she did not care for. Clara would have jerked away her hand and reminded him to mind his manners. Judy merely giggled again and tried to extract her fingers from his sweaty clutches.

Chang intervened, distracting Lord Selby by asking if he cared for something from the suitcase he was carrying, the one Mr Wimpole had supplied. Inside the case, Clara was not surprised to see a large assortment of illegal substances.

Clara would have been appalled at the sight. Judy merely smiled blithely.

Clara was finding playing being the dopey girl on Chang's arm was already causing her some discomfort. She was not used to keeping her opinions to herself, and was struggling to avoid saying something that would mark her out as someone other than the pretty, insipid girl she was playing.

She did not have much practice at behaving in such an 'un-Clara-like' fashion and it was starting to wear on her nerves.

Lord Selby selected a syringe containing some form of liquid. Clara watched him while pretending not to watch him. It crossed her mind that if they could ensure the house guests were sufficiently drugged and drunk then the rest of their escapade would be easy. They would just have to take the time to sneak through the house and find what they needed while everyone was lying around in a stupor.

It was a plan – of sorts. Clara wondered if Chang had had a similar idea.

"Always a pleasure to have you at one of my gatherings," Lord Selby was beaming at Chang, who had just informed him there was no charge for the syringe, seeing as it was Lord Selby's open invite that allowed him to be there. "I always say, Judy, that no party is the same without Chang and his little assortment of goodies."

Clara was distracted from taking a glance at the other guests in the room by Selby addressing her again. She turned in his direction and smiled broadly, giving a girlish chuckle that sounded terribly inane to her ears.

"He brings such pretty friends with him, too," Selby reached out and curled a finger under her chin.

Clara wanted to bite his finger to the bone, and was perilously close to doing so, when Chang had the wisdom to intervene.

"Might you introduce me to your other guests, Lord Selby, I do not think I have had the pleasure of their custom in the past."

Selby's attention wandered, and Clara took a firm step back from him, to make it harder for him to reach out towards her again. Selby started to reel off the names of the guests to Chang, who was listening intently.

Clara decided she would like some distance to recompose herself and stepped over to the side of the room where there was a table lined with drinks. She was not usually a drinker, and she did not think this would be a good time to start. Clara with her inhibitions loosened was prone to being even more contentious than her usual self. She settled for some tonic water she noticed in a siphon and sipped it slowly to try and ground herself.

"I don't know you."

Clara glanced up at the purring voice in her ear and saw another woman. This one was older than her but aiming for a similar look, with her platinum blonde hair set with a shingle and a somewhat excessive amount of make-up – at least to Clara's eye.

"Judy," Clara smiled brightly and offered her hand.

The woman stared at it, as if she had been offered a snake, then pulled a very poor excuse for a smile and shook Clara's hand. The distaste pouring off the woman was plain.

Well, Clara was not there to make friends, and she would be glad to keep whoever this person was at a distance.

"Lady Selby," the woman said in that same purring voice.

Clara cursed her luck. She had just managed to offend the lady of the house.

"You have come with Mr Chang?" Lady Selby asked, there was a definite edge to her voice.

"Yes," Clara responded, wondering if there was any answer she could give that would deflect some of the woman's visceral hatred.

"The day my husband offered him an open invitation to any of our gatherings is a day I rue," Lady Selby dropped what limited mask of politeness she was attempting to portrait and revealed her true feelings. "You can tell your little Chinese friend I do not want him here with his drugs, and I shall do everything I can to have him out of this house and banished for life before the weekend is through."

"Oh dear," Clara said, giving an uncomfortable laugh. "That is a lot to remember, could you write it down for me, maybe?"

Lady Selby muttered something under her breath about stupid women bringing the country to ruin (and on any other occasion Clara would have been quite inclined to agree with her) then she snapped at

'Judy.'

"Just tell him I want him out of this house," Lady Selby repeated. "And what I want, I get."

Clara nodded along with this information, her smile never leaving her face.

"I can remember that. Sorry we are a bother," she gave an inane giggle, and it had the effect she had hoped of driving Lady Selby away in despair.

Clara was beginning to see there could be some advantages to playing the stupid airhead, at least when it came to dealing with stuck-up over-opinionated women such as Lady Selby.

Then she had a terrible thought that she too might be one of those stuck-up over-opinionated ladies, when she was not playing her part. She would have had a similar poor opinion of any 'Judy' who came her way. She felt horrified at the revelation and promised to try to be a better person in the future.

Chang had disappeared among the guests for a while but now re-emerged and was clearly looking for her. Clara caught his eye, and he moved over to where she was alone for the time being. There proved to be a sufficient number of young and rather stupid girls in the room to avoid Clara drawing too much attention, and so she was spared being fawned and pawed over by the older men in the room.

"Lady Selby has your number," Clara said in a hush as Chang drew close.

"She has always detested me," Chang agreed. "What did she say?"

"She is going to do everything in her power to get you thrown out of the house and banished for good before the weekend is over."

Chang nodded his head thoughtfully.

"She could be a problem to us. If she is intent on getting rid of me, she will also be watching me like a hawk."

"There goes my plan of suggesting we get every guest so drunk and drugged none will notice what we are up to. Lady Selby doesn't strike me as the sort of person who would allow herself to succumb to any sort of influence."

"You almost sound like you admire her," Chang was amused.

"Not admire, but I do appreciate a woman who knows her own mind and isn't easily led. Let's be honest, Lord Selby is a fool to take what you are selling."

"You would not care for a pick me up?" Chang attempted to look hurt.

"I am well aware of the effects of the drugs you sell, so the answer is most definitely a no."

"Has anyone ever told you, you are rather boring?" Chang huffed.

"No one who cared not to have a hatpin shoved in their leg."

Clara raised an eyebrow at him, reminding him of one of their earlier meetings when she had done just that. Chang had the sense not to press the matter.

"We should head up to the room Lord Selby has given us and freshen up. It is late and everyone is already half-cut."

Clara glanced around the room, noticing how many of the guests were slumped against walls, or laughing inanely. Chang was right, they were half-cut.

"Not all of them are staying for the night, but when those that are go to bed, we will need to take a look around this house," he added.

"Pity we could not spike their drinks and make sure they could not trouble us," Clara said, holding her glass of tonic water close to her face, so no one could see her lips moving.

"Devious as always, Clara."

"Judy," Clara hissed at him.

Chang was confused for a moment and then realised what she was saying.

"Of course, Judy," then he offered her his arm and she took it.

Chang guided them out of the drawing room and towards the staircase to head upstairs. Clara sensed someone watching them and turned her head a fraction, pretending to be glancing at her dress. Out of the corner of her eye, she glimpsed Lady Selby watching her. Clara did not like the intensity of the woman's stare or the glimmer in her eye. She had a worrying feeling Lady Selby was going to be a lot of trouble for them. Far more trouble, in fact, than her husband.

"I feel like there is a dagger in my back already," Clara muttered to Chang.

He grinned merrily.

"Welcome to my world," he snorted. "I feel like that all the time."

"How do you endure it?"

"Easy," Chang chuckled. "I think about the money!"

Chapter Twenty

C lara lay on the bed in the guest room, her shoes discarded on the floor while Chang sat at the dressing table going through his suitcase of drugs.

"They have underestimated how much I can sell," Chang grumbled as he went through the contents, writing out a list on a piece of paper he had found in a desk opposite the bed. "I could sell twice this much, easily."

"Perhaps they do not wish you to overdo things?" Clara said.

"You were the one who suggested it would be best if the guests were all drugged out of their heads," Chang reminded her.

"Drugged or drunk," Clara corrected. "In any case, we are not going to be here the whole weekend. I don't think that would be wise. So, sell everything you can and make sure the guests are too high or tight to know what we are doing."

Chang turned in his chair and glanced at Clara.

"Something worrying you?"

"Lady Selby," Clara replied. "She is no fool and she will be watching our every move."

"She must sleep sometimes," Chang snorted.

"You are not taking this seriously enough," Clara tutted at him.

"Lady Selby could be a great danger to us. She might have servants in this house who are loyal to her and will report anything they see."

"Servants are not a problem," Chang shrugged. "They don't mind a little something too."

He produced a brown bottle of pills which he tipped back and forth.

"You intend to drug the staff as well?" Clara asked in amazement, before she considered the implications. "Good idea. We just need to have them all drink from something laced with sleeping powders and they will be out of our hair."

Chang stared at her.

"Is your plan to drug everyone in this house?"

"If I can manage it," Clara replied.

Chang turned back to his suitcase.

"Well, in that case you may be disappointed. I don't think I have enough here to result in the level of incapacitation you are hoping for."

Clara *was* disappointed. She frowned.

"Tell me about the guests who are staying here. You said you didn't know some of them?"

"Quite a few of them are new faces to me," Chang admitted. "They are from the North, and do not spend much time in London, so are not around my usual social circles. Most of the parties I attend are in the south of the country. There is another lord here, his name is Russell. He seems rather hare-brained; I think he has just inherited the title and a lot of money and is trying to make friends. Lord Selby will be interested in him because of the possibility of help with any financing he needs, rather than because he thinks the fellow is much of a supporter of his cause.

"There is a Mr Dodd, who is something of an iron magnate. He would do very well if the country were at war again. I didn't get to speak to him, but I had the impression he has a number of factories and was making shells during the war."

"Terrible man, thinking of profit over the loss of life a war would cause."

Chang shrugged, as if this were rather meaningless to him. Considering the sort of business he ran, in many ways he was not so far removed from Mr Dodd.

"There was a fellow by the name of Rankin who is another industrialist who can make a fortune in a time of war and would prefer if peace had never come to this country. Those are the key people here. Some of the others were hangers-on, who had popped over for the evening but were not staying. Russell, Dodd, and Rankin are the actual houseguests."

"What about the people Wimpole mentioned?"

"Not here. I get the impression his information is not as up to scratch as he thinks," Chang replied. "None of the people he mentioned to me are present, unless they are coming tomorrow."

Clara was not sure if that was a good or bad thing, the smaller the number of guests, the easier it might be to slip away and avoid them.

"What about the women on the arms of the men staying here?" Clara asked.

"Only Dodd has a wife. She is young, too young for him really, but I suppose she is thinking about money too," Chang shook his head, as if he might have suddenly developed a conscience.

Clara was about to mock him when she recalled his late younger sister. Chang's one weakness was his sister, and his protectiveness towards her had nearly been his downfall. It seemed he still tended to have brotherly feelings when he saw women of a certain age flaunting themselves at men. There might not be much that was noble about Chang, but in this regard Clara admired him, and did not wish to mock him.

"Do you think any of the other women could be a risk to us?"

"Hard to say," Chang confessed. "They were all very much like 'Judy' when I spoke to them, but they could be playing a part. They seem to have been invited by Lord Selby to give company to the men, though possibly I should say they have been paid to be here."

"Those sorts of women," Clara said darkly.

"At least they should not be terribly interested in us and may even be a useful distraction. They can peddle their form of vice, while I peddle mine."

Clara was not sure what to say to that. She suddenly felt tired and wished she was at home. She had never wanted to be a spy, to play such ridiculous games and to feel so scared at the possibility of being uncovered. Yet here she was, doing exactly that.

She did not like the anxiety it was causing her, and the tension running through her body. It was bad enough she was scared at what might happen if they were discovered, but to know that any escape was virtually impossible because of Mr Wimpole and his goons hanging around outside only made it feel worse.

Somewhere outside the room, a clock struck one in the morning. Chang glanced up, then rose and headed for the door of their room. He opened it a fraction and listened intently. Clara watched him without saying a word. The house had gone noticeably quiet since they had come up to the room. Earlier, she had been able to hear the chatter of voices and the general hum of a social gathering, now there seemed to be a stealthy silence creeping over the entire building.

Chang stood for several moments, just listening. Then he looked to Clara.

"I think everyone is abed."

Clara climbed off her own bed, ignoring her shoes. High heels would make too much noise as she moved around the house. Better to go in her stockings. She tiptoed to the door and stood just behind Chang.

He was still listening carefully but appeared to be satisfied that no one was stirring. He nodded to Clara and then slipped out of the room. She took a deep breath, regretting every decision she had made in the last twenty-four hours, and followed him.

The corridor was inky black, the shadows deep. No one had lit any lamps, and the corridor had no windows to offer a hint of light. Chang had been given a guest room close to the end of the corridor, meaning they would need to go past all the other guest rooms to reach the stairs. Clara felt as though this was a nightmare she was living in, but Chang was apparently enjoying himself. He still had a smile on his lips as he began to creep down the corridor.

Clara followed him, sticking to the carpet in the middle of the floor and hoping none of the boards beneath their feet creaked. As they passed by each door, they heard various sounds coming from the houseguests within. In one room, a man snored so loudly the windows seemed to rattle. In another, it appeared one of the ladies Lord Selby had invited was earning her keep. Clara cringed as she heard the sounds of their activities and sorely wished she could eradicate them from her mind.

They reached the head of the stairs without incident, though Clara had been ready with the excuse that they were looking for a bathroom if anyone had appeared. It might not have worked, these sorts of old stately homes did not necessarily have internal bathrooms, but it was better than any other excuse she could think up.

Chang was first down the stairs, and Clara followed him, creeping about as if she were a mouse in a room full of sleeping cats – which was not so far from the truth.

They reached the bottom of the stairs and were about to walk across the tiled floor of the front hall, when Chang waved a hand at Clara, and pressed her suddenly against the wall where there was a block of shadows to hide them.

Clara was not sure what had caused his panic, until she heard footsteps and saw a servant walking across the hallway, carrying trays laden with dirty plates and glasses away to be cleaned.

Chang was pressing her rather hard against the wall, and he had placed his hand over her mouth, which she did not like one bit. She would have bit his thumb, except she could not risk alerting the servant to what was occurring. She waited until the servant had departed, and Chang removed his hand before she berated him.

"Why did you cover my mouth?"

"Habit," Chang snorted at her. "And you might have asked a question, you do that sort of thing."

"I have enough sense not to in these circumstances!"

"Then why are you arguing with me and risking alerting people to our presence?"

Chang's sharp whisper silenced Clara because she was acutely aware he was correct. In the quiet of the night, even a hushed conversation was noticeable. She cursed herself for being so careless, but promised she would have words with Chang once they were safely back in their room.

Chang moved away from her, now slipping across the tiled floor. He had left his shoes behind too, deciding he could sneak around better in his socks. He paused in the middle of the hall and stared into the shadowy doorways that led to the servants' area, then he waved to Clara. She joined him, wondering why she was letting him lead the way, then recalling that he had more at stake than she did and if the worst occurred, she could probably feign ignorance of what he was up to.

Or rather Judy could feign ignorance if he were caught. She would profess to being an innocent dupe who had just come along for the party and who would think otherwise?

Chang headed to the nearest doorway, and she followed, noting he seemed to know his way around the house. She knew Chang had been here before, but to know the layout of the property so clearly suggested he had spent quite some time exploring it in the past. She would have to ask him about that too when they were safely back in their room.

She followed down one corridor after another, trying to keep track of where they were going, until they finally came to a room which seemed to be at the back of the property. The hallway was pitch black, which made it even plainer that there was a light glowing within the room.

"Damn it," Chang hissed under his breath.

Clara came close to him to see what the matter was.

"That is Lord Selby's study," Chang told her.

"Looks like someone has been in there tonight," Clara nodded. "But it could just be they have left the fire to burn down?"

Chang nodded his head, though his face suggested he was not convinced. Bottling his nerve, he went to the door and carefully turned the handle. There was a slight creak, but nothing more, then he pushed the door open, and they peered into the room.

As Clara had guessed, there was a fire burning down in the fireplace, casting its pleasant orange glow over the room. Unfortunately, there was also someone sitting in an armchair before the fire. It was Lord Selby, and he was sound asleep, lightly snoring, but in his lap was a large cat, which lifted its head as the door opened and glanced in their direction looking like it might meow.

Chang hastened to depart the room, not wanting to risk the cat alerting its master to their presence.

"No good," Chang shook his head to Clara.

Clara sighed, there was nothing else they could do but return to their room.

"We still have two days," Clara reminded him.

But the look on Chang's face echoed her own concerns. Two days suddenly seemed like no time at all, and the last thing Clara wanted was to be stuck in the forced employment of Mr Wimpole for any longer than necessary.

Chapter
Twenty-One

O'Harris woke before dawn and could not get back to sleep. He went down to the kitchen and made himself a cup of tea, while he considered his plan for the day ahead. The only clue they had was the letter with the mention of Lord Selby's party in it. That had to be significant, why else would the kidnappers have attempted to burn the letter? He had to think like Clara, and he knew what she would do.

He made his way to the library and retrieved from one of the shelves a directory for the county, then it was only a question of going through the index to look for Lord Selby's name. It revealed there were two entries for the gentleman. The first was a brief article about the local district, which mentioned Lord Selby as a person of significance who occasionally resided in the locale. O'Harris carefully read the details, not sure if any of it would be important.

Lord Selby had inherited his title in 1902 when his father had died. The title itself was old, dating back to the Tudors, though it had not been continuous and had briefly fallen out of use when a distant relative had become a political liability. The title had then been reinstated in the early nineteenth century.

Lord Selby was a keen investor in the industrial growth of the county and had shares in a number of important factories in the area, as well as further afield. The article listed some of the enterprises he was involved in from coal to copper, and then described the significant contribution Lord Selby had made to the war effort, turning over some of his factories to munition production, and putting a sizeable amount of money into the development of a type of tank that had ultimately been taken on by the military.

Lord Selby had been a key player in arming the country during the war, and the article keenly paraded his patriotism. Outside of being someone who knew about tanks and shells, the article went on to mention that although Lord Selby's ancestral estate was further in the north of the country, he spent a considerable amount of time in a smaller mansion located not far outside Brighton, close to a number of his business enterprises.

O'Harris flicked to the second entry which gave the address for Lord Selby's Brighton mansion where he spent the majority of his time. The compilers of the directory had been considerate enough to list not only the acreage of the estate, but the number of bedrooms, bathrooms, and overall rooms it contained. Along with listing the servants that were employed there at the time the directory was compiled, which was just after the last war.

O'Harris was not interested in whether Lord Selby employed three footmen, or had ten bedrooms, he just wanted to know where his house was.

Now he had an address, and he would travel to it as soon as Tommy was awake to discover if Clara was being held there. Lord Selby was already his primary candidate for being her kidnapper. Though his motive eluded him. Even so, he would make sure the man paid for his actions.

He heard the household rising, and determined he would head to the breakfast room, where everyone would gather for the day, and announce his discovery. He found Tommy stood by the window, his hands behind his back, his body rigid with the tension he was feeling.

"Tommy, I know where we need to head next," O'Harris announced as he entered the room.

Tommy spun around and listened keenly to O'Harris explain his discovery in the directory. Before O'Harris had finished, others were joining them. Tommy suggested they wait until everyone was there to save the captain from explaining himself a dozen times over.

O'Harris knew his brother-in-law was correct with the suggestion, but he was having a hard time keeping quiet when he was desperate to get out on the road.

"Where is Annie?" he asked Tommy to distract himself.

"I am here," Annie appeared in the doorway, carrying a tray of food.

Tommy jumped up to help her, though she scolded him with her eyes as he snatched the tray from her.

"You are to eat well before we leave this house," Annie informed O'Harris and her husband. "Clara needs us all at our best, and you cannot go play hero on an empty stomach."

O'Harris felt his belly suddenly grumble as if in agreement with Annie and he decided he could not argue. He took a plate of food, as did Tommy, and the rest of the fellows around the table joined in.

Annie sat beside her husband and helped herself to her own portion.

"Now, John, tell us what you have discovered?" Annie said once everyone was settled.

O'Harris had not realised Annie knew he had wanted to say something. He smiled at her, reminded that she was as worried as everyone else about Clara; she just had the sense to remain practical.

"I was thinking about the fragments of letter we discovered last night that mentioned an invitation to Lord Selby's party. That along with the items of clothing that had recently been bought, suggest Clara has been taken to this event, for what purpose I cannot fathom, but I think it is as good a place as any to look for her," he took a pause before he laid out his plan. "This morning, I looked up where Lord Selby lives in the local directory. While his main house is some distance away, he has a smaller residence which he frequently uses nearby, and I think it is logical for us to go there next and look for Clara. We can worry about the deeper questions concerning this matter, such as why she was taken, after we have found her."

Tommy nodded keenly, it made perfect sense.

"We shall do as we did last night and arrange two parties of rescuers. We have no idea what we shall find, but we do know that whoever has Clara is prepared to go to great lengths to keep her," O'Harris added.

"Should we bring guns, Sir?" one of the men down the table asked.

O'Harris hesitated; while his gut reaction was to say no, it had suddenly occurred to him that the people holding Clara were likely to be extremely dangerous and a gun to hand would not be a bad idea.

"I don't like guns," Annie said quietly.

"We have no idea what we are heading into," Tommy reminded her. "It may be necessary to fight for Clara."

Annie frowned deeply, her own appetite now evaporating.

"We shall be armed," O'Harris said decisively. "We shall place guns in the boots of the cars, but we will only use them if it becomes necessary. We cannot risk starting a fire fight and hurting Clara."

"What about Inspector Park-Coombs?" Annie said. "He should know where you are headed."

O'Harris almost refused, not sure he wanted the inspector around to see what he and his men got up to. They would never do anything particularly illegal, but they might bend the rules of law to ensure they reached Clara safely. Annie was looking at him intensely, and he knew he was not going to get away without agreeing to Park-Coombs being present.

"We shall take the inspector with us, so he can arrest the fellows responsible," he said to appease her.

"I shall make up a fresh hamper for Clara," Annie said firmly. "She will be hungry and thirsty, I am sure."

Tommy cast a look in her direction, a hint of unease in his expression, but he said no more until the breakfast was over and everyone was either preparing for the day at the home, or for the drive out to rescue Clara.

Annie started to tidy the plates on the table, even though there were servants ready to do it – she simply could not help herself. O'Harris had unfolded a map on the table and was working with Jones and Tommy to plot out the route they should take to Lord Selby's house.

O'Harris noticed that his brother-in-law was not paying full attention, his mind elsewhere. Abruptly, Tommy took a deep breath, then reached out for Annie's hand as she was about to pick up a teacup.

"You are not coming today, Annie."

Annie froze; it was like she had literally turned to stone beneath his hand. After several tense seconds, she turned her gaze towards him.

"Why not?"

"It might be very dangerous," Tommy told her calmly. There was no point getting agitated and starting an argument. "I cannot risk you, and you know that. You have to look after yourself by staying here."

Annie gave up upon reaching for the teacup and sat down in the chair she had so recently vacated.

"I can't Tommy, this is Clara we are talking about."

"Clara would not want you to risk yourself for her," Tommy said softly. "Nor the baby. Clara will be furious if you come on this rescue adventure."

Annie placed a hand on her slowly growing stomach.

"I want to be there when you find her. I want her to know I came for her."

"She will know that," Tommy reassured her. "Because we will tell her what you did, but Clara will be more upset if anything happens to you than if you are not there. And you know that."

Annie stared at the table, not sure how to respond.

"I just don't know if I can sit around here waiting to know if she is all right," Annie said at last, her voice barely a whisper. "What if something terrible has happened? What if I wait here all day only for you to come back and tell me Clara is..."

"Clara is too stubborn to die," Tommy told her firmly, now clasping her hand tightly. "You are in the best place by being here, and we shall get word to you as soon as we know anything."

"Even if you get to this place and discover Clara is not there?" Annie asked.

"Even then, we shall not leave you in suspense."

Annie thought about his words for a while, her free hand rubbing at her belly.

"You are right, of course. I have to stay here," Annie gave a shaky sigh. "You will be very careful, won't you, Tommy?"

"Of course!" Tommy leaned in and kissed her cheek. "You don't have to worry about me."

"I couldn't bear it if you didn't come back," Annie said, a tear rolling down her face. "I couldn't bear to lose you and Clara."

"No one is losing anybody," O'Harris told her firmly. "I promise you."

Tommy hugged Annie as tightly as he dared.

"We shall all be home this evening, you wait and see."

Annie sniffed.

"Don't make promises you are not sure you can keep."

Chapter
Twenty-Two

C lara stood before the full-length mirror in the bedroom admiring her appearance in the clothes Irving had bought for her. She had to admit the man had a good eye and had judged her size perfectly. The day outfit was more tasteful than the evening one, but it still had a lot of glamour about it. She fancied she looked rather good in the dark olive-green dress, and the deep red jacket that accompanied it. She was still unhappy about the stole, however, and was content to leave it lying on the bed for the time being.

"Ready for breakfast?" Chang asked her.

He was not in a good mood. After their foiled attempt to find the documents the night before, they had come back to the room to regroup and consider what to do next. Chang had moaned and groaned about his bad luck, and made a fuss about everything, until he had finally conceded defeat and fallen onto the bed, fully clothed, and grumbled his way to sleep.

Clara had lain on the far side of the bed, (which was thankfully enormous and afforded them plenty of room without getting too close to one another) and stared at the ceiling, trying to fathom how she had ended up in this mess. Since she had no night clothes, she lay in the evening gown she had worn, pulling a blanket over her to keep out the chill, wondering how she would ever explain this to O'Harris and Tommy.

She could barely explain it to herself.

Clara finished neatening her hair, still trying to get used to its shortness, and turned to follow Chang from the room and head downstairs. They had heard people stirring in the other rooms and assumed they would soon all be heading down for breakfast.

Chang picked up his suitcase of delights. Clara was surprised he would consider taking it down to breakfast, until she realised he was thinking he could sell drugs to give the previous night's customers a boost for the morning. No doubt some of them were feeling rather worse for wear and would appreciate something to perk them up.

Clara thought it was amazing how people abused their bodies. They had one physical form to live out their days in, and they treated it appallingly, without considering how that might impact them in their later years.

Or maybe they did not care to reach their later years?

Still pondering the oddness of people, especially people with money and no excuse other than boredom and a general disaffection with life to destroy themselves, she followed him downstairs.

"You seem to know this house very well, Chang."

"It's not my first time here," Chang replied.

"Even so, your knowledge of the floorplan was quite impressive."

"Clara, ask the damn question you want answered, and save us the bother of all this pussyfooting around."

"Judy," Clara corrected him, wondering how Chang ever managed to navigate his own criminal world if he could not recall her dummy name. "Have you explored this house before?"

"Yes," Chang answered sharply.

"When?"

"About a year ago," Chang answered. "I was here for another party, and I took myself for a late-night stroll around the house. I never sleep well in a strange bed, and it is always prudent to know the ways in and out of a property."

"I will give you a point for forethought and cunning," Clara nodded at him. "I am also very impressed at your memory."

"It doesn't pay to forget how you can escape from somewhere, just when you might need that knowledge," Chang huffed at her. "I am surprised you are not more familiar with such a practice."

"I rarely need to know such things," Clara replied. "At least not to the extent you do."

They were in the front hall and crossing to the breakfast room where they could hear the clink of cutlery. Lowered voices suggested some of the guests were present, but were not feeling bold enough to speak loudly, probably suffering the effects of hangovers from the night before.

As they were closing on the room, the giant cat they had noticed the night before came out of another doorway and bumbled over to them. The feline was rather fat and looked as though it lived its life largely to be fed titbits and take naps in any patch of sunlight it could find. It greeted Clara happily and she rubbed its head.

"Charlie knows a cat person when he meets her," Lord Selby had appeared behind his pet and smiled at Clara. "You have made a friend, Miss Barlow."

Clara stood up from stroking the cat.

"I do love animals," she simpered at Lord Selby. "Chang says he will buy me a puppy, isn't that right, darling?"

She nudged Chang who had a face like thunder. Somehow he mastered his expression so by the time he turned to look at Lord Selby, he appeared on top of the world.

"I have promised her that, anything for my lady."

"A gentleman to a fault is our Chang," Selby chuckled. "I say, whatever was in that syringe last night was good stuff."

Selby patted his shoulder affectionately.

"Best night of sleep I have had in years."

Chang chuckled back, only Clara noticing the concern in his eyes. What had Mr Wimpole supplied him with? If he did not know the efficacy of his own drugs, then how could he work out how much to give people? He could be at risk of over or under dosing them and leaving their espionage in a tricky position.

Chang's concern never made it beyond a slight crinkle at the corner of his eyes, and he was joking with Lord Selby as they were shown into the breakfast room.

There was a lavish assortment of food laid out for them on a sideboard. Clara caught the distinctive aroma of kippers – a fish she had never been charmed by due to the considerable amount of small bones that had to be navigated to consume it. There were platters of bacon, eggs, sausages and toast, and a jug of freshly squeezed orange juice which took Clara by surprise. She had consumed fresh orange juice on very rare occasions in high summer when it was available but had never seen it in a private house. She wondered just how wealthy Lord Selby was to be able to buy in large amounts of oranges just for the sake of juicing them for his guests.

Where did a person even get oranges at this time of year? It was only the start of summer, and Clara associated them with Christmas when a small orange was customary in a stocking.

She did not question the bounty, however, and helped herself to food and orange juice just as Chang did. Clara was not surprised to discover that her belly was in control that morning. She had eaten little over the last couple of days and a good detective never worked at her best on an empty stomach. Her mouth was almost watering as she contemplated the food before her.

"Who are the people at the table?" Clara whispered to Chang when she had the chance.

Chang lifted his head a fraction as he replied.

"Mr Dodd is the funny looking fellow wearing that unappealing mustard coloured suit. Just to his right is Mr Rankin."

Clara caught a glimpse of a man who reminded her of a walrus with a very gingery red moustache and not a strand of hair on his head. Mr Rankin was unappealing on the eye, but the girl sitting next to him was very pretty and fawned over him. She was currently mopping at his waistcoat with a napkin where he had dropped a blob of butter.

"No sign of Lord Russell, then," Clara noted.

"Or of Mrs Dodd," Chang replied.

The only women in the room were Clara and the girl who had accompanied Rankin. Mr Dodd did not look upset by the lack of his wife and was putting away his breakfast quite happily.

Clara took up her plate of food and followed Chang to the table. They sat opposite to Rankin, with Dodd at the foot and Lord Selby at the head of the table. The overweight cat sauntered to its master and plonked itself down at his feet, clearly ready for the food about to come its way.

Clara began to butter a piece of toast, taking the time to observe her fellow diners. She was unsure how Judy would start a conversation, but she knew full well how Clara would – Clara would barrel in with both feet and demand answers.

She was desperate to say something, but no matter how she spun an opening question in her mind, it sounded wrong. Not 'Judy' enough.

Luckily for her, the girl who was pandering to Mr Rankin took an interest in Clara when her male companion turned his attention to Mr Dodd and began asking him about certain stocks and shares they had in common.

"My name is Ginny," she held out a hand for Clara to shake.

Clara did so gladly.

"Judy," she responded.

"I have not seen you at one of these parties before."

"I have never been before," Clara admitted.

Ginny looked her up and down, the appraisal in her expression blatant.

"You are a bit old to be only just starting out."

Her words cut through Clara like a knife, and Chang was so taken by surprise that he nearly choked on a kipper he had been in the process of eating.

Clara turned from the hard gaze of Ginny, who had gone from friendship to rivalry in an instant, to start slapping him hard on the back – harder than was strictly necessary, in fact, because she was hurt and felt this was all Chang's fault.

Chang started to cough harder in his effort not to laugh.

"Is the fellow all right?" Mr Dodd asked.

"Fish bone in his throat," Clara responded, giving Chang one last vigorous slap on the back.

He sucked in a lungful of air, tears streaming down his face.

"My dear, your tender attentions have worked their magic yet again," he choked out.

Clara gave him a cold smile.

"All it took was a good slap."

Ginny was watching them with a strange look in her eyes. Clara had now had the time to compose herself and take her on. She turned back to the woman.

"I do not precisely understand what you mean by starting out. Would you be so kind as to elaborate?" Clara gave Ginny her most innocent smile.

With all the diners' attention on Chang, Ginny now found herself surrounded by silence and all ears on her words. She hesitated because hinting at something, and being blunt about it, were very different things.

"I think you misheard me," Ginny said quickly.

"I am pretty sure I did not," Clara replied.

Ginny looked frozen as she tried to think of something to say, fortunately she was to be provided with a distraction by shrieks from upstairs. The screaming voice of a woman rang down the stairs and disturbed them all from their breakfast.

"Lord Russell is dead! Lord Russell is dead!"

Chapter
Twenty-Three

N o one moved.

Clara glanced at Chang, every detective fibre in her body insisting she rise at once and go to see what had just occurred. Chang gave her a stern look, indicating she was not to move.

At that moment, Mrs Dodd stumbled into the breakfast room. She looked dishevelled and was dressed only in her nightgown with a dressing robe over the top, which had fallen open and flapped behind her as she ran like angel wings.

"Did you not hear me?" she demanded of the room at large.

Lord Selby had a strange look in his eyes, as if he had no idea what to do. He glanced around the diners in a panic. It was no good, Clara was going to have to do something.

Mrs Dodd was standing in the doorway, desperate for help, her chest rising and falling as she contained the hysteria building within.

Clara made a decision.

Ignoring the scowling glance Chang gave her, she rose from the table and went to Mrs Dodd.

"Show me," she said to her softly, and with an arm around the woman's shoulder, she walked with her back to the dead man.

Mrs Dodd took Clara upstairs and along the corridor. Outside a door that Clara recognised as the one she had heard some very passionate sounds coming through the night before, Mrs Dodd froze and hesitated.

"He is in there," she said quietly.

Clara squeezed her arm in an effort to be reassuring, then entered the bedroom. There was no sign of the girl that Lord Russell had been with the night before, though Clara noted a discarded stocking near the bed. She found that curious, as she could not imagine the girls who had been brought to the house to entertain the men were the sort to be able to simply throw away stockings.

Lying in the bed on his back was Lord Russell. The young man had a pronounced overbite as his head rolled back against the pillow, his nose pointing at the ceiling. Clara checked his pulse, noting that his skin was ice cold. He had been dead some time.

Resting one knee on the bed so she could reach over better, she began an examination of the young man. There was staining around his mouth that looked like vomit, and she wondered if he had choked to death after his excesses of the night before.

She was beginning to take a closer look at the corpse when she heard someone else in the doorway.

"What is going on?"

Clara looked up and saw that Lady Selby had arrived. She looked as grim-faced as the night before, and her clear distaste for Clara was plain on her face. She was only just out of bed, and without her make-up she looked a lot older and much more time-worn. She could almost be described as haggard.

"Lord Russell is dead!" Mrs Dodd declared, still sounding close to succumbing to hysterics.

Clara wondered just what had caused the woman to enter this bedroom so early in the morning looking for his lordship. She must have been seeking him out, there was no other reason for her to have entered his lordship's room.

"What is she doing over him?" Lady Selby demanded, pointing a finger at Clara.

Clara was tired of these games.

"I was an auxiliary nurse during the war," she responded.

"I suppose they were desperate for people," Lady Selby scoffed.

Clara ignored her because she had just noticed something peculiar about Lord Russell's torso. The man had fallen back on the bed fully dressed, which had struck Clara as strange considering the sounds she had heard coming through the door the previous night.

But it was when Clara touched his jacket that she realised there was something hard beneath it. When she flipped open the lapel, she discovered that Russell had not died by accident. Someone had shoved a thin, brass letter opener into his side and up beneath his ribs. They had pushed the item at an angle, and in so deep, that the fall of the jacket had disguised the murder weapon from a casual glance.

The lack of blood on the bed was explained by the murder weapon still being in place and plugging the wound, but no doubt Lord Russell had suffered severe internal bleeding. He had probably been too intoxicated to realise what was happening to him and so had failed to get himself help.

"We have a problem," Clara said to the women in the doorway. "Lord Russell has been murdered."

Lady Selby stared at her in astonishment, then marched across the room as if she would slap Clara.

"Surely not! It must have been an accident. It was that ghastly

Asian's fault with his suitcase of poison!"

As she arrived at the bed, Clara opened the jacket so she could see clearly what had happened to the unfortunate lord. Lady Selby gasped.

Mrs Dodd now ran into the room to see for herself what they were looking at. When she saw the letter opener jabbing into the side of Lord Russell, she fell to her knees and started to weep.

Clara already had a suspicion about the connection between the girl and the deceased peer, but her sudden tears confirmed it.

"Lady Selby, this is a matter for the police," Clara informed the lady of the house.

"No!" Lady Selby said fiercely.

"A man has been murdered in your home. We both know you cannot cover that up. Not when the gentleman in question is a peer of the realm. His family will ask questions."

Lady Selby's eyes were fixed on the letter opener. The shock had turned her already haggard face into the horrific visage of a mythical gorgon. She just needed some snakes around her head to complete the look.

"I need to speak to my husband," she said, departing the room in a hurry.

Clara abandoned the bed and helped Mrs Dodd to her feet. In the immediate moment, she was content to allow others to worry about the demise of Lord Russell. From all she had been told, he was probably not a great loss to the country, and if he *was* a conspirator in this scheme to start another war, it was probably best he was out of the way. But she was intrigued by who might have killed him and why.

Was someone else in the house concerned about the conspiracy here and determined to rid the group of one of their key members or was there another motive behind the crime?

"Mrs Dodd, why don't you come to my room and sit down."

Clara escorted the sobbing woman to her own bedroom at the end of the hall. Mrs Dodd was a tiny thing, light as a feather in Clara's grasp. Her hair, just like every other woman's at the event, was bobbed, shingled, and dyed that awful platinum blonde colour Clara was growing to detest. Her eyebrows, however, revealed that she was a natural brunette. Clara almost had to carry her into the room, and deposit her in the padded chair before the dressing table. Mrs Dodd's eyes fell on the suitcase that Chang had left sitting there after the audit of his stock.

"I need something to take off the edge!"

She started to fumble with the suitcase, which Chang had taken the precaution of locking before they went down to breakfast.

"You need nothing from there," Clara told her firmly, taking her hands. "I shall get you a glass of water to begin with, and then we shall talk."

Clara fetched a glass from the bedside cabinet and filled it with water from the jug standing just next to it, bringing it back to Mrs Dodd to sip. Then she brought over another chair and sat down before the woman.

"Tell me why you were in Lord Russell's room this morning."

Mrs Dodd dipped her head.

"Isn't it obvious," she sniffed, pulling at the edges of her dressing gown, and hauling it back onto her shoulders.

"I prefer not to make assumptions," Clara told her.

"You would be the first around here to behave that way," Mrs Dodd huffed. "We were having an affair. We have been these last six months."

Clara had supposed something like that to be the case.

"Were you with him last night?"

"For a little while," Mrs Dodd confessed. "While my husband was lying unconscious on our own bed. Then I had to return to him so he would not realise I had been gone."

Mrs Dodd rubbed at her eye, smearing the remains of her mascara from the night before.

"This morning, my husband rose first and left the bedroom. I waited until I was certain he was downstairs and absorbed in eating his breakfast, then I headed to Lord Russell's room to wake him," Mrs Dodd gnawed on the edge of her thumb as she remembered that moment. "Poor Bertie didn't answer the door, and I could hear nothing from within. He had consumed rather a lot of *stuff* last night and I was a little concerned about him. He had passed out after..."

Mrs Dodd hesitated to finish her statement, though Clara knew exactly what she meant.

"I had left him passed out on the bed. I was worried about him then, but I had to get back to my husband. When Bertie did not answer my knock this morning, my worries increased, so I opened the door and hurried inside, which was when I saw him lying on the bed."

Mrs Dodd sniffed back further tears.

"I knew he was dead at once. I could just sense it, then I went over to him and shook his shoulder, and he was stone cold."

She began to weep again. Clara rested a consoling hand on her arm.

"I am so sorry, Mrs Dodd," she said. "It must have been a terrible shock."

"I thought he had overdosed," Mrs Dodd whispered, the words almost too terrible to say aloud. "But now you say someone murdered him?"

"You saw the letter opener in his side, he was stabbed and that wound killed him," Clara had never seen a reason to be anything other than blunt when stating the facts. "Someone in this house took advantage of Lord Russell being unconscious and killed him."

Mrs Dodd shuddered at the news.

"How could this have happened? Why has this happened?"

"I do not know," Clara replied. "But we have to convince the Selbys to summon the police. A murderer cannot go free."

Mrs Dodd lifted her eyes and stared into Clara's.

"I don't know who you are, but I am so grateful you are here," she said, leaning forward and embracing Clara. "You were the only one in that whole room who listened to me and helped me. If you had not stood up, who would have?"

"Someone would have, eventually," Clara replied.

She gently patted the woman's back.

"Thank you," Mrs Dodd pulled away and dabbed at her eyes again. "I... I think I will get dressed. If the police are coming, I want to be ready for them."

"I am going to make sure they come," Clara informed her.

Mrs Dodd nodded her head, reassured by Clara's calm authority, then she departed from the room. Clara was standing up to return to the breakfast room and demand something was done, when Chang stormed in and shut the door behind him.

"We need to talk."

"You are going to berate me for going to Mrs Dodd's aid, and I do not care."

"No, we really need to talk," Chang threw up his hands. "Lord Selby has just had a big argument with his wife, and they have agreed to call the police. I understand his lordship has been murdered in their guest room?"

"Yes."

"Then what on earth are we going to do now?"

Clara glanced towards the window.

"Well, I don't know about you, but the second Inspector

Park-Coombs arrives I am going to place myself under his charge and tell him everything that has gone on the last couple of days."

"You really think that will work?" Chang looked desperate.

Clara was not used to seeing him so spooked.

"I think it will place Mr Wimpole in a pickle, and I intend to make him suffer for all he has done."

"What about the safety of the country?"

"Oh, on that regard, I think now is the perfect opportunity for you to go find those documents everyone is interested in."

Chang stared at her.

"You are serious."

"I am. I shall keep everyone together and busy while we await the police, and you will search the study."

Chang groaned to himself, but there was a certain logic to Clara's suggestion, and they might not get another chance once the police were there.

"This is crazy!" he hissed at her.

"No crazier than anything else we have done so far this weekend," Clara shrugged.

Chapter
Twenty-Four

I nspector Park-Coombs nodded his head as Tommy and O'Harris explained their deductions and stated they were going to Lord Selby's country estate because it was the logical next step. He had arrived in the police car, (the only one his particular constabulary had) with four constables, after O'Harris had telephoned to say he thought he had an idea as to where Clara might be.

Now he bundled his men back into the car and followed the captain's lead as he drove out, Jones was behind the inspector in a third car. Tommy and the other men from the home were distributed uncomfortably between the two vehicles. There was an atmosphere of tense anticipation as they headed out.

Park-Coombs was slightly alarmed by the number of men who were getting into the two vehicles, there seemed to be a lot more of them than was necessary, but he had the sense to know he could do nothing about the matter. O'Harris would simply drive off if he tried to protest and, in truth, he would be glad of the back-up when they went to Clara's aid. He was angry on her behalf as well and wanted to see her safely home.

Had he known that there were hand pistols loaded into the boots of the cars, he would have had something to say, but O'Harris had made sure to pack them before he arrived.

O'Harris led the charge, having memorised the map directions to Lord Selby's address. Tommy sat in the passenger seat beside him, trying to convince himself that Clara would have been sensible enough to cooperate with her captors, and not irritate them into doing something rash. He loved his sister dearly, but he was also aware of her shortcomings, and she was very good at causing people to lose their temper.

It was as if she just could not help herself.

They had driven for a while, following the back roads without seeing anyone, when suddenly Tommy spotted something. Tucked behind a hedge, partly down a country lane, was a black car with white wheels.

"Look at that!" Tommy nudged O'Harris.

The captain needed no further hint. He pulled his own car in front of the lane, blocking in the suspect vehicle and was jumping out before the engine had quite stopped. His men followed, bundling out either side of the car.

Tommy jumped out of the passenger seat, his door directly opposite the lane and their targets. As they all rushed towards the vehicle, the two men inside it looked at them in astonishment. They tried to get out and escape, but the lane was rather narrow, and their car doors would not open fully, being jammed against the hedges either side. In the chaos that followed, O'Harris' team gained the upper hand, and within moments they had the two strangers tightly clasped and secured as their prisoners.

Park-Coombs joined the commotion around the time it was all

coming to an end. His police constables hastily formed a cordon to prevent the two suspects running away, though with the amount of irate former soldiers surrounding them there was slim chance of them attempting an escape.

One of the fellows was tall and lanky, with greying hair and an expression on his face that suggested he would gladly kill them all. The other was a solid-set man, with bandy legs, who looked like he could take all-comers in a fair fight. They were a proper pair of thugs and Tommy found himself mentally shuddering at the sight of them. If it was men like these who had taken his sister, he truly feared for her wellbeing.

"I am Inspector Park-Coombs of the Brighton Constabulary, and I have heard talk of men in a car just like yours abducting a young lady," Park-Coombs stormed towards the two men, bristling with authority.

His anger was palpable, and while it might be better restrained than that of O'Harris – who looked like he wanted to beat the men to a pulp – it was no less dangerous for being constrained by the limitations of his rank as a policeman.

Neither of the two suspects spoke.

"You are not going to say anything? You are under suspicion of kidnapping," Park-Coombs reminded them.

The two men glowered at him.

Park-Coombs gave a dramatic sigh.

"Whoever you are, I am going to throw the book at you, and I sorely doubt your employer will be able to stop me."

Again, the men did not react. Their stony silence was beginning to trouble even the usually implacable Park-Coombs.

"You realise what you have done, don't you?" he stepped nearer to the two men. "You have upset what is in essence an entire army platoon by stealing that woman. You are being held by men who served our country nobly, who have seen the very worst humanity can do, and who have already had their fair share of blood on their hands. And you stole from them a young lady they think rather fondly of. What do you suppose they are going to do to get her back?"

Still no words escaped the men's lips, but the stockier one cast a sidelong look at the man to his side, the first hint that he was nervous.

And he was right to be nervous, for O'Harris and his men were furious. They turned fearsome gazes upon their captives, their eyes calling for blood. There was no sign that there would be mercy at their hands, except if their suspects talked.

"I am going to go back to my car and make a few notes," Park-Coombs said loudly. "You will keep an eye on these fellows while I am gone, yes? I might need my constables to assist me with some of my spelling, so I shall take them with me. Terrible speller, I am, terrible."

Park-Coombs fixed his gaze onto the suspects.

"While I am gone, I am sure you will take good care of these two. I dare say, I shall be making my notes so loudly I shan't even be able to hear if you call out for me. Come along, constables."

The inspector turned away, his constables following, and immediately the two suspects felt the hands upon them tightening. O'Harris stepped before them, arms folded over his chest, Tommy was just at his side. The captain was not a brute, and torture was not in his repertoire, but his captives were not to know that, and the look in his eyes was dangerous.

"What shall we do with them?" O'Harris said to his brother-in-law.

"I can think of a few tricks I learned at the front to get a man to talk," Tommy said, lying through his teeth, but doing a good enough job of it that the smaller of the two men pulled away from him.

"No one here to help you," O'Harris took a pace closer, stretching his arms as if preparing to strike. "I fancy you are rather expendable in the eyes of your employers. Can't imagine they will worry themselves about what became of you, right?"

O'Harris had hit a nerve. The men did know that in the event of any trouble they were on their own. Mr Wimpole had been very clear about that. The knowledge no one was coming to the rescue and that they were surrounded by a dozen men with military training, and a taste for blood, finally cracked the stockier of the two men – the one who, ironically, had looked the toughest.

"We never laid a finger on her!"

"Shut up, Stan!" the tall fellow hissed at his comrade.

Stan was not about to shut up. He knew when he was outnumbered and fighting a losing battle. Why should he take a beating for the sake of a man who would cast him to the wolves if the need arose? It wasn't as if they were even being paid very well for their work, and he couldn't say he terribly cared about their mission. He just was in it for the ready cash.

"She is safe as houses," Stan persisted. "No harm done."

O'Harris stepped forward until he was towering over Stan, who proved to be a good head shorter than him.

"You kidnapped my wife, and you try to tell me there was no harm done?"

Stan gulped.

"It was just for a while, just to help convince *him* to help us. Really, it was that other fellow's fault."

"What other fellow?" Tommy asked.

"The Chinese bloke," Stan continued. "He was the one they were interested in. He was the one they needed to help us."

"Chinese bloke?" Tommy paused for a second, then nudged O'Harris hard. "They have to mean Brilliant Chang!"

"Then we were right that he is involved," O'Harris groaned.

"He turns up like a dirty penny," Tommy shrugged. "So, they needed Chang's help and for some reason they thought Clara could convince him?"

Stan nodded his head vigorously. His cohort was trying to pretend he was not there, and not a party to his friend giving away all their employers' secrets.

"I don't care why they did this," O'Harris snapped. "I want to know where Clara is right now, so I can go and fetch her."

"They are not far up the road," Stan said. "At Lord Selby's summer estate."

"Then what are you doing here?" Tommy asked him.

"Watching, in case either of them try to escape without doing their job," Stan explained as fast as he could. "We have orders to shoot Chang if he bolts."

"There is a rifle on the back seat of the car," one of the men told O'Harris.

"You were going to shoot my wife!" O'Harris shouted in Stan's face.

"No! No! Only Chang! We only had orders to shoot Chang if he tried to flee!"

O'Harris was not impressed.

"You could have used the gun on us," Tommy reflected, thinking they had had a lucky escape.

"Never would have taken out all of you, would I?" Stan snorted at him. "I would have been caught all the same and in even more trouble. We should have bolted sooner."

"You shouldn't have kidnapped my wife!" O'Harris growled at him. "I take things like that very personally!"

O'Harris was scary when he wanted to be, and as he towered over Stan, the full force of the man who had once flown the skies and dodged the enemy was shone upon him. Stan gulped and trembled.

"It was a mistake, s-s-sorry!"

"Enough with these two, we need to find Clara," Tommy was the voice of reason. "We shall make sure these two can't escape, and head for Lord Selby's home."

The tension evaporated from O'Harris as he came back to the moment. They were close to finding Clara and he did not want to waste any more time.

"Get them in my car," he said to his men. "Use whatever you can find to tie their hands and feet. Time we moved on to catch their employers and bring my wife home."

Chapter Twenty-Five

C lara had dropped the act of pretending to be airhead Judy Barlow, it was serving her no purpose anymore. She rounded up Lord and Lady Selby, Mr and Mrs Dodd, and Mr Rankin in the breakfast room. Mr Rankin's lady friend had made herself scarce as soon as she learned there was a dead body upstairs. Clara was annoyed she had departed – she was just as much a suspect as anyone else – but there was not much she could do about it.

In any case, she had a hunch she already had the killer trapped in the breakfast room, she just had to work out who they were.

A message had been sent for Inspector Park-Coombs, but his arrival would take some time considering the distance they were from Brighton. In the meantime, Clara was going to keep all the suspects in one place and let Chang get on with finding the secret documents.

Chang had reluctantly agreed to her plan, seeing as it was about the only hope they had left of gaining the documents and getting out of the place. She liked to suppose she had played on his conscience to achieve the result, but in reality she knew she had merely played on his powerful sense of self-preservation. If he wanted out of this nightmare, he needed those documents.

Clara now faced the room of people, standing before the door and observing them as if they were each and every one a killer. No one was arguing with her, too shocked and still a little too doped and hungover from the night before to be able to formulate an argument.

"How could this have happened?" Lord Selby said quietly.

He had repeated that phrase at least three times already, and it was plain his wife was sick of it and, by extension, him.

"Which of you knew Lord Russell before he came here?" Clara asked the room.

"Why is she asking us questions?" Mr Rankin glanced at the others.

"Because, Mr Rankin, I am about the only one here who is able to keep a cool head. You do realise the seriousness of this situation? A man is lying dead upstairs, someone stabbed him, someone from this household."

"It must have been the girl he was with last night," Mr Dodd muttered.

Mrs Dodd trembled and cast her eyes at Clara, begging her not to mention the woman Russell was with was right in the room with them. Clara saw no benefit in mentioning her indiscretion just yet, especially as Mr Dodd had a prime motive for killing his lordship. If he knew his wife was having an affair, then getting him to slip up and admit it would be a good start to proving him a potential murderer.

"This is ridiculous," Lady Selby declared. "No one among us would have done such a thing."

"Lady Selby, what justification can you give for that statement?"

Lady Selby stared at Clara in shock.

"I beg your pardon?"

"You made a statement that no one among you would have stabbed

Lord Russell, and I wondered what you base that supposition upon."

"I know we are not murderers!" Lady Selby chuckled.

She looked anxiously around the others in the room.

"People like us do not murder other people."

"I am not sure that is a statement that would hold up in a court of law," Clara countered. "I find that anyone can do just about anything if they are pushed far enough."

"Where is that bloody Chinese fellow?" Mr Rankin now bellowed. "He has to have done this! Foreigners are always out for the blood of good Englishmen!"

Clara narrowed her eyes at him. Xenophobia was one of her least favourite prejudices, though she could safely say she disliked them all.

"Chang has an alibi in me, and also he has no motive," Clara replied. "He is currently waiting for the police."

"You mean he is hiding his wares so that he is not discovered to be a cheap and tawdry drug peddler!" Lady Selby snapped at her.

"That too," Clara smiled in her direction. "But let us get back to last night. Lord Russell imbibed a number of substances in full view of everyone. It would be safe for the killer to assume he would be unconscious when they entered the room and killed him."

"Why was his door not locked?" Mr Dodd demanded. "Or did the killer have the key?"

"Lord Russell's companion left in the night," Clara said carefully. "She could not have locked the door as she left, as that would have meant taking the key with her."

"There you go, it was the girl who did it!" Rankin pointed out. "Case closed. Don't even need the police."

"Why did she do it?" Clara asked him.

Rankin, who was a barrel of a fellow and not dreadfully bright, hesitated.

"What?"

"Why would his lady friend kill him?"

"Easy, to rob him!" Rankin looked pleased with his solution.

"Except, as far as I can tell, his lordship was not robbed and considering he was passed out on the bed, there would have been no need for a thief to waste time killing him."

Rankin's confidence evaporated.

"But it has to be one of the girls, who else?"

"Lord Russell was fully clothed when he was found dead," Clara now said. "Yet, last night, I know full well he was engaged in activities that would have required him at the very least to have removed his trousers and underwear."

"How could you know that?" Lady Selby narrowed her eyes at her.

"Because I went to the bathroom and heard noises from behind his door," Clara returned the stare. "I know what such noises imply. I am speculating that someone dressed Lord Russell, seeing as he was unlikely to have been in a fit state to dress himself. This person likely also killed him. Such kindness paired with terrible violence is curious."

"Maybe the person did not want the fellow to be found with his trousers down?" Mr Dodd suggested. "It would be horrible for the police to waltz into his room and find him undressed as well as dead."

"The dead generally do not care about such things," Clara remarked. "But the living do, especially those who have a strong connection to the victim."

Clara's eyes went to Mrs Dodd, who was not looking in her direction. The obvious person to care about Lord Russell being found with dignity was her, but Clara could not say why the young woman would have wished to murder him.

"This is preposterous. Why are you asking us all this?" Lady Selby demanded. "You are just a cheap woman who was brought by that horrible drug dealer."

"Hardly cheap," Clara snapped at her. "But that is beside the point. The real irony is that if someone had attempted to end Chang's life it would have made better sense than this. You hated Chang, after all, Lady Selby."

"My dear?" Lord Selby glanced at his wife.

He still looked dazed, as if whatever he had taken the night before had yet to wear off. Clara wondered just what had been in those syringes Wimpole had given Chang.

"Why shouldn't I despise him?" Lady Selby squawked. "That awful man brings poison into this house. It is bad enough you insist on having those girls come here to entertain your friends, but to have *him* as well. I feel like I live in a bordello, with an opium den on the side, just to make things even more unbearable."

Lord Selby blinked his eyes, unsure how to respond.

"It upsets you that much?"

"Of course it upsets me! Why wouldn't it? You are bringing us into disrepute. I dread to think what the servants tell people about us! My mother, God rest her soul, would be devastated if she knew."

Lord Selby was too dopey to be much shaken by her statement. He had an expression on his face that Clara had once witnessed on a goldfish. The sort of glazed, boggled-eyed look of something that was not really thinking at all.

"I am done with all this! I am going home!" Rankin rose from his chair and took a determined step towards Clara.

She had expected something like this, and was surprised it had taken so long for anyone to try to leave. She was ready to stop him.

"You cannot go until the police have arrived and spoken to you."

"Why ever not?"

"I have already told you, you are a suspect," Clara informed him calmly. "This is a police matter, and they will expect you to all remain here until they have had the chance to speak to you."

"Nonsense!" Mr Rankin took another firm step forward; he looked ready to drag Clara out of the way if he had to.

Clara stood her ground. She was fully herself now. Judy was just a bad dream and had disappeared to be replaced by a woman with an iron backbone, one who had been through quite enough recently.

"You would do very well to sit down, Mr Rankin. If you knew half the things I do about what is waiting for you outside, you would be much more concerned about your safety and be very glad the police are on the way."

Rankin hesitated; it was the edge to Clara's voice that had done it. He stared at her, trying to determine if she was joking, or trying to bluff him. Her serious expression told him he ought to listen. His gaze switched to Lord Selby.

"What is going on?"

"I don't know!" Selby shrugged.

"Lord Russell's murder is serious," Clara persisted. "But we are all aware of the other secrets this house holds, and there are people outside these four walls who know it too and would do anything to get inside here and rip the place apart."

"What do you know?" Lady Selby jumped from her seat.

Out of the people in the room, only Mrs Dodd looked confused about what was going on, and the things people were talking about in odd asides and vague inferences.

"I know enough," Clara informed her. "And you would be best advised to sit down and wait for the police. You have no reason to trust me, but right now, I do not want those individuals who are watching this place crashing in because they think they have an excuse with Lord Russell's murder."

"You are saying there are spies outside?" Rankin demanded.

"Spies, assassins," Clara shrugged. "This is a dangerous game we are playing, and there are people who would very much like to see you all pay with your lives."

Clara was frustrated enough to be prepared to reveal what little she knew about Mr Wimpole, especially if it kept all her suspects where she wanted them. Let them think that there were people just outside the door ready to murder them, it would not take much to convince them. They were already paranoid, wary of the secrets they were keeping, and now a man was dead. Not so farfetched to think others could die if they did not obey Clara.

She also wanted them to think she was on their side, so they would cooperate with her. It appeared her efforts were working. Certainly, Rankin had gone pale and hastily returned to his seat. Lady Selby was staring out of the window, across the grounds, as if hunting for danger with her gaze.

"I knew this would happen," she said sorrowfully, before slapping her husband's shoulder, hard. "I knew you would let this happen with all your partying and excesses! I told you that was not the way to run these things!"

Lord Selby said nothing, he did not seem to be entirely following events.

"The police are going to be ages, at least we should make ourselves comfortable in the drawing room," Mr Dodd suggested.

It was an innocuous statement and perfectly rational, but Clara did not want them leaving the breakfast room. The second she was not keeping them corralled, one of them might wander off to the study and discover Chang. She was about to say something, trying to come up with an excuse to make them stay, when she caught a glimpse of a car pulling up the driveway.

Lady Selby saw it too.

"The police are here already!" she groaned.

Rankin, looking like he wanted to bolt, startled up from his seat and then sat down again uneasily. Clara, however, was smiling, for she had recognised the car, and she knew it was not the police.

She felt a surge of pride and joy at the sight of her husband's favourite Bentley rolling towards the house, knowing he had sought her out, just as she knew he would, and had done a fine job of it too.

Behind him was a second car, and a moment later, a third hove into view.

"I think the entire police division has been summoned!" Mr Rankin declared as he hastened to the window.

Clara saw her opportunity and was not going to miss it. She bolted out of the door she had been guarding and locked it before anyone could stop her. Removing the key and placing it in her pocket, she heard her prisoners banging on the door, demanding to be released.

Clara smiled to herself. It was very satisfying being the one locking people up and not the other way around. Now it was time to deal properly with Mr Wimpole, and she was looking forward to seeing his face when he felt the full, righteous indignation of Clara O'Harris.

Chapter
Twenty-Six

O'Harris pulled up outside the grand house and jumped out of the car. No servants rushed out to greet him. He was not expected and what servants the household had were camping out in the kitchen, determined to avoid getting any further involved in the drama than was absolutely necessary.

Tommy jumped out of his side of the car and within moments, the whole force they had brought with them was disembarking. Inspector Park-Coombs joined them as they stood before the house.

"I shall lead the way, if you don't mind, police authority and all that."

O'Harris was in half a mind to storm the house, when someone gave a shout that there was a person in one of the ground floor windows yelling at them. The captain started to rush towards the window when he saw it was a female figure who was hammering on the glass. Naturally, he assumed it was his wife. He did not have to get too close to see the woman was not Clara, and that she was accompanied by several men in smart casual attire.

"You don't have to worry, John, I locked them in there."

O'Harris swung his head to the right and saw Clara emerging onto the front steps of the house. It took him a moment to recognise her with her new, short, blonde hair, but his instincts reacted faster than his mind and he was rushing towards her before his thoughts had truly caught up with the situation. He grabbed her up into his arms and embraced her so hard Clara gasped.

"I am perfectly all right," she promised him.

O'Harris refused to let her go, though he did give her the room to breathe. As Tommy, the inspector, and the men rushed over, O'Harris clasped her closer, breathing hard into her shoulder.

"What did they do to you?" Tommy said, staring at his sister.

"It is a long story," Clara replied, peering around her husband's shoulder. "What the inspector needs to know is that two men claiming to be working for the government kidnapped me and they are lurking somewhere about this estate. They have two cars."

"We found one of their cars," Tommy said. "We made sure to disable it before we came to find you."

"They could still get away," Clara frowned. "But I rather fancy they might have a vested interest in hanging around a while longer. There is something in this house they want, and they won't give it up without a fight."

"What about those people locked in that room?" O'Harris finally pulled back a fraction so he could look into his wife's face.

"Oh, they are a different matter entirely. I think one of them murdered one of the other houseguests last night, but I am not sure which. Also, they may be traitors to this country plotting to bring about another war, which is why Wimpole is interested in this whole affair."

"A murder?" Inspector Park-Coombs frowned, struggling to keep up with everything that was going on.

"I had a feeling you were not here because you had been officially summoned," Clara nodded at him. "You arrived too soon, and with the cavalry."

She popped up on her toes and kissed her husband's cheek as she said this. O'Harris was grinning from ear-to-ear.

"It is good to see you well, Clara, I was so scared."

"To be honest, for a while I was pretty scared too. But then I became angry and that carried me through," Clara paused. "Please tell me you found the poor dog?"

Tommy laughed.

"Should have known you would be more worried about the dog than yourself. We found him, he is safe and well at your house."

Clara sighed with relief.

"I was furious when I realised they had just left the poor creature behind to die when they took me. I have a lot of things to say to Mr Wimpole."

"First things first," Park-Coombs stepped forward. "You need to explain all of this to me, so I understand who the real criminal in this matter is and precisely what I am investigating."

Clara concurred.

"John, I would suggest a search is made of these grounds to try to locate Mr Wimpole and his assistant Irving, but you must be very careful. They are armed."

"We can handle that."

Clara glanced over at the voice and saw that it was the stoic Jones, their chauffeur and mechanic, who had spoken.

"Leave it to us," he said this for the sake of O'Harris who could only nod in return.

He was feeling emotional at having Clara back and did not want to leave her side, let alone release her from his grasp. He was scared that if he did, she might suddenly disappear again.

"Let's go inside and discuss this," Park-Coombs repeated. "Where is Mr Chang, by the way?"

"How did you know he was involved?" Clara said, her turn to be surprised.

"Mr Wimpole's associates were rather helpful," Park-Coombs waggled his moustache.

"Well, I am hopeful Chang is busily searching through Lord Selby's study for incriminating papers. Though, it is possible he has decided to take his chances with this distraction and has absconded, or even that he has found those papers and taken them to Wimpole as he was ordered to do. It is all rather complicated."

"You really need to explain everything properly to us," Tommy informed her.

The four of them headed inside, while Park-Coombs instructed his constables to guard the suspects in the breakfast room. Jones and the other men headed out on their own operation. Once Park-Coombs was out of sight, Jones discreetly went to the back of his car and produced the hand pistols for the men.

They were not going to take any chances.

Clara showed them through to the drawing room where the night before she had met with the rest of the guests as Judy Barlow. She was not entirely surprised to see Chang in there, sitting by the fire, legs crossed, and helping himself to a glass of whisky.

"Oh good, you are alive," he said as Clara walked in.

"Did you find the documents?" Clara asked.

Chang indicated a pile of papers beside him.

"You would not believe the things I found. Lord Selby is so stupid he wrote down everything. I really despair of the British criminal."

Clara said nothing but walked over and picked up the papers. She turned and showed them to Park-Coombs.

"These are the reason I was kidnapped."

"By him?" O'Harris pointed a finger at Chang and looked like he was thinking of eating him.

Chang merely smiled back.

"No, Chang was a prisoner as much as I was. We were both pawns in the game Mr Wimpole was playing. He wanted these papers which are proof that Lord Selby and the other men in the breakfast room are working together to bring about another war for their own profit."

"What a terrible thought," Tommy shuddered. "They would condemn us all for money."

"Hardly novel, it is what people do all the time," Chang shrugged.

"It is what *you* do," Clara huffed at him.

"I am really glad we no longer have to work together," Chang snorted back at her. "Captain O'Harris, has anyone ever said to you, your wife has very strong opinions and is something of a bully when she wants a person to do something for her?"

"I am always glad to hear Clara's opinions," O'Harris said firmly, glowering at Chang.

"Hard to imagine you being bullied," Park-Coombs sniffed at Chang.

"I find it hard to believe also, and yet here I am, having had that exact thing happen to me," Chang spread his arms in an expression of his amazement. "Honestly, I really do not know what to make of it all."

"Time for that explanation," Park-Coombs hinted.

"Right," Clara said. "I suggest we all sit."

She proceeded to explain to them in detail the events that had befallen her from the moment she had heard a dog crying for help.

Aside from Chang occasionally elaborating on elements of the saga that only he was present for, she told the story herself, aiming not to miss anything out. When she was done, everyone was silent, taking in what she had told them.

"They really thought they could kidnap you to get you to work for them?" O'Harris said. "Why not just ask you?"

"Apparently they did not think that would work. Quite frankly, I think all this espionage business has gone to their heads and they don't know their up from their down anymore," Clara shook her own head. "They didn't want anyone to see them talking to me and so tried to orchestrate a meeting when I was alone, and when that failed, they lured me into a trap. Of course, I point blank refused to help them at that point, which was when they resorted to kidnapping me."

"They sound like lunatics!" Park-Coombs declared.

"Most such people are," Chang replied. "Anyone with an ounce of sense would not want to get involved."

"I am still not entirely sure how legitimate this whole enterprise is," Clara added. "Mr Wimpole says he is working for the government, but I am not convinced. It would not surprise me if there were something else happening. But the point is we have the papers, I am free, and Lord Selby is exposed for being a warmonger."

"And everyone is happy," Chang said through clenched teeth.

"You are not?" Clara asked him.

"You forget, I have been promised a bullet to the head by dear Mr Wimpole, and I don't have the confidence you do he shall just forget his threats now his plot has been rumbled."

Chang looked sorry for himself; Clara was almost sympathetic.

"What about this murder?" Park-Coombs asked. "You say Lord Russell was stabbed?"

"Yes, by someone who apparently cared enough about him to put his clothes back on before they departed."

"Then it has to be Mrs Dodd," the inspector said firmly. "A lover's tiff, perhaps."

"Perhaps, and yet I am not so sure," Clara responded. "The letter opener is a curious choice of weapon, not something that would have come to hand easily in the bedroom."

"Is there a writing desk in the room?" Park-Coombs asked.

"That letter opener came from Lord Selby's study," Chang intervened before Clara could answer. "I am sure I saw one just like it in that room."

They all paused, if he was right, then that would suggest the killer had deliberately gone downstairs to retrieve the murder weapon before using it to slay Lord Russell.

"Well, I suppose as I am here, I ought to solve this murder," Park-Coombs slapped his knees and rose from his chair.

"Until Mr Wimpole is in custody, I am going nowhere," Clara added. "He is dangerous and cannot be allowed to go free. I have an idea how we can lure him out."

"Oh no," Chang grimaced. "I had a worrying feeling you would say something like that."

"You will be even more worried when I tell you who we are going to use for bait," Clara grinned at him.

Chapter Twenty-Seven

C hang hated the idea, as Clara had predicted.

He hated it so much he refused to agree to it, and when Clara began to badger him he stormed off up to the guest bedroom and locked himself inside.

"He will think about it, realise I am correct, and agree," Clara said confidently.

"You seem to have come to quite the understanding with Chang," O'Harris said, raising an eyebrow at her. "Just when did you marry him?"

"Haha," Clara pouted at him. "I would probably have murdered the fellow by now if I were forced to call him my husband, it was bad enough playing this little game and hanging off his arm. I had to giggle inanely instead of telling people exactly what I thought about them."

"You must have found that extremely hard," Park-Coombs said, his moustache mostly hiding his amusement.

"How long did your façade last?" Tommy asked his sister with a chuckle.

Clara sighed.

"Right up until Lord Russell was murdered, though it was starting to slip a little before then. One of the women who were here to entertain the men last night inferred I was rather too old to be hanging off Chang's arm."

Tommy widened his eyes in mock horror.

"How did you bite your tongue?"

"With difficulty," Clara said, missing that he was mocking her. "Unfortunately, that woman appears to have departed when she heard the police might be coming, otherwise I would have had strong words with her about demeaning her fellow woman, and also about her career choices."

"Probably just as well she escaped," O'Harris said to Tommy, who barely hid his grin of amusement.

Clara now realised they were making fun of her.

"Might I remind you that just an hour ago you had no idea of where I was and were beside yourselves with worry over me, and now you are laughing at me."

"I was pretty confident you would be all right," Tommy said, trying to make his face serious. "Never thought I would see the day you let someone cut your hair short, though."

Clara gave a shudder.

"I hate it so much," she grimaced.

"It isn't all that bad," O'Harris consoled her, leaning forward and kissing the top of her head. "I won't say it suits you, because you will be furious, and I shall be glad when it grows out, but you are still very beautiful."

"Sweet talker," Clara sighed at him, then she put her arms around him. "I was really glad to see you arrive."

"You seem to have had things in hand, as usual. I was a bit late to act the white knight riding in on his fearless steed."

"I was scared half to death most of the time," Clara grumbled. "But I was angry also, and that meant I could not really think about things too hard, as all I wanted to do was punch Mr Wimpole's lights out."

"Hopefully, you will still get the chance," Tommy told her.

"Should I call the men back from their search for Wimpole?" O'Harris asked.

"No," Park-Coombs shook his head. "Wimpole will expect the search, to call them back abruptly will make him suspect something else is planned. If Clara's trap is going to work, it has to seem as if we believe Wimpole has escaped."

"The inspector is right, to play Wimpole's game we have to think the way he does. I am sure he is a little mad," Clara added.

"He thought he could use you to get what he wanted, clearly he is very mad," Tommy said with no sense of irony.

"Well, if I can't go about arresting Mr Wimpole, I suppose I ought to begin solving this murder," Park-Coombs twitched his moustache and glanced out of the drawing room door which had been left open when Chang had made his exit. "How long have those people been hammering on that door opposite us?"

"Since we got here," O'Harris replied. "The servants appear to have made themselves scarce."

"I don't blame them, knowing what must have been going on in this house, they don't want to get caught up in the madness," Tommy snorted. "Do you think Lord Russell died as part of Wimpole's plan?"

He had asked the last of his sister. Clara shook her head.

"I cannot see how that would serve any useful purpose. I think it is more important to note that Mrs Dodd was having an affair with Lord Russell, which would give her husband a good reason to want him dead."

"I shall bear that in mind," Park-Coombs said, starting to leave the room.

"Wait for me," Clara pulled herself out of O'Harris' arms and hurried after the inspector.

"Really, Clara?" Tommy asked her.

"I have nothing else to do," Clara responded to him. "And that awful Lady Selby was most derogatory about me, and I wish to demonstrate just who I really am to her."

"I fear she already knows," O'Harris whispered as an aside to his brother-in-law.

Tommy nearly burst out laughing again.

"We might as well follow them, old man, nothing else to do, and you know what Clara is like when she has a bee in her bonnet," Tommy replied.

The two men wandered behind the inspector and Clara as they headed across the tiled foyer towards the breakfast room.

When they had first been locked inside, the irate suspects had hammered keenly on the door, assuming someone would come speedily to free them. When that had not happened at once, their hammering had become even more urgent, especially when Lady Selby discovered the windows were also locked.

A raging argument had begun between her and her half-stoned husband, who was still catching up with what was occurring. To emphasise her fury, Lady Selby had started to grab up cups and glasses from the breakfast table and hurl them at her husband's head. After he had taken a sharp blow from a saucer, he had realised he ought to try to dodge them.

Meanwhile, Rankin and Dodd were taking turns to pound on the door, while Mrs Dodd sat at the table and tried not to cry and smear the remains of her make-up any further. Her husband had said nothing about the fact she had been the one to find Lord Russell. He had either not connected the dots or was too absorbed in their current situation to react. Either way, she knew at some point they were going to end up discussing it, and she was not looking forward to the argument that would follow.

Time had mellowed them all, and Lady Selby had run out of cups to throw. Now, having been stuck in the room for close to an hour, they were left with occasionally kicking or yelling through the door when they thought someone was close by, or when their earlier anger sparked again.

It was into this state of exhausted resignation that Park-Coombs waltzed with Clara just behind him. Tommy and O'Harris lingered in the doorway, to make sure no one attempted to leave.

Park-Coombs looked around the room, taking in his suspects. Clara was not surprised that it was Lady Selby who spoke first.

"This is unspeakable! I have been locked up in my own home! Your superiors will hear about this!"

"My dear lady, you have a lot more to worry about than being locked up in this room after what I have learned has been occurring here this weekend," Park-Coombs said calmly. "I assume you are Lady Selby?"

"I am," Lady Selby declared. "And I have no idea what you are talking about. This was just a regular weekend party."

"With an array of drugs being sold by a notorious criminal, upmarket prostitutes on hand, and now a dead man," Park-Coombs remarked, being careful not to mention the papers that were the reason Clara was there.

"She has been telling you all this!" Lady Selby pointed a finger at Clara. "You cannot believe a word she says! She is just as bad as the rest of them!"

"Precisely what do you mean by that?" Park-Coombs asked gently; when questioning a suspect he typically acted amenably, it usually threw them off guard. "That she is a lady of questionable morals, or an accomplice in the drug dealing you permitted in your home, or both?"

Lady Selby hesitated, realising that in her efforts to demean Clara she was perilously close to incriminating herself and her husband further. She shut her mouth sharply, though her furious glare never left Clara.

"The real matter at hand," Park-Coombs continued, "is that there is a dead man upstairs, and he was murdered by someone in this household."

"Chang!" Lord Selby burbled. "You should arrest him. He did it!"

"I have already spoken to Mr Chang, and while he is certainly a criminal and a man of very low moral fibre, he had no reason to murder Lord Russell. I understand he had never even met him before last night."

"They must have argued, over money," Lord Selby persisted.

In his addled mind he fancied if he could get the inspector to concentrate on Chang, the rest of them could go free and be out of the house before lunchtime.

"Chang does not argue with people over money," Clara responded. "He has far better things to do with his time. And killing Lord Russell would not result in him being paid."

Lord Selby did not seem to heed her argument, his blank look suggested most of his brain cells were still failing to fire.

"Then it must have been one of the women who was here last night," Lady Selby intervened. "Lord Russell must have taken one up to his room."

"So, you are admitting there were ladies of questionable employment here?" Park-Coombs made a note in his trusty notebook.

"I never suggested money exchanged hands!" Lady Selby threw up her arms in exasperation. "But these things happen. A lover's tiff!"

Mrs Dodd gave a sudden loud sniff, trying to hold back the tears from falling. Her husband did not move in her direction, it was hard to say if he had even noticed her distress, he was too absorbed in his own worries.

"The person who murdered Lord Russell behaved in something of a peculiar fashion," Clara spoke. "It would seem, after they had stabbed him and left him to die, they felt a pang of concern about him being discovered half-dressed, and therefore they returned and put his clothes on. This suggests someone who cared about him enough to wish to preserve his dignity. And that implies this crime was committed by someone who was close to Lord Russell."

Mrs Dodd glanced up at Clara, her eyes wide. Maybe she thought Clara was implicating her, or maybe she was considering this new information in light of what she had been doing with Russell in the early hours of the morning. Either way, she looked surprised.

"If we are all satisfied that this was not the actions of a casual acquaintance of Lord Russell, might we get down to the real heart of this matter," Park-Coombs said to the room. "I need to have a long chat with all of you, to discover where you were last night and just what you know about this crime."

Chapter
Twenty-Eight

A s they wanted to interview the suspects alone, they decided to use the chamber next to the breakfast room, which was an underused sitting room filled with old family portraits. O'Harris and Tommy agreed to keep everyone who was left behind in the breakfast room in order, while each individual suspect was escorted in turn to the sitting room and questioned. Clara joined Park-Coombs.

They began their interviews with Lord Selby who, as the head of the household, seemed a logical first choice, though Clara had severe doubts he would be able to offer them any useful information.

They escorted Lord Selby themselves to the sitting room and seated him in an old armchair that creaked beneath him. He was still struggling to process what was occurring, and once more Clara wondered how this man could be behind a scheme to start another war. He did not look capable of keeping secrets, that was for sure.

"How do you come to know Lord Russell?" Park-Coombs began.

Lord Selby glanced around the room, taking note of the paintings. "Haven't been in here in years," he mumbled to himself.

"Lord Selby," Park-Coombs snapped the man's attention back onto them. "How did you know Lord Russell?"

"We move in similar circles," Lord Selby explained. "We both have our fingers in the industrial pies of this country. We were at the same meetings and so forth. His father was a good sort, really keen on promoting the use of British iron and steel. Shame he passed on so young. His son is all right, but a bit wet behind the ears. He will learn, in time, I suppose. I am something of a mentor to him."

Lord Selby grinned at them proudly and it was plain he had forgotten the young man was dead.

"Lord Selby, Lord Russell was found deceased this morning, remember?" Park-Coombs told him.

Lord Selby's face went through quite the performance of emotions as some part of his rational mind managed to click in and recall that Lord Russell was deceased.

"Oh dear," he said. "His family will be devastated."

"Perhaps you would care to tell me about last night," Park-Coombs decided to try a different approach. "When did you last see Lord Russell?"

Lord Selby considered for a while.

"I don't know the exact time, as I was a little tight," he gave an apologetic chuckle. "But it must have been gone midnight when I last saw him. He was speaking quietly with Mrs Dodd. Funny, isn't it, how I always think they would have been better suited to each other than the man she actually married? Anyway, Mrs Dodd became distracted because her husband went to sit down on a chair that did not exist and ended up on the floor roaring his head off with laughter. We all laughed a lot, it was very funny."

Lord Selby smiled at them, trying to express how amusing the scene had been. The stony expressions on his interviewers' faces told him to give up the effort.

"After that, Mrs Dodd collected her husband and took him up to bed. Mrs Dodd is a good gal, never touches a drop of… well, she sticks to her sherry and the odd drop of gin. She helped her husband upstairs, and Lord Russell went to assist her. Mr Dodd is not easy for one person to carry along, and Mrs Dodd is rather a small thing. That was the last I saw of them, carrying Dodd up the stairs, one on either side of the old oaf."

"When did you go to bed?" Clara asked him.

Lord Selby shrugged.

"Who knows? I wasn't checking the time. It could have been ten minutes or two hours after they had gone upstairs. I don't really remember much after Dodd was carried away, truth be told."

Lord Selby scratched at the side of his head, as if the sudden knowledge of his lapse in memory were troubling him. Then his smile returned.

"I slept like the dead!"

He laughed, oblivious to how crass his comment was.

Clara glanced at the inspector, who just shook his head a fraction. Lord Selby was useless to them. Even if he had somehow managed to rise from his drugged state and wander into Lord Russell's room after Mrs Dodd had departed, what would be his motive for killing the man?

"Were you aware that Mrs Dodd was having an affair with Lord Russell?" Clara asked.

It was time to get to the meat and bones of the matter, and Clara could not keep that particular thing a secret any longer. It was far too likely that the affair could have been the trigger for the murder, one way or the other.

"Was she? Good for her," Lord Selby nodded his head approvingly.

"She married Dodd for the money. Let's face it, he is an ugly fellow and far too old for her. Fat, too. She was much more suited to a young man like Russell."

Lord Selby now gave a chuckle.

"It would have made more sense her killing her husband so she could marry his lordship, don't you think?"

They were going to get no more from the man, not at least until he had finally come down from whatever he had consumed the night before. Park-Coombs took him back to the breakfast room and reappeared shortly after with Lady Selby. The woman had the same scowl on her face that had not left her since Clara had first met her. She turned it on Clara, as if it might work better this time than before. Clara smiled back.

"Lady Selby, perhaps you could confirm a few things your husband said?" Park-Coombs asked as he pointed out a seat to her.

She sat, and the inspector settled in a chair opposite, beside Clara.

"I would not pay much heed to what my husband says," Lady Selby declared quickly, obviously anxious about what her husband might have said while away from her. "He gets a little carried away at these parties of his and consumes too much alcohol."

Park-Coombs made no response to this, pretending to flick through his notebook.

"Do you recall the last time you saw Lord Russell?" he asked.

Lady Selby hesitated, trying to decide if the truth or some sort of fabrication would be best, but as she had no idea what her husband had said, she settled for being honest.

"Lord Russell assisted Mrs Dodd in taking her husband upstairs to their room. The man had completely disgraced himself trying to sit down on a chair that did not exist and then laughing his head off as he slumped on the floor," Lady Selby pulled a face at the memory.

"You do not care for your husband's parties," Clara remarked to her. "Or his friends."

"I do not like them, no," Lady Selby declared. "My husband has never understood the value in restraint, and he attracts similar people to him. However, it is his household, and I must merely abide with his decisions, even if I dislike them."

"You do not drink or take drugs, then?" Park-Coombs asked bluntly.

Lady Selby narrowed her eyes at him.

"I drink gin with tonic water, which is about the only thing that gets me through these terrible evenings. As for the other things you mentioned, I know nothing about drugs or drug taking. I have never seen it occur in my home."

"Of course you haven't," Park-Coombs said, his tone bordering on the cusp of sarcasm. "When did your husband go to bed?"

"It was about one in the morning," Lady Selby declared at once. "He probably does not remember the time, considering the state he was in. I helped him upstairs and put him to bed."

"Was he the last to leave the party?" Park-Coombs asked.

"Surely, she has told you everything?" Lady Selby pointed at Clara.

Her vicious expression clearly implied Clara was not forgiven for being associated with Chang.

"Chang and I went up to bed around midnight," Clara said calmly. "Once it was apparent he could not do anymore business because the others were simply too far gone. I believe we were the first to leave, in fact."

Lady Selby stared at her, clearly she had not remembered they had departed first. Maybe she was not as clear-headed last night as she liked to suppose.

"Mr Rankin went up to bed after Dodd had been removed. He was on the arm of that girl whose name escapes me. My husband was alone then, and I thought it best to get him up to bed. So yes, he was the last."

"You were both the last ones," Clara reminded her.

"Yes, if you wish to put it that way," Lady Selby shrugged.

"Do you share a bedroom with your husband?" Park-Coombs asked in that innocuous way that caught people off guard.

Lady Selby stiffened.

"No, I do not. He snores."

"Then, once he was in his room, you parted ways?"

"My husband did not rise from his bed after I placed him there, of that I am certain," Lady Selby said hastily. "For a start, he was too inebriated, and secondly, I locked his door when I left him."

"You locked his door?" Clara said in surprise.

"Sometimes he sleepwalks, and it is inconvenient," Lady Selby shrugged again. "He fell down the stairs once. So, I lock his bedroom door, and I do not unlock it until I hear him moving around and know he is truly awake."

"You must be a light sleeper to hear him so easily," Park-Coombs observed. "From a different room, no less."

"I have the room just next door to his and, yes, I do sleep badly. If I manage a couple of hours a night, I am more than pleased," she waited for them to challenge this statement.

Neither of them did.

"Did you hear anyone else moving about after you had placed your husband in his bed?" Park-Coombs asked.

Lady Selby hesitated and then decided there was something she needed to say.

"I was aware that Lord Russell had a woman in his bedroom. There were noises coming from the apartment, to indicate what was going on. I assumed it was one of the girls he had been speaking to earlier."

"It was Mrs Dodd," Clara said.

She was watching Lady Selby's face intently. The woman didn't even flinch.

"Was it now?"

"You did not know?" Clara asked.

"I did not," Lady Selby said firmly. "But I am hardly surprised. You saw the man she married. He was bad enough before they were wed, he has only gotten worse. Honestly, women have to put up with an awful lot if they want a husband with wealth and power."

"I take it you are referring as much to yourself with that statement as Mrs Dodd?" Park-Coombs asked.

"My marriage was arranged by my parents, and my opinion on the matter was not sought," Lady Selby replied. "No doubt some would consider that scandalous, but my parents were of a generation who fancied they knew what was best for me. Thank goodness they are both now deceased, so they do not have to see the wreck of a man their son-in-law became."

"You detest your husband," Clara observed.

"I detest what he has become. He was not always so absurd and decadent," Lady Selby sighed. "I suppose life wore him down."

"You could divorce him," Clara pointed out. "People do these days."

Lady Selby snorted derisively.

"People like me do not. He is my husband and that is that. One day, hopefully soon, he shall take one evening cocktail too many and save me from this nightmare, but until then, I shall continue to endure him. Now, if you are done with me?"

She rose from her seat implying that *she* was *done* with *them*. Park-Coombs let her go, with an assurance she would head straight back to the breakfast room and send them Mrs Dodd next. He was not concerned about her obeying, as he had O'Harris and Tommy outside the room.

"She clearly hates her husband," Park-Coombs remarked to Clara when the woman was gone.

"It would make more logical sense if he was the one who was murdered," Clara agreed.

"Still three suspects to go," Park-Coombs checked his notes. "One of them must have done it."

"Right at this moment, I am no closer to deciding which one, however," Clara sighed.

Chapter Twenty-Nine

M rs Dodd dabbed at her eyes with a handkerchief. She had spent far too much time that morning crying and her eyes were red raw, her throat ached, and her head pounded.

Poor Bertie was dead!

She would never get over it. In the grim world she found herself living in, he had been her ray of sunshine. She might even have dared to say she was in love with him, and now he was gone.

She sat before the inspector and Clara and gnawed on her lip.

"You have to find who did this," she said, trying to control the tears that threatened yet again.

"We are aiming to," Clara promised her.

Out of all of their suspects, the least likely killer was Mrs Dodd, though she did fit all their criteria.

She cared enough about the man to want to preserve his dignity, and they knew she had been with him the night before. But the choice of the murder weapon and her motive were still questions that lingered.

"Lord Russell helped you to get your husband up to his bed?" Park-Coombs began.

"He did," Mrs Dodd nodded. "My husband was terribly inebriated, among other things. He ended up on the floor and it was time I got him into his bed before he did anything else stupid."

Mrs Dodd sighed.

"Might I ask, why did you marry him?" Clara enquired.

"I suppose Lady Selby told you it was for the money?" Mrs Dodd said grimly. "I cannot deny that was part of my decision, but at one time I actually thought I loved him. I worked in one of his factories during the war, making munitions for the soldiers. He often came to visit and see how we were doing. He used to give little speeches and read out excerpts from the newspaper about how useful our shells were at the front, to give us encouragement. I always thought he looked rather smart in his suit.

"You might not have noticed, but he is really a rather warm person. Quite kind, in his own way. We started to talk and slowly became friends, which then turned into something more. When he proposed to me, I was quite convinced I loved him, and it was not about his money.

"Some of the other girls sneered, thought I was just being mercenary, but I swear I did care about him. I still do care about him. It is why I hate seeing him make a fool of himself. But, since the war, he has not been the same. The factories were making a fortune when there was a great need for munitions, but afterwards, when the economy slumped, his factories began to struggle. The products he made before the war were not so popular, and people did not have the money to spend on them anyway. He had to close two of his factories, which he felt awful about as it put people out of work, but he had to do it or ruin himself.

"Around that time he met Lord Selby. They started talking, and he said Selby saw a way forward, and understood the crisis he was in. That was when we started attending these weekend parties, and my husband began to follow Selby's lead in consuming anything that was offered to him."

Mrs Dodd grimaced.

"He is not the man I married anymore."

"When did you start the affair with Lord Russell?" Park-Coombs asked.

"I suppose it was late last year. He started coming to Lord Selby's parties and we were introduced. He was closer to my age than any of the other men and we used to talk a lot. Poor Bertie always felt awkward among the others, he thought himself very naïve," she sniffed and looked about to weep.

"Did your husband suspect?" Park-Coombs asked before she descended into tears.

"I don't think so," Mrs Dodd shook her head. "We were discreet, and we only came together when my husband was so out of his mind he could not have known a thing."

"Did anyone else know?" Clara asked.

Mrs Dodd pulled a face.

"Until recently I would have said no," she replied. "But, last night when I was leaving Bertie's room, I bumped into Lady Selby. She had to have guessed where I had been. She was right outside in the corridor, almost as if she was about to enter the room herself. It was very odd."

"What was she doing there?" Park-Coombs wondered.

"I asked her the same," Mrs Dodd replied. "She said she could not sleep and was taking a walk to check on her guests. It did not seem logical, but I was too worried about what she might be thinking about me to pay heed. I hurried to my own room and was there the rest of the night."

Mrs Dodd sucked in her lower lip.

"My husband knows nothing, and I would really appreciate it if you didn't tell him. I think it would break his heart."

Mrs Dodd had no more to tell them, so they sent her back to the breakfast room and summoned her husband instead. Mr Dodd was now pretty much sober and very concerned about the events of the night before and the implications for him.

"I did not realise the drugs were illegal," he said the second he sat down. "I am not a man of the world, I just assumed it was what one did at these parties."

Clara did not believe a word of that lie, but she had no need to question him on the matter.

"What do you remember about last night?" Park-Coombs asked him.

Dodd scratched at his head.

"Not a lot, really," he said, abashed. "I had a little too much, you see. I get carried away. Honestly, when I woke up this morning I felt so ill I thought I was dying. My wife told me to take an emetic, which I did, and it helped a little. Then, oddly, I felt really hungry, so I came down to breakfast. Thought some fresh coffee and bacon would do me the world of good."

"Your wife remained in your room?"

"She said she wanted to sleep a little longer. She rarely takes breakfast," Dodd replied. "Sorry, but I really can't tell you much about last night. I don't recall seeing Lord Russell after probably around ten, but then I don't recall seeing anyone beyond that time."

Park-Coombs took a deep breath.

"How well did you know Lord Russell?"

"Only vaguely," Dodd answered. "He seemed a nice fellow, but a bit dim about industry. He had inherited his father's factories on the man's death. Lord Selby had been friends with his father and extended that friendship to his son. He was coming along nicely under Selby's guidance, I would say, really getting the hang of things. Terrible to think he was murdered."

Park-Coombs took another deep breath, bracing himself for the question he now had to ask. There was no easy way to get around it, and he knew he was about to destroy a marriage, but the truth was what it was.

"Did you know your wife was having an affair with Lord Russell?"

Mr Dodd, if he did know, was a remarkable actor because he looked as if a blow had struck him in the belly. The colour actually drained from his florid skin and his flesh sagged. He seemed like a man who had just seen his world collapse around him and Clara did not think that was something anyone could fake.

"No, I did not," he said in a shaky voice. "Is that true?"

"It is," Park-Coombs responded. "Your wife was with Lord Russell before he was murdered."

"Then, you are wondering if I killed him?" Dodd said. "Out of jealousy."

He shook his head.

"I am not the killing sort. And, if I am honest, I have known these past few years I am a disappointment to my wife. I disgust her now, whereas once we were so close. I can see why she picked Russell over me."

"You are taking this rather well," Clara said to him.

"I see the man she sees every day in the mirror," Dodd replied. "I despise him, so why should I expect her to feel any differently? I am ugly, and fat, and I drink too much, and take substances that leave me out of my head. I do that largely because I am so unhappy about myself and my life. Why should I expect her to put up with that and not have a little pleasure in her life? If he made her happy, good for him."

Dodd hesitated.

"Oh, my poor flower, no wonder she is so devastated. I haven't been paying attention to her. I have done her such a great disservice," Dodd put his head in his hands and groaned.

Neither Clara, nor the inspector, had anticipated such a response.

"You are saying you would not have accosted Lord Russell in anger?" Clara asked.

"No," Dodd replied. "He was doing what I could not, caring about my wife. Oh, I have been such a fool!"

With that declaration, Dodd began to weep into his hands, and they could get no more sense from him. He kept sobbing over his 'poor little flower,' and how he had failed her, and that was the extent of what they could achieve.

They sent him back to the breakfast room and asked for their last suspect.

Rankin entered the room looking fed-up.

"I saw Lord Russell help Mr Dodd to his room and that was the last I witnessed him alive," he said without sitting down. "I went to my bedroom with a lady friend shortly after, and I was in my room the rest of the night until I came down to breakfast."

"I see you have been speaking with the others," Park-Coombs muttered.

"I had no grievance against the young man, I barely knew him," Rankin continued. "If that damn woman had not run off, she could confirm to you that I was with her all night. Now, if we are done?"

"Just a moment," Park-Coombs raised a hand to stop the man departing. "You did not leave your room at all?"

"No," Rankin snapped.

"Did you hear anyone outside your room?" Clara asked him, thinking about the mysterious Lady Selby wandering the corridor.

"No," Rankin repeated.

"Did you know that Lord Russell was having an affair with Mrs Dodd?"

"No, and I did not care," Rankin shrugged. "I had my own business to attend to. What Lord Russell did in his bedroom was purely up to him."

Rankin looked at them in a surly fashion.

"Are we done?"

Park-Coombs held up one finger to indicate he should be patient, then made a pretence of going through his notebook looking for something. He did this purely to annoy Rankin and to waste his time.

"Well, Mr Rankin, it seems we have all we need from you."

Rankin grumbled under his breath about the tiresomeness of the police and then left the room. Alone together, Park-Coombs leaned back in his chair and glanced at Clara.

"I want to see the body. I have a hunch who might have done this, but without evidence we have nothing."

"Agreed," Clara said. "I will show you to the corpse."

Chapter Thirty

L ord Russell was stretched out on his bed as Clara had left him earlier that day. He still had his head thrust back and his mouth open. His skin was going grey, and he was stiffening rock hard with rigor mortis.

"I should really summon Dr Deáth," Park-Coombs said as he leaned over the body. "But I would rather not drag anyone else into this just yet."

"Cause of death is pretty obvious," Clara moved back the flap of the jacket and revealed the letter opener.

"And Chang said he had seen a letter opener like that in Lord Selby's study?"

"He did, and the one thing Chang is not is a liar, at least not about something like this. He is also very observant."

"Wouldn't surprise me if the fellow was considering it as a weapon when he laid his eyes on it," Park-Coombs huffed. "Chang strikes me as the type to look around a room and pick out objects he could use offensively before he thinks of anything else."

"A fair point, Inspector, which leaves us with the question who would have gone down to that study and picked up the letter opener?"

"You told me that you saw Lord Selby in his study sound asleep,"

Park-Coombs remarked. "Yet, he said he went up to bed."

"He also said he recalled very little about the evening, and that I believe," Clara replied. "It is entirely possible he has forgotten he fell asleep in his study. At some point, he either took himself up to his bedroom or someone helped him, and as he woke up in his bed, so he supposes he went there straight away."

"And if there was someone in the study who helped him upstairs to bed, then they could have picked up the letter opener," Park-Coombs nodded. "The question is, why would they do that?"

"They did not do it by chance," Clara theorised. "They were already thinking about using it. Maybe they even went to the study because they wanted the letter opener?"

"And then they saw Lord Selby and decided to help him up to bed, which implies it was someone close to him. You see who I am thinking of?"

"Lady Selby," Clara nodded. "She has been my prime suspect for a while. She was outside this room when she ought not to have been, and she lied about helping her husband to bed, failing to mention he fell asleep in the study."

"She would have known about the letter opener," Park-Coombs added. "I am going to suggest she witnessed Mrs Dodd emerging from Lord Russell's room and decided to kill him, let us surmise she was jealous. She went down to the study to fetch the letter opener, as it was the only weapon she could think of that was close to hand. Unluckily for her, she found her husband there and decided she ought to help him up to bed. She took the letter opener, nonetheless, and once her husband was safely in his bed, she went back to Lord Russell and dispatched him."

"We don't have a motive," Clara pointed out.

"Logically, she was in love with him, or maybe even having an affair with him like Mrs Dodd, and she was beside herself with jealousy when she saw the young lady emerge from his room. She knew she could not compete with Mrs Dodd's youth and beauty."

"It was a pure act of vengeance, then?" Clara considered the idea. "After which, remorse kicked in and she was upset at the idea of Russell being seen partly unclad and so she redressed him."

"It fits the facts as we know them, but we cannot prove it," Park-Coombs rubbed his chin. "We have nothing that can indicate to us Lord Russell was having an affair with the woman."

Clara took a turn around the room, glancing around the scene to find something that would help her resolve the case. As she did so, her foot caught on something, and she kicked a loose stocking out from under the bed. She recalled seeing that stocking earlier, when she had entered the room at the summons of Mrs Dodd. She had thought it must have belonged to one of the ladies who had been hired to entertain the menfolk, but had found it odd it had been so carelessly discarded.

Now she knew it had not belonged to one of those women. Clara picked up the stocking and took a closer look. The stocking was new and undamaged. Whoever had abandoned it here, it was not because it had been laddered and therefore unusable. It could have belonged to Mrs Dodd, but Clara could not fathom why the woman would be so careless with the article if she was so keen to keep her affair a secret.

Even if she had forgotten it the night before, she had plenty of time between the discovery of the dead man and summoning Clara to retrieve the stocking, so no one ever knew it had been there. That she had completely ignored it, suggested to Clara it belonged to someone else.

Clara stared at the inspector.

"We need to get Mrs Dodd and Lady Selby up here at once."

Instructions were given to O'Harris and Tommy, and they escorted the respective ladies upstairs. Lady Selby's face had hardened into a look of hatred as they were brought into the bedroom where Lord Russell's corpse lay. Mrs Dodd just looked despondent.

"I am sorry to ask you to stand in this room again," Clara said to them. "But I think I can at last resolve who was in this room with Lord Russell and murdered him."

Clara glanced between them, looking for a reaction, but receiving not so much as a hint of one from either.

"Mrs Dodd, could you tell me the type of stockings you wear?" Clara asked the woman.

Mrs Dodd looked at her in bemusement.

"I wear Pretty Polly's sheer ladies' stockings."

"In what colour?"

"Flesh tone. They are virtually invisible," Mrs Dodd responded.

"Would this be one of those stockings?"

Clara handed over the item she had retrieved from under the bed and Mrs Dodd examined it.

"This is too dark," she replied.

"Did you notice this stocking when you were in the room earlier? It was lying on the floor."

Mrs Dodd surprised Clara by nodding her head.

"I saw it."

"You made no comment on it?"

Mrs Dodd shrugged.

"You shall think me a fool, but I was fully aware that Bertie entertained other women. We only saw each other occasionally and he used to say to me he had needs. He arrived here the night before last, a day earlier than everyone else, and I assumed he had one of the girls Lord Selby had supplied in his room that first night. I noticed the stocking when my shoe rolled under the bed as I was getting dressed but made no comment on it."

"It was not under the bed when I came in here to look at him," Clara pointed out.

Mrs Dodd took a deep breath.

"I pulled it out," she said. "You see, I assumed it was one of those girls who killed him. I could not think who else would have done it, and before I came down the stairs screaming, I pulled out the stocking so that others would see it."

Mrs Dodd met Clara's eyes calmly.

"I want his killer found. He might not have been true to me, but he did not deserve to die, and I shall see justice done for him."

Clara nodded her head and then looked towards Lady Selby.

"Are you so eager to find out the truth, Lady Selby?"

Lady Selby had grown pale, and her eyes were fixed on the stocking.

"I wonder," Clara said, "if we were to search your room, would we find stockings matching this one? More to the point, would we discover you were missing one?"

Mrs Dodd turned sharply to the older woman beside her.

"You?"

"I imagine, Lady Selby, that one stocking going missing would not trouble you greatly. You probably had a hunch where you had left it, perhaps that was why you were lurking in the corridor last night, intending to go into Lord Russell's room and search for the missing item. Or perhaps you had come to see if he required company? It must have been quite a shock to see Mrs Dodd leaving the room, and to realise you were not his lordship's one and only. Unlike Mrs Dodd, I don't think you would have reacted to the betrayal with such equanimity."

Lady Selby's eyes had become glazed, and Clara was amazed to realise the woman was actually close to tears. She had not thought she had such emotion in her.

"He said he was in love with me," Lady Selby forced the words out through gritted teeth. "He made me all manner of promises."

"Bertie said silly things when he was in bed with a person," Mrs Dodd sighed, proving she had a somewhat more worldly head on her shoulders than the older woman at her side.

"He had no right to toy with me like that!" Lady Selby hissed. "No right!"

"Then, you were in this room the other night?" Clara nodded her head. "You were having an affair with him, and then you discovered you were not alone. Filled with anger and fury, you went downstairs and found your husband's letter opener, which you then used to stab Lord Russell. But remorse kicked in almost immediately and you detested the thought of the man you cared about being seen with his trousers down, so you dressed him."

"You cannot prove anything with a stocking," Lady Selby snapped. "I will not confess!"

"We actually have more than just a stocking," Park-Coombs told her. "We know you repeatedly lied to us, including when you failed to tell us you had helped your husband from his study to his bed. You deliberately made it sound as if you had brought him upstairs directly from the party."

"How do you know that?" Lady Selby asked in astonishment.

"I have a sound witness," Park-Coombs replied.

Lady Selby's eyes flashed to Clara.

"You were poking about my house?"

"I wasn't killing people," Clara shrugged. "That's for sure."

"Combined with the evidence of the stocking, the murder weapon being one you had to know about to fetch, and that the person who killed Russell clearly cared about him deeply, I think I can make a pretty good case against you, Lady Selby."

Lady Selby scowled at them all.

"I would like to see you just try! My husband will pay for the best barrister he can find, and no court of law will convict me!"

"Your husband has his own problems to worry about," Clara said darkly.

Lady Selby did not understand the inference but something about Clara's expression caused her to hesitate.

"Lady Selby, I shall have to detain you for the time being, until I can have you removed to the station for further questioning," Park-Coombs said politely.

Lady Selby glowered at him, but she had no more fight left in her. That had mostly gone when she had seen the man she loved, the man she had betrayed her husband for, consorting with another woman.

"I am going to my room," she declared to them, before storming off.

O'Harris watched her leave to be sure that was where she went. Park-Coombs nodded once he heard her slam the bedroom door.

"I shall have a constable stationed outside her door," he told Clara.

"I cannot believe she did such a thing," Mrs Dodd looked teary. "What an awful woman!"

Clara wanted to say something about how Lord Russell had treated the women in his life being a contributing factor to the crime; not that she thought he deserved to be murdered, but he had not been terribly honourable, or even nice, to the ladies he courted. She decided now was not the time.

"Mrs Dodd, while this matter is resolved, I wish everyone to continue to remain here," Park-Coombs said to the grieving woman.

Mrs Dodd frowned at him.

"Why?" she asked.

"Because we have another crime to resolve as yet," Clara said grimly. "We just need to persuade a certain person to come out of their room to help us."

Chapter Thirty-One

"Chang, stop cowering in there. We both know you are going to do this," Clara stood outside the locked bedroom door with her arms folded.

Park-Coombs was trying to hide his smile as he watched her confront the criminal mastermind, who had hidden himself away in a sulk like a teenage girl.

"How do you get away with saying things like that to him?" he asked.

"Because he knows it is the sort of thing I do," Clara shrugged, before returning to shouting through the door. "Look, Chang, the episode with Lord Russell has given us an opportunity we did not have before. We can tell Wimpole that the police were not here because of him or us, but because of the murder, and that will buy you the time you need to lure him properly into our trap."

There was still silence from the other side of the door.

"Maybe he has fled the house?" Park-Coombs suggested.

"He is inside," Clara said firmly. "He just doesn't want to admit I am right."

They waited another few seconds before Clara began again.

"Chang, please, I want to get home, but before that I want to wipe the smug smile off Wimpole's face. If we do not resolve things here and now, then he is going to keep coming after you and, maybe, me. If nothing else, he will do it to be vindictive because he is that sort of fellow. I personally would prefer to know he was behind bars, or at the very least so discredited he cannot do anything like this again."

There was movement inside the room. Park-Coombs went to say something, but Clara held up a hand to stop him. For an instant, silence returned, and the inspector thought Chang was continuing to ignore them, then the door opened, and he stood before them.

"I hate you," he informed Clara, though there was little venom in his tone.

"I am sure you will get over it," Clara replied. "I have discussed with the inspector our plan. He is going to appear to drive off with Lady Selby to take her back to the police station. The other cars will depart, leaving just a handful of people inside and making it seem as if the police truly only arrived because of the murder of Lord Russell. With Wimpole's two men already prisoner, he only has Irving to help him keep watch, and with any luck they heard the screaming from within earlier today."

"He might also have witnessed your reunion with your husband, which will make him aware of what is going on," Chang reminded her.

"True, but he still wants those papers, doesn't he? So we have to play him at his own game. You are going to go to the rendezvous spot, as you were told to, with the documents, but we will be waiting to capture Wimpole."

Chang narrowed his eyes.

"How?"

"O'Harris and some of his men will position themselves in places they can keep watch and run in to intercept Wimpole when he appears," Clara explained.

Chang snorted dismissively.

"He will notice them."

"He is probably in hiding right now to avoid the extensive search party that spread across the grounds," Park-Coombs countered. "If we get people in place before he returns, he shall not know they are there."

"Too much of a risk," Chang shook his head.

"I am prepared to let you have a gun, as well," Clara told him.

Chang perked up.

"Really?"

"Wimpole does not know that we have guns with us. I did not know until my husband explained he had rounded up some service pistols when he came on the hunt for me. He rather seemed to take the matter a little too seriously and thought I was being held by armed criminals."

Park-Coombs gave her a look of astonishment as she dismissed O'Harris' concerns.

"He took the matter *too* seriously?"

"There is never a need for guns," Clara protested. "They only guarantee someone is going to get shot."

Chang was chuckling under his breath, enjoying Clara's temper being deflected onto someone else.

"Anyway, we have guns," Clara continued. "Far too many guns. But I am prepared to give you one. Wimpole has no way of knowing that you will be armed, and therefore, if he tries any funny business, I am sure you will be able to handle him."

Knowing he would be armed for the encounter did soothe Chang to a degree.

"What if Wimpole sends Irving alone? I am guessing his dogsbody won't be good enough for you?" Chang said.

"You must insist on handing the papers to Wimpole directly. I am sure you can make it sound convincing that you will not trust Irving with them and want to be sure Wimpole sees you upholding your side of the agreement."

Chang nodded his head.

"Very well, I am not happy about this, and I think your plan has a lot of flaws, but I shall attempt it. I want to get away from this house and back to my usual life."

Park-Coombs started to speak; Clara cast him a sharp look.

She knew full well the inspector was thinking he had a prime opportunity to arrest Chang while in possession of illegal substances, and usually Clara would agree with him. But Chang had been given those substances by Wimpole who, on this occasion, was the greater danger. She needed Chang's cooperation, and he would not give it if he thought he was about to be arrested.

"What were you saying about Lady Selby?" Chang asked.

"She murdered Lord Russell," Clara explained. "Bit of a love triangle going on. She was upset to know he was also sleeping with Mrs Dodd."

Chang raised an eyebrow but said no more.

"If you ask me, this whole conspiracy has gone down the toilet this weekend without any need of Wimpole's games," Park-Coombs spoke. "Lady Selby is something of a driving force behind her husband, there is no way he could have kept such secrets without her assistance. Then one of their main conspirators is dead, killed by her. Two people have been taken out of this plot, and I suspect the others will struggle to hold it together."

"Having seen how Lord Selby and Mr Dodd behave, and their excessive consumption of illegal substances, I do not think they are going to be able to plot anything of much use in the future. Even if they could, they would get themselves so wasted they would likely reveal their secrets to someone else," Clara agreed. "I am beginning to wonder if they were ever really the threat Wimpole imagined them to be."

"Wimpole is a paranoid man," Chang concurred. "He could easily have sunk into his own world of madness far enough to see enemies where there were merely fools."

"I want to know precisely which government department he works for, secret or not," Clara felt her anger returning. "And I shall be having words about the kidnapping of innocent civilians for these schemes. Those sorts of things cannot be allowed in England."

"Heaven help the British secret service when Clara lands on their doorstep," Chang grinned.

Clara knew he was mocking her, but she was prepared to let it pass.

"That is settled then," Park-Coombs declared. "I am going to arrest Lady Selby and depart. I will summon Dr Death to come for the body now we have solved the crime. He should arrive within the next few hours. Once I have departed, I shall return in secret."

Chang gave the inspector a look that implied he did not think the man capable of doing anything secretly. Park-Coombs ignored him.

"We shall reconvene in Lord Selby's study this evening," Clara confirmed. "About the papers Chang found, they are proof of Lord Selby's own dubious activities, and I imagine you would like them, Inspector?"

"I would, indeed," Park-Coombs grinned. "Would be quite a coup for a humble coastal inspector to unravel a plot to start another world war."

"Why not just give him the papers now and have him arrest Lord Selby, then the whole affair will be over, and Wimpole will have no need of me?" Chang protested.

"I already told you. I can see Wimpole being the vindictive sort, and I do not think he would like someone to steal his thunder. If the inspector is seen to have succeeded while Wimpole remains a free man, then I suspect he will come after one of us to have his revenge."

Chang thought about Clara's words, then nodded his head.

"You are right, unfortunately. The man is clearly unstable."

He groaned to himself.

"Just hurry, Inspector, I want to get this over and done with."

Park-Coombs needed no further prompting. He went to summon Dr Deáth, the police coroner, and start their charade. Clara waited until he was out of hearing before she turned to Chang.

"Thank you, Chang, for everything."

Chang looked at her in amazement.

"I beg your pardon?"

"Despite your snide comments and crass manner, you have been watching out for me, not just here this weekend, but in the past too. I believe Wimpole was telling the truth when he said he chose to kidnap me because he thought you would protect me. I don't know what I have done to warrant your consideration, but I do appreciate it."

Chang grumbled to himself.

"You helped me with the situation concerning my sister, and I shall never forget that," he muttered. "But that does not mean you can interfere in any of my future business plans."

"I would not dream of it," Clara promised him. "Unless, those plans interfere with something I am doing."

Chang huffed.

"Any chance of a sandwich before I walk out and risk my life?" he asked. "I barely ate anything at breakfast, and I am famished."

Clara had to admit she was feeling a pang of hunger too. In all the excitement of solving the murder of Lord Russell, she had forgotten about her own needs, but now she was being reminded she had barely eaten for the last couple of days. Running on nervous energy would only take a person so far, and now she definitely needed some food in her belly to help her over the last hurdle.

"I am sure I can whip us up a sandwich if we just find the kitchen," Clara said to Chang. "I might not be Annie, but I have some basic culinary knowledge."

Chang gave her a long look.

"I shall make the sandwiches," he declared. "You might manage to burn them or something."

"You cannot possibly burn a sandwich!" Clara scoffed.

Chang was already walking away down the corridor.

"You would find a way," he declared over his shoulder. "You might be a great detective, but your skills in a kitchen are diabolical."

"How would you know?" Clara snorted.

"You forget, I have spent time with Annie," Chang gave her a sly smile. "Besides, I just spent a whole day in a kitchen with you, and all it did was bring me more grief."

"That is hardly fair," Clara said, coming behind him. "I wasn't cooking."

"Just arguing," Chang said. "Like right now. Can you do nothing but argue with me?"

Clara opened her mouth to counter his comment, then realised he was once again mocking her and compelling her into proving him right. She scowled.

"Once this is all over I shall be very glad to see the back of you, Brilliant Chang."

Chang grimaced.

"I can safely say the same about you!"

Chapter
Thirty-Two

E vents unfolded as Clara and the inspector had planned. The coroner arrived before Park-Coombs departed with Lady Selby and went through the usual procedures to secure, and then remove, the body. Dr Deáth had nothing to add to what Clara already knew about the death of his lordship. He confirmed the only wound on the body was that caused by the letter opener, and it seemed very much the case that the man had suffered internal bleeding and bled to death. His condition would have been worsened by his state of deep intoxication, which prevented him from seeking medical help.

He had probably died without ever regaining consciousness.

It was not a happy thought for anyone, and Lady Selby was beside herself as she was escorted to the inspector's police car. She had had time to regret what she had done, and to realise how foolish she had been. Lord Selby watched her departure from the front steps of his home. He was finally becoming sober from the night before and the realisation of what had happened was sinking in. He was contemplating a future without the steady hand of his wife to keep him on track, and it was not a pleasant notion.

Lady Selby had been his anchor, and without her he was not sure how to carry on. With any luck, the conspiracy to create another war had ended as surely as if the plotters had all been arrested.

Mr and Mrs Dodd, and Mr Rankin, had already left the house in their own cars. Mrs Dodd had given a statement to the police, and it would be necessary for her to bear witness against Lady Selby in a future trial, but Park-Coombs had decided he no longer needed to prevent her from departing with her husband. Mr Dodd, much to everyone's surprise, was being most caring of his wife in her distress, blaming himself for her seeking out comfort in the arms of another man. He fawned over her as she headed for the car, making promises to improve himself and turn their lives around.

Clara wondered if this was the wake up call he needed, or whether his promises would simply evaporate once time and distance from this crime had intervened. Ultimately, it was not her problem.

With the house party gone, and his wife disappearing in a police car, Lord Selby went up to his room and completely forgot about those who remained at his home. Clara, O'Harris, Tommy, Chang and some of the remaining rescue party collected in the study to discuss their next move.

While Chang was dismissive of O'Harris being capable of organising a trap for Wimpole, the captain was confident in his abilities. Most of his men had been involved in ambushes of some description during the war and were capable of being stealthy. O'Harris cleared Lord Selby's desk and made up a crude map of the gardens and the position of the pavilion where Chang would meet with Wimpole. He pointed out key spots where people could hide.

He had had spotters positioned upstairs and on the alert all day, looking out for any sign of Wimpole and Irving. After the search of the grounds had thoroughly scared the two men off, the spotters had lain in wait to see them return. Wimpole was not as cunning as he liked to imagine. O'Harris' men had found a spot near the wall of the grounds where a number of cigarette ends had been discarded. Quite clearly, this was where someone had been lurking. Irving was a heavy smoker, so he seemed the likely culprit, though no doubt Wimpole was stationed close by.

The moment either of the two men returned to the garden, O'Harris' spotters would spy them and report in.

Chang followed the arrangements O'Harris made with his mouth firmly shut, pretending he was not impressed by the efforts the man had gone to. Clara watched him surreptitiously, satisfied that his silence and lack of sarcastic remarks indicated a newfound respect for her husband. But Chang would never confess to such a thing out loud, and he was determined to be as surly as possible during the whole affair.

He was still in a sulk that Clara had been right when she said they had to do something to rout out Wimpole if they ever wanted peace of mind.

The final element of the puzzle had been determining where the household staff had hidden themselves, and whether they would be a complication in their plans. As it turned out, when Clara and Chang reached the kitchen, they discovered the servants had all disappeared. They clearly had more sense than their employers and were alert to the illegal nature of the things occurring in the main house. With the arrival of the police, and whispers of a dead man, they had quickly made their exit and not a single one was to be found.

This might be a problem for Lord Selby, but it suited Clara and the others. Having fewer witnesses around also meant fewer chances of their trap being revealed before Wimpole was safely in it.

All there was left to do was wait for the inspector to return and the spotters to let them know that Wimpole had reappeared.

They sat together in the study, perching wherever they could as there was only one armchair and another chair behind the desk. O'Harris was scanning through the documents Chang had discovered.

"Really makes you despair to think that a fellow Englishman would be intent on starting a war again," he said as he flicked through the documents. "How could anyone consider it after the horrors we witnessed?"

"No doubt Lord Selby never witnessed them," Tommy snorted. "Probably never went to the front as he was considered too important with his factories back in England. Sort of fellow who has no clue as to the suffering of others."

"It makes me almost depressed," O'Harris said, glancing up towards Jones who was stood by the window of the study watching the dusk fall. "All the efforts I am making to help men who have been damaged by the last war, and here is this man sitting in his position of privilege looking to start it all over again."

Clara reached out for his hand.

"John, there will always be men like that, we just have to do all in our power to prevent them from achieving their goals. You must not let it depress you."

"It is hard not to, Clara. I feel as if there are too many people of influence who do not give a damn about the suffering of the ordinary folk, as long as they can gain more wealth, power, or fame."

"I agree, it is a terrible, terrible thing. But there are also a lot of good people doing all they can to stop those warmongers," Clara reminded him. "I am one of them. I did not agree to this mission because I was afraid of Wimpole. I agreed because I realised this was actually rather important and I could not turn my back on it and walk away. Yes, it was my means of escaping Wimpole's grasp, but it was also something I believed needed to be done."

"Had we known how stupid the people behind this scheme were, I think I would have agreed a lot faster," Chang remarked. He was happily smoking a cigar he had found in Lord Selby's desk, having claimed the armchair by the fire. "Then again, I really did not want to do what Wimpole told me to do."

"When it comes to contrariness, I suspect you and my sister are rather matching," Tommy said to him, earning him a stern glare from his sister.

"When this is over, I want just a couple of minutes with that Wimpole fellow and his companion, Irving," O'Harris said, grinding his teeth.

"You are not allowed to punch them, dearest," Clara told him softly. "That is my department."

O'Harris caught the smile on her lips and his mood lightened.

"I am so glad you are safe. I knew you were tough, old thing, but even so I was scared for you."

"I was a little scared as well," Clara admitted. "Though once I met my captors properly, and saw Chang was also at their mercy, my fear was replaced by outrage. Which is why Wimpole is all mine."

"I want to know how Wimpole knew the correct dress size to go out and buy you new clothes," Tommy said idly.

"That was Irving, in fact," Clara frowned. "That seedy little fellow apparently has a good eye for ladies' dress sizes. He must have guessed, but he was alarmingly accurate."

"How dare he look at you and guess your dress size," O'Harris rumbled.

"He could have done a lot worse, Captain," Chang replied.

O'Harris cast him a stony glare, no love lost between the two. He would never accept Chang's presence like his wife did, even though he was secretly glad to know Chang had had an eye on Clara and was ready to aid her if needs be.

They were distracted from their talk by the return of Park-Coombs.

"Slipped in through the gates and kept to the shadows," he told them as he entered the room. "No one about, I am sure of it."

"Wimpole should still think that his men are watching the front of the house," Clara said. "Unless he took the time to seek them out and found the car empty, but I doubt it. He would have had to double back to do so and that would have risked running into the search party."

"Well, we are banking on a lot of luck tonight," Park-Coombs acknowledged. "But it will have to do. Any sign of Wimpole or Irving?"

"Not so far," O'Harris said. "I am mildly concerned they are leaving it this late."

"They will be back," Chang grumbled. "I have a feeling they are too desperate to simply run off and forget about the papers they want."

As if he had talked them up, a voice called down the staircase. One of the spotters was heading as fast as he could to the study to let them know that he had spotted two men at the far wall of the estate. He had been using binoculars, and though the figures were too distant to make out clearly, the way they were cautiously moving through the bushes made him fancy they could be no one other than Wimpole and Irving.

Either that, or a pair of thieves had picked that very night to try their luck.

"Ready for action?" Park-Coombs asked.

"All my men are in place," O'Harris informed him. "We just need

Chang to lure Wimpole close enough to strike."

Chang muttered something indecipherable under his breath.

"Give them half an hour to settle down," he added, louder. "Then I shall go outside and meet my fate."

He focused his attention on Clara.

"I was promised a gun."

Clara nudged her husband, who reluctantly reached into the waistband of his trousers and produced a service pistol. It happened to be the one he had flown with during the war. He handed it to Chang.

"It only has three rounds," he said. "Most of the guns we brought with us are old pieces that were not loaded."

Chang gave him a look of disapproval.

"They were from my uncle's old gun collection," O'Harris became defensive. "He was a military historian, and he liked handguns, but most were either deliberately deactivated or there is no ammunition for them. They were more for show than to be used."

"Oh John," Clara smiled at her husband. "Do you know how happy that makes me to know you brought unloaded guns?"

"You would have been deeply upset if I shot someone," O'Harris told her sheepishly. "But I would have taken a potshot if I needed to."

"You two are appalling," Chang said, sounding as if he might gag at the pair of them. "If I were married and someone kidnapped my wife there would be hell to pay, and I would turn up with a dozen men armed with rifles."

O'Harris ignored him. Clara merely smirked.

Chang sank into his chair with the pistol, scowling to himself, though it was hard not to suppose he felt just a little jealous of the affection between the two.

Chapter
Thirty-Three

T he evening drew on and a fine drizzle decided to grace the night. This displeased Chang even further when he realised he was going to get wet standing outside waiting for Wimpole. But there was nothing else for it, and as the clock on the mantelpiece chimed a quarter past seven, he rose from his seat in silence and took a bundle of papers.

They were not the real papers that Wimpole wanted. They were dummy ones that had been scraped together from Selby's desk. Chang was to do everything in his power to prevent Wimpole from taking a proper look at the papers before the trap could be sprung.

He slipped the pistol into the waistband of his trousers and headed out of the study, towards the back of the house. Clara and the others followed at a short distance. The spotters were back in the attic, ready to signal if they noticed any signs of danger, such as if it looked like Wimpole was going to renege on his word and shoot Chang.

Chang was acutely aware of that as a strong possibility and was not convinced he was going to live through the night. He had not made mention of his concerns to anyone – it would not be the first time he had fancied his life was in peril – but it was making his belly ache, nonetheless.

The annoying thing was he could see no other way forward. Clara was right, even if they escaped with the police, Wimpole was liable to come after him simply out of revenge. The man looked like the type to hold a grudge, and Chang would rather face him with the knowledge he could die, than to have a bullet shot through his back months from now when he was not expecting it.

Chang lived most of his life wondering who was out to get him and whether this day was to be his last, he did not need to add Wimpole to the list of people looking to end his existence.

Chang paused briefly in the kitchen of the house. A short passageway beside it led to a back door. He knew once he was through that door he was at the mercy of O'Harris' men and the trap they had set. Clara was to remain in the kitchen and watch from the safety of indoors.

"Good luck, Chang," she said to him just before he left.

Chang was pleased to see the seriousness on her face. For once she was not going to deflect her fears with jokes or bravado. He appreciated that, and her words. He nodded to her, avoiding looking at her husband who he was sure would scowl daggers at him, and then exited the house.

The drizzle seemed surprisingly chill as it hit his bare head. He hunched his shoulders, hands in his trouser pockets partly to keep them warm and dry, partly so he could feel the reassurance of the pistol, then he hurried across the garden. He passed bushes where he knew men were lurking, lying prone on their bellies and ready to spring out just as they might have done during the war. He kept his eyes focused ahead on the pavilion which was slowly looming out of the dark.

The structure was painted grey, with a dark blue roof, and it seemed to merge into the shadows of dusk. Chang hopped up the three steps into its open interior, glad to be out of the rain at least. He cast his eyes across the garden, looking for any sign Wimpole had noticed him. Then he lifted one hand out of his pocket and made the prearranged signal with a mirror and the flicker of a torch he had brought from the house.

Then Chang simply waited, using the glimpses of the moon he could see through the rainclouds to judge time passing. A shiver of cold ran down his spine and a droplet of water fell off the end of his nose.

When this was over he was going to have a long, hot bath, with no one badgering him about doing the right thing for the good of the country.

Chang stood in the pavilion for over an hour. He could not judge the time precisely, though he knew it felt forever. He imagined Clara back in the warmth of the house, watching the minutes ticking by on the kitchen clock. How long would she leave him out here, before deciding Wimpole was not going to come? Or would he be the one to get fed up first and head back to the house, grumbling about being drenched to the bone?

He hoped it would not come to that. He really wanted this to be over tonight.

Chang waited and waited. He suspected he was being made to endure this torment to satisfy Wimpole that he really had something, or maybe just because Wimpole wanted to see him suffer. When finally there was movement in the shadows of the grounds, Chang hardly believed his eyes. He blinked several times before he was convinced that someone was walking towards him.

As he peered into the dark, he realised there was not just one person heading his way, there were two – one walking almost perfectly behind the other.

Chang could guess that Irving was leading the way, in case he tried anything stupid, and Wimpole was following. Chang would have loved to produce the pistol and shoot them both, but he was not entirely confident that O'Harris was telling the truth when he said the gun had three rounds in it. For all he knew, it was unloaded. He had not had the opportunity to inspect the gun himself, not daring to take it out and look at it in the pavilion in case Wimpole or Irving were lurking nearer than he realised and spotted him.

Now he took a deep breath and wondered if it would be his last, as Irving drew closer and closer. Neither of the approaching men seemed to be armed, at least they did not have their arms raised and pointing at him. That bought him some time and told him they did not intend to just shoot him on sight – at least, not just yet.

Irving's grim features became clearer as he moved into the pavilion, though everything was too shadowy to see much. Wimpole was a few steps behind him.

"What on earth has been going on?" Wimpole hissed at Chang, making it sound as if he was personally responsible for the chaos in the house.

"Lady Selby murdered Lord Russell in a jealous rage over Mrs Dodd," Chang explained bluntly. "They had to summon the police."

"We saw them! Why were they searching the grounds?"

Chang had thought up an excuse to cover this scenario.

"The servants made themselves scarce after the cry of murder went up. The police thought one of them might have been responsible. Honestly, the hysteria in that house today has been absurd."

"What about the drugs?" Irving asked quietly.

"They don't know about them," Chang said firmly. "It took some doing, but I made sure no one spoke about my purpose here. It has been a difficult day."

"Enough of that," Wimpole waved a hand to indicate he was done with discussions of the murder of Lord Russell. "Do you have the papers?"

"Yes," Chang said, producing the papers from under his jacket.

There was a brief moment when Irving tensed, as if he expected something else to be brought out, but Chang was careful not to let either of them see the gun in his waistband.

"I actually retrieved these in the early hours, but with all the police at the house I could not come out here to meet you."

"We had to make ourselves scarce, anyway," Wimpole replied. "Too many people around. Still, you have done well Chang, considering the difficult circumstances."

Wimpole held out his hand and Chang handed the papers over. There was no way that Wimpole could read the papers in the darkness, but Irving had a torch, and he now turned it on, shielding the light it created with his body, so no one watching from the house might see.

Wimpole peered at the first page. Chang felt his nerves twitching as he wondered where O'Harris' men were. Surely the captain had not left him out to dry?

His hand slipped to the gun.

"This paper appears to contain figures," Wimpole said.

Chang knew it was an innocuous accounts sheet he had pulled out of the desk, which mainly detailed Lady Selby's household expenses and recent clothing purchases.

"This is very good, Chang, follow the money and see where it leads!" Wimpole said, clearly not paying great heed to the contents of the paper.

Irving, however, was not so easily fooled and was now looking down at the paper.

"Sir, I am not sure..."

Chang was reaching for the pistol, knowing Irving was about to ruin the plan, when five men came surging out of the bushes and raced towards the pavilion. Chang had not seen the signal for their sudden attack, but he was glad it had been given.

Wimpole looked up in amazement at the sight, while Irving reacted rather predictably by grabbing for something at his waist. He had a pistol too and was reaching for it when Chang moved a fraction faster and, with a click, held his own gun to Irving's head.

"Do not move," he said with icy coldness.

Irving froze.

"What is happening?" Wimpole demanded as three of the men grabbed at his arms and restrained him.

The others joined Chang in capturing Irving.

"He has a gun," Chang told them, and someone reached forward and pulled the weapon from Irving's jacket pocket.

"Put your hands up!" someone cried out.

Irving quietly obeyed. He cast a look of pure hate at Chang, who merely smiled in response.

"Tables have turned," he grinned.

"I am on official business for the government," Wimpole was shouting. "I have the papers to prove it!"

His pleas were falling on deaf ears. The men were pulling his hands behind his back and securing them with rope. Irving's hands were similarly pinioned, and then both men were being escorted back towards the house.

"Tell Mrs O'Harris, she will pay for this," Irving said sinisterly to Chang.

"Tell her yourself," Chang snorted back. "She wants a few words with you."

Wimpole bleated protests all the way back to the property and was still trying to claim he was only doing his job when he arrived in the kitchen and was pushed into a chair. Inspector Park-Coombs now appeared before him.

"I am going to arrest you for kidnapping and holding people hostage," he told Wimpole.

"I have authority from the British government to do what must be done!" Wimpole declared.

"I have a feeling they won't be in a rush to rescue you," Park-Coombs smiled. "They won't want it known that the British government condones the kidnapping of innocent civilians. I have a feeling you have overstepped your mark."

"Really, who are you?" Wimpole now demanded, trying to find his authority again.

"Inspector Park-Coombs," Park-Coombs informed him. "A dear friend of Clara O'Harris."

Wimpole's eyes drifted past the inspector to see that Clara was stood by the kitchen range, a look of sheer fury on her face.

"You!" Wimpole snapped.

Clara stormed forward and without a word slapped him hard across the face.

"I am not usually one to resort to violence, but from the moment I met you, I have wanted to do that to you. I shall make sure you are sent to prison for this Mr Wimpole, and you will not see the light of day for many a year to come."

Wimpole looked dazed.

"But, I was only trying to protect my country!"

"You went about it all the wrong way," Park-Coombs snorted.

"Another time, try just asking for Clara's help, it usually works out better in the end."

Chapter
Thirty-Four

I nspector Park-Coombs called for the police car, and it arrived swiftly. Wimpole and Irving spent the time while they waited protesting their arrest, trying to convince the inspector they were on the same side.

Or at least that was what Wimpole attempted to do. Irving largely stayed silent, occasionally throwing in comments to help his employer, but otherwise choosing to shoot sour glances at the people in the room. Clara suspected that, out of the pair, he was the more dangerous, and the one more likely to ultimately seek revenge.

"If it makes you feel any better," Park-Coombs told Wimpole at last when he finally grew sick of his excuses. "I am going to arrest Lord Selby on charges of espionage. I have all the proof I need."

"No!" Wimpole declared in horror. "He was mine! You cannot take this from me!"

"You should have thought about that before you began kidnapping young ladies from the side of the road," Park-Coombs replied.

Wimpole argued further, but he achieved nothing. When the

car came he was bundled with Irving into the back seat while Park-Coombs went to arrest Lord Selby.

His lordship had been sleeping and was bemused to be woken and informed he was being arrested. He could not comprehend what was going on as he was escorted down his own staircase and to the waiting car.

"I am not sure you appreciate who I am," he said as he was dragged outside. "I think you have made a mistake."

His protests were still ringing in the air as the vehicle drove off, leaving behind his houseguests to take care of his home. Clara glanced around the empty tiled hall, thinking how just a couple of days before she had walked into a party atmosphere here – now one man was dead and four people arrested.

"Do you think they will arrest Dodd and Rankin too?" Tommy asked, coming to stand beside his sister.

"I think it depends on what is in those papers that Chang discovered," Clara replied. "And how incriminating the evidence. But with Lord Selby arrested I consider the conspiracy to be largely at an end. He was the lead in all this, with his wife his able assistant."

O'Harris appeared from the drawing room, where he had been giving a debrief to the fellows who had assisted them that day.

"They are pleased as punch with themselves," he smiled as he approached his wife. "Not only have they rescued you, but they caught your kidnappers and saw a man who was conspiring to start another war arrested."

"I am pretty certain I was already largely rescued by the time you arrived," Clara pointed out.

"Don't take this glory from them," O'Harris shook his head at her. "They will live off this for months."

Clara sighed; yes, they would be telling everyone how they had rescued her, coming to her aid as she was held at the hands of evil fiends. And people would find that a lot more believable than supposing they had waltzed up when Clara had already confined the conspirators, was on the cusp of solving a murder, and had already determined how she was going to turn the tables on her kidnappers.

Well, she could let them have their glory, it did not matter to her.

"We should head home," Tommy stretched his arms and yawned. "I think we would all benefit from sleeping in our own beds and Annie needs to know we succeeded."

Clara had not precisely forgotten about Annie, but in all the chaos her friend had been rather sidelined in her mind. Now she realised how agitated she must be feeling, especially with the long delay in the return of her husband and friends.

"We must get back to Annie at once," Clara determined. "She cannot be left to wonder any longer."

"Might I get a lift back to Brighton?" Chang appeared behind them, carrying Lord Selby's obese cat in both arms.

"I assumed you would like one, old man," O'Harris said to him politely. "You are welcome in the car. I have to say you did a good job and held your nerve right up to the last."

"And you didn't shoot Irving in the head, which must have required all your restraint," Clara teased him.

Chang glowered at her.

"You know full well they were wrong, don't you?" he snapped.

"About what?" Clara asked innocently.

"About me protecting you," Chang snorted.

"Well, of course!" Clara laughed. "I do a perfectly fine job of protecting myself."

She turned away and sauntered out of the door with her husband. Tommy cast a glance at Chang, there was a moment of silence between them.

"What about the cat?" Tommy finally asked.

"Lord Selby is being arrested, so it shall need someone to take care of it. I have always been partial to cats," Chang replied.

Tommy shook his head at him.

"I have no idea what to make of you, Chang."

"I have the same feeling about your sister," Chang responded.

Tommy paused thoughtfully for a second.

"But, if you are keeping an eye out for her, and making sure some of the worst elements in the criminal world are not out for her blood, well, I am grateful."

Chang sighed.

"Shut up," he declared.

"She is grateful too, but she will never admit it, because that would imply she cannot look out for herself, and you know how Clara feels about saying something like that."

"All too well," Chang grimaced.

"Good man," Tommy nodded at him, before heading towards the door.

"Precisely who is locking up this place after we leave?" Chang asked.

"O'Harris found the housekey, he will make sure of it," Tommy replied.

Chang looked around the hallway. It was a rather pleasant house, nice and isolated, yet easy to watch the grounds for intruders.

The sort of house where a man who likes to get away from London and his criminal endeavours every once in a while could find useful. And it was not so far from Brighton, after all.

"You say O'Harris has the key?" Chang called out as he followed after Tommy.

They arrived home in the early hours. Annie had been waiting for them, determined to stay up as long as she could to anticipate their arrival. However, slumber had eventually caught up with her as she sat on a sofa in the front room. She woke at the sound of wheels on the gravel of the drive and the flash of headlights through the window to discover that someone had been caring enough to place a blanket over her while she rested.

Standing up and holding the blanket around her, for the house felt cold at this time of the night, she hurried to the window and looked out.

She recognised the cars that were pulling up before the house and her heart pounded as she hoped – no, prayed – that inside one of them was her sister-in-law.

She was not alone in noticing their arrival. Several of the staff and men at the home, who had been left behind and were also eagerly awaiting news, hastened down the stairs to stand in the front hall and see who had returned.

Annie was at the head of them and opened the front door. She paused anxiously in the doorway and looked across the drive.

The driver's door of the first car opened and O'Harris emerged. The car was pulled around so that Annie was opposite the passenger side, and so she could not see who was climbing out of the rear on the driver's side until their head bobbed over the top of the car. But all she saw was a woman with short fair hair, and her heart sank.

Tommy emerged from the passenger side at the front of the car, stretching his back and looking a little stiff from his adventures. Annie tried to see the expression on his face, but she was distracted by the appearance from the back door of a familiar figure.

Brilliant Chang stepped out of the car and glanced up at the house before him. Annie felt her heart soar. If Chang was there, than surely Clara was too.

She hurried down the steps, blanket trailing her like a cloak. Tommy met her, a smile on his face.

"Everything is all right. Clara is safe."

"Where is she?" Annie demanded.

Clara now appeared from around the side of the car and Annie got a good look at her hair.

"Oh my!"

"I was undercover Annie," Clara declared. "But not willingly."

She tapped her bob.

"I am hoping it will grow back swiftly."

Annie felt light-headed at the sight of them all. She embraced Clara and wept on her shoulder, then she embraced Tommy, so relieved he was back safe and sound. Next to be hugged was O'Harris, then, to everyone's surprise, not least his own, Annie hugged Chang.

"What are you doing here?" she demanded as she embraced him.

"It's a long story," Chang replied.

Annie stood back and lightly slapped his arm.

"Is this all your fault, Mr Chang? We have had words before about your wicked ways."

She pointed a finger at him. Chang opened his mouth to protest then realised there was not much he could say to deny the truth.

"It was, indeed, my fault," he explained to Annie. "But it was not quite what you imagine."

Annie wagged her finger at him, then sighed.

"Well, at least you are all alive and well. You need tea and something to eat, and probably cocoa."

Annie began to fuss about the things they would need to eat and drink to restore them after their adventure and hastened back indoors with Tommy at her heel as she threatened to cook up a banquet for her returning friends.

"You never mentioned she was pregnant," Chang whispered to Clara as they headed to the house.

"Well, she is," Clara responded with a shrug. "Don't upset her, she is more temperamental than ever."

Chang's eyes went wide, and he pulled a face as if he were deeply alarmed.

"I shall endeavour to be incredibly careful."

Clara would have liked to have gone straight to bed, but she could not deny the enthusiasm of her friends and joined them in the kitchen as Annie whipped up drinks and food, with Tommy clucking at her side, trying to prevent her from doing too much. Clara supposed that she did need to unwind a little before she made her way upstairs. She had a feeling that when her head hit the pillow all she would do was think about her ordeal and very little sleep would come her way.

O'Harris sat beside her at the table and slipped his arm around her.

"For a while there, I was afraid I might never get to do this again," he said softly.

Clara leaned into him.

"I never doubted you would find me," she said. "I knew you would come for me."

"They didn't make it easy, but I guess I have learned a lot from being married to a great detective."

Clara chuckled.

"I am not sure I am a great detective! A great detective would have worked out that someone was trying to kidnap them."

"Don't run yourself down, you did remarkably today," O'Harris hugged her closer and then fell into silence watching the endless debacle that was Tommy trying to control Annie's urges to feed them every dish she could think of.

"Any minute now he is going to push his luck," O'Harris said quietly.

In that instant, Annie spun on her husband.

"Thomas Fitzgerald, will you please get out of my way and allow me to cook! I was not the one out all day and night with no word! I have been worried sick about you all, and now I am going to look after you all!"

"Sorry, Annie," Tommy said meekly. "I just want to help so you don't overdo things."

"Well, then, go get the fresh milk from the larder!" Annie waved him away and Tommy headed off on his errand.

Chang had watched the drama unfold without comment. Now a smile graced his lips.

"That is what being married is like, then?" he said to no one in particular.

"Not all of us, old man," O'Harris interjected.

Chang gave a snort.

"It is not for me, anyway," Chang laughed. "I don't think I could ever find a woman to match me. And where would the fun be if I didn't have someone who could give me a run for my money?"

His eyes briefly flickered onto Clara, then he was rising from the table and asking Annie if there was anything he could do for her.

"I don't understand him at all," O'Harris said.

"I doubt Chang understands himself half of the time," Clara responded, before leaning her head into her husband's shoulder and closing her eyes. "I daresay that is part of his charm."

Chapter Thirty-Five

C hang was gone by the following afternoon, saying he had to get back to London and discover what had happened to his 'business' while he was gone. Clara was not sad to see him depart. He was simply too complicated a fellow and she always felt as if he made her see the world a little more bleakly than she liked.

Clara was just glad to be home. She spent the morning in bed resting and enjoying the comfort of her own blankets. When that became tiresome – because there was only so much rest Clara could endure – she headed downstairs to see what everyone was doing. The house was surprisingly quiet. She supposed many of the men were recuperating as well from the events of the last few days. She ventured into the library to see who was around.

One of the nurses was just standing up from tending to Colonel Bradley, who was hunched in his usual chair. She smiled at Clara as she departed, whispering in passing that she was very glad to see her safe and well.

Clara walked over to the fireplace beside the ageing colonel, returning to reality with a bump. When all was said and done, and talk of espionage was at an end, there was still the everyday struggles to consider. Such as the colonel and his increasingly difficult family.

"How are you feeling, Colonel?" Clara asked the man, not expecting a reply. "I apologise for failing to read to you for a few days. It has been a rather trying time. I shall make amends…"

Clara never expected to see the colonel move so swiftly. He was out of the chair in a moment and wrapping his arms around her. He embraced her heartily and sobbed softly on her shoulder.

"I heard them say you were kidnapped by evil men."

His voice was a croak from being so little used. Clara patted at his arms, feeling his weight nearly toppling her. The colonel was not entirely steady on his feet.

"Evil men did kidnap me, but they soon discovered they had bitten off more than they could chew."

The colonel simply cried, a lifetime of sorrow suddenly pouring forth. Clara had no idea why her disappearance would trigger this sudden outpouring, why this was the thing that finally brought the colonel back to the world. She was just glad to know that the colonel had never been as far gone as they had imagined.

He had been listening. He had known what had happened.

"I am safe now, Colonel," Clara reassured him. "The men who did this have been arrested."

The colonel sagged, carefully Clara helped him back into his chair. For a moment she was fearful he might revert to his prior state, become the hunched solemn form she was used to, but he did not. He looked up at her with old, but bright eyes.

"You look tired," he said, fussing over her now. "You should go back to bed."

"I was growing bored."

"You must rest," Colonel Bradley insisted. "Promise me you will."

Clara paused.

"I shall if you promise me you will keep talking? I want to have a proper conversation with you when I next come down."

Colonel Bradley pulled a strange expression. Clara realised he was trying to recall how to smile. When he at last mastered the art, he beamed at her with the kindest of smiles. Clara could not help but smile back.

"I shall be waiting, my dear," the colonel promised her.

"I have a fine story to tell you," Clara replied.

"Once you are fully rested," Bradley insisted.

Clara was happy to obey him. She realised her eyes had welled with tears of relief and joy at the sight of the colonel speaking again. She squeezed his hand.

"You have a lovely smile, Colonel."

"My dear, until I met you, I had forgotten there was anything to smile about."

Clara followed the colonel's orders and returned to bed, though this time to lie on top of the blankets in her clothes. She watched the sun roll through the sky out of the window and found herself ever so glad to be able to watch it in the freedom of her own home.

O'Harris brought her up afternoon tea. He was looking tired himself, but he would never admit it as he fussed around his wife.

"Why don't you lie down beside me?" Clara suggested, wanting him to rest too.

"Maybe later, I have a lot of work to catch up on," O'Harris refused gently.

Clara sighed.

"Always one of us is working too hard."

"True," O'Harris nodded.

He was placing a tray on the bed when a dark, ginger creature bounced up beside him and nearly made off with the top slice of toast. O'Harris saved it just in time.

"Hey you! I thought I shut you in my study!"

Clara laughed at the sight of the little dog who now bounced all over her gleefully, tail wagging furiously.

"Oh it is you!" she declared. "Do you remember me? Sorry I did not get you out of that awful pit, but I made sure to give the fellow who put you there a good slap."

The dog licked her face enthusiastically and then settled down in the bed beside her, nesting in the blankets with a clear intention of remaining.

"Did you find out who had lost him?" Clara asked her husband.

"Sadly, no one is claiming the little fellow. He was sold to Mr Wimpole cheaply by the man who bred him because he is gun shy."

"How could anyone consider you something to be sold cheaply," Clara petted the head of the spaniel. "Fortunately, you find yourself now in a big house with a huge garden, so you have nothing to fret about."

The spaniel responded by digging itself further into the blankets and resting its body right beside her.

"I suppose that settles things," O'Harris laughed.

He finally gave Clara her tray.

"Tommy called up your old friend, Captain Steadfast, a little while ago."

"From the secret service," Clara nodded. "What did he say?"

"He was appalled, naturally, about what had happened and promised it had not been authorised by his department. He is going to look into things and find out who was behind Wimpole, but he did admit we would probably never hear any more about it as it would be an inside matter."

"They like to keep their mistakes to themselves," Clara nodded. "Well, at least he is aware."

"The inspector rang also and says he has been busy all morning talking to his superiors about the various cases he has suddenly found himself with. Lady Selby is probably the easiest of the lot, but Lord Selby's involvement in espionage is causing quite a stir and he thinks questions may even be asked in parliament."

"As long as the situation is in hand and no one else is going to get hurt, that is all that matters," Clara decided. "Really, John, do sit down beside me. It is such a pleasant afternoon with the sun coming through the window. It shall not hurt you for half an hour or so."

O'Harris could not resist her pleas and laid down on the blankets beside her. The spaniel glanced up to be sure he was not about to be moved from his spot right next to Clara, then went back to sleep.

"All is well that ends well," Clara said, taking up a scone and buttering it. "Except my hair. I hate it so much."

"It will grow out," O'Harris promised her.

"I feel like I shall have to hide away until it does," Clara gave a shudder. "Of all the things he did, cutting and dying my hair is the second most reprehensible thing about my ordeal with Mr Wimpole."

"What is the first?" O'Harris asked.

"The use of a dog to lure me into his trap," Clara said. "And then abandoning the animal there."

As she spoke, she carefully broke off a small piece of the scone and fed it to the dog.

"By the way, does he have name?"

"Not as far as I know," O'Harris responded.

Clara gave the dog a good look. He stared back with big black eyes and his tail flailed merrily.

"He seems so happy despite everything," Clara said.

"You could call him that."

"What?"

"Happy," O'Harris grinned. "The name suits him."

Clara looked down at the spaniel.

"Do you care to be called Happy?"

The spaniel's tail pounded and then he reached up a paw and nudged her hand. Clara pulled off another small piece of scone and fed it to him.

"Then that is settled," she said. "It appears, John, I have a dog now."

"It appears so," O'Harris replied, smiling from ear to ear.

He rested his head back on the pillow and sighed as the sunlight through the window fell on him.

"Very glad to have you safely back, old thing."

"Very glad to be back," Clara replied. "Would you care for a scone, Annie has sent me too many, as usual."

When Clara received no response, she glanced at her husband. O'Harris had fallen asleep, the tension and the apprehension of the last few days finally catching up with him. Clara smiled as he breathed deeply and slumbered.

"It is very good to be back where I belong, Happy," she informed the dog. "Very good, indeed."

Enjoyed this Book?

You can make a difference

As an independent writer reviews of my books are hugely important to help my work reach a wider audience.
If you haven't already, I would love it if you could take five minutes to review this book.

Thank you very much!

The Clara Fitzgerald Series

Have you read them all?

The Woman Died Thrice

The eighth mystery

Murder and Mascara

The ninth mystery

The Green Jade Dragon

The tenth mystery

The Monster at the Window

The eleventh mystery

Murder on the Mary Jane

The twelfth mystery

The Missing Wife

The thirteenth mystery

The Traitor's Bones

The fourteenth mystery

The Fossil Murder

The fifteenth mystery

Mr Lynch's Prophecy

The sixteenth mystery

Death at the Pantomime

The seventeenth mystery

The Cowboy's Crime

The eighteenth mystery

The Trouble with Tortoises

The nineteenth mystery

The Valentine Murder

The twentieth mystery

A Body Out of Time

The twenty-first mystery

The Dog Show Affair

The twenty-second mystery

The Unlucky Wedding Guest

The twenty-third mystery

Worse Things Happen at Sea

The twenty-fourth mystery

A Diet of Death

The twenty-fifth mystery

Brilliant Chang Returns

The twenty-sixth mystery

Storm in a Teacup

The twenty-seventh mystery

The Dog Theft Mystery

The twenty-eighth mystery

The Day the Zeppelin Came

The twenty-ninth mystery

The Mystery of Mallory

The thirtieth mystery

Death at the Sun Club

The thirty-first mystery

The Disappearance of Emily Potter

The thirty-second mystery

Bright Young Dead Things

The thirty-third mystery

The Price of Honour

The thirty-fourth mystery

Murder on the Silver Screen

The thirty-fifth mystery

Also by Evelyn James

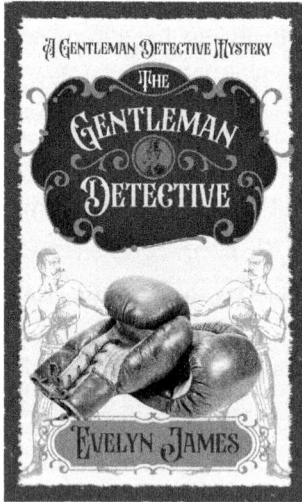

The Gentleman Detective

Norwich 1898.

Colonel Bainbridge is wondering if it is time to hang up his magnifying glass when a pugilist dies unexpectedly, and an innocent man is accused of his murder.

Distracted by trying to save a friend from the noose, Bainbridge finds himself investigating the murky world of street fighting and match fixing.

Can he determine who really killed the boxer Simon One-Foot or will a innocent man end up swinging for a crime he could not have committed?

The Gentleman Detective is the first novel in a brand new series from the creator of the Clara Fitzgerald Mysteries, Evelyn James.

Start your investigation with Colonel Bainbridge today!

Available on Amazon

About Sophie Jackson

Back in 2003 I decided to take a leap of faith and become a full time writer. Little did I imagine that all these years later I would have authored over 100 books (I lost count somewhere around 2021!) and would be connecting to my readers as an independent author.

I am delighted that you picked up my book today. My goal whenever I write something is to bring alive another time and place and to captivate my readers.

Writing about ghosts combines two of my passions – a fascination for the paranormal and the history of the British Isles – in a way that no other form of book truly can. Ghost legends as much as being spooky and entertaining (whether you believe in them or not) also provide insight into the lives and mindsets of our ancestors. The way people react to ghosts in different time periods is as interesting as the ghosts themselves.

In writing these volumes my goal has been to bring these legends to life, to explore their origins and, where possible, to discover the real people behind a ghost story. The research for this has been exhilarating as well as sometimes sad, for the reality is that every ghost story begins with a death, often a tragic and untimely one.

Thank you for choosing to read this book, I truly hope it was as much pleasure to read as it was to research and write.

If you would like to get in touch you can contact me at **sophiejackson.author@gmail.com** or check out my website **www.sophie-jackson.com**

Printed in Great Britain
by Amazon